Livie's Lilies

A Novel

by Garrison Somers

Illustrations by Shelly Hehenberger

BLOTTER BOOKS

Published by **The Blotter Magazine**, Inc.
Text copyright 2017 by Garrison Somers
Illustrations copyright 2017 by Shelly Nehenberger
First Printing 2017

Somers, Garrison 1957 -
Livie's Lilies
ISBN 978-0-9839022-8-7

Published in the United States by
Blotter Books
an imprint of The Blotter Magazine, Inc.
1010 Hale Street, Durham, NC 27705

Printed and bound in the USA

Livie's Lilies

by Garrison Somers

For my wife,
my daughters,
my sisters,
and my mom.

Chapter One

Her first name was Olivia and her last name was Bien which is French for *good* and she had long light brown hair all the same length which wouldn't stay out of her brown eyes. No one called her Olivia, though, except occasionally the little voice in her head that quietly talked to her when she was thinking and sometimes argued with her as well. They called her Livie, or more often "Livie! *Stop it!*" or "Livie, *don't!*" In fact, someone was always telling her "no!" If yelling at her was a measurement, she was probably anything else in the whole wide world *except* good.

She was often in the way, probably because no one paid attention to her, but also just as possibly because she was shorter than anyone else in her family. This made sense because she was the youngest, and she had one dress only and one pair of *sabots* – very uncomfortable shoes with wooden soles. Her knees seemed to be eternally scabby because she knelt on them a lot and her dress dirty because she ran full-tilt all of the time no matter where she was going or what she was doing. Running, she had to admit, gave Livie great joy. Running was almost but not quite like flying. But as her Papa said,

"Oh! You, Livie! Quit galloping around the yard. Slow down, before you break your neck!" Papa Bien had said this more than once, probably more than a thousand times, each time his face frowning, his voice always growling and gravelly, like the mean dog that Olivia's brothers kept tied out by the stone cattle-byre. "Can't you do what you are told? Livie, no!"

So with that scolding, and remembering she did sometimes go around a corner of the house too fast and her knees told that story, she would skid to a walk, and say, "*Oui*, Papa. Yes, Papa." Olivia would force herself to walk for about a minute (or maybe even a little bit less than a minute but longer than a moment) before she would be off on another thought, racing through the farmyard with her hair whipping in the wind that she herself made. Racing, perhaps, to the tilted little field where tomatoes grew ripe and red-yellow, because Maman needed four of them and right now! - and *of course* that was why Olivia had been running in the first place. For certainly you see that only when Maman had her tomatoes, or potatoes fetched from the cold-storage bins in the stone cattle-byre, or curved yellow squash from the vines that wrapped around a cedar pole in its own place, could Olivia - Livie - slow down for a moment and let her thinking catch up with her.

And so what kinds of things did Livie think about? Well, she wondered about the whole wide world, about which she knew nothing. Nothing! What made the wind blow when Livie wasn't running? And what made tomatoes grow? And how confusing was it to have a cattle-byre on their farm and not have cows, just as it was strange to have a mean dog with no name living on the farm.

"I should imagine that he might sometime have a name," Livie said at supper. Oh, she had said this, or something like this, many times before. In fact, by now she had learned to always speak as if she were just making conversation; never, ever telling her older brothers, Jean-Charles and Guillaume, that they were wrong. "I can't just go on calling him Mean Dog. Everything ought to be named. Don't you think so?" But even her casualness didn't help her brothers understand.

"Livie, no. Actually what I am thinking is that you should be good and quiet and mind your own business," Jean-Charles barked, through a mouthful of Maman's bitter-tasting supper soup.

Livie didn't wince because this, too, had happened before. Jean-Charles, tired from working and in a bad mood, would often snap at her. Or perhaps Guillaume would say something of a similar sort, missing her point completely, because the idea was that any creature no matter how mean and nasty should have a name, not that it was her mean and nasty dog, which it wasn't. And how many times had she brought this up? More times than Livie could recall (although she was quite competent already at adding sums.) Her brothers, who were twins and much older than she, alternated between bites of food in arguing with her about it.

To prove her point, Guillaume added, "Just eat your supper, if you please," with a great deal of grumpiness intended to complete the discussion.

And of course this caused Papa to loudly enter the fray with, "You're not the *Maman!* Not the Mother at all!" and then Maman retorted, "and of course neither are you," at Papa, which as it also almost always did, sent the family spiraling into an argument about who worked each day under the hot sun to put food on the table and some tiny quantity of coins in the mattress, and who slaved over a fire and why couldn't some people remember to keep their muddy boots outside instead of tracking across the floor?

And so that was one good reason that they didn't have cows, Livie supposed, because on reflection how much more so would the arguing be worse if there was also cow manure on Papa's and her brothers' boots?

"Oh for pity's sake, just finish your supper and go to bed," were always the final words, uttered by Papa and Maman nearly simultaneously and somehow the sum of their two voices, a raucous mix of frustration, anger and exhaustion at a poor meal once again spoiled, was worse than the two voices individually considered.

Livie spooned the soup into her mouth and swallowed almost without chewing in order to avoid any spanking that she may or may not have earned with what seemed to her such a simple question. As carefully as one can do such a thing, she galloped up the stairs. And leaning back on her straw mattress, causing it to huff under the weight of her body, Livie again wondered about things. How her bed was comfortable, she had stuffed it full all by herself with clean dry straw brought in from the cattle-byre. The mattress smelled good, like lying in a field of hay, even though it crackled a little beneath her. This little room of hers was warm, warmer than outside and warmer still because the kitchen fireplace chimney went up one stone wall, and its heat radiated into the room. The rough-wood walls had been white-washed long ago, but the paint had faded into pictures that Livie could sometimes see with her eyes open just the right amount. The little window at the end of the room let in the early spring breezes. It also glowed with the evening light, as days steadily grew longer and warmer.

No one had told her that this was so, that days changed with the seasons, but she was old enough to have seen it. And not that she didn't sort of enjoy winter, even with its long, dark, cold nights and crisply gray and frosty days, but summer was better. She looked forward to its arrival. There were more things to do, more places she was allowed to go, as long as she stayed out from under foot. Apparently being *under foot* was her worst fault. Worst because it was bothering someone when they were busy. Even more so than asking questions.

She tossed away thoughts about the fuss at supper, for it was almost always like that; Papa grim and tired from working all day outside on the farm, Maman grim and tired from working all day in the house. And her two older brothers were just grim and tired. *And perhaps even though you, Olivia, aren't grim and tired,* said The Voice In Her Head, *your family is grim and tired with you.*

Yes, yes, she thought. Grim and tired. My goodness, I understand! Our life is difficult. But what's wrong with asking a question? Why, indeed, do we have a cattle-byre but no cows? More to her original point, why would no one name the mean dog? She shook her head and the straw beneath her crackled a bit more.

But in truth there was so much that she didn't understand. No, she corrected, this was her worst thing – that she didn't know why things were the way they were. Or what things were. She'd heard of school, but had never been. She'd watched seasons change, days lengthen and shrink, but didn't know why they did. Why it got cold, then warm, then cold again over and over. How was it that the moon constantly changed shape but the sun did not. Why could leaves fly on the breeze but chickens were just terrible at it.

And what it was that made wherever she, Livie, happened to be *under foot*.

"I think I'm not always under foot," she told her mother the next morning, when, first thing, Maman scolded her out of the kitchen and away from the cooking fire. Her mother, shaking her head in exasperation and waving a wet wooden spoon must have thought differently.

"Do you want a hot pot of wash-water to dump on your head? No, I shouldn't think so. Or how about if you tip tonight's soup? And the fire might burn you! Not to mention there would be no supper for the family. What do you think Papa would say about that? Now, *get!*"

Certainly, Livie didn't want a pot of hot wash on her head. Or tonight's soup, either. Both would be equally bad. So she found herself outside, alone, for now out from under foot. She stood in one place, turning in a slow circle. In front of her, the Bien house with its stone foundation, heavy wooden upper walls and tiny glass windows. Everything topped with a thick, gray thatch roof and high above a tall stone chimney topped with a fired-clay pipe to keep burning embers away from the thatch. Turn to see the oak trees deeply shading the farmyard's edge, and then out to the rye field where the grain grew that Papa would sell in town, where other farmers would sell their goods as well, to shop-keeps and townsmen and their wives. Good sour rye for baking bread. Beyond that a stone wall that marked the oat field; oats for meal, for mush, for feeding ducks to fatten them up. Turn again, to see the farmyard; the well, Maman's gardens, the stone and thatch cattle-byre. Within the cool darkness of the cattle-byre were storage bins for bales of straw and barrels of grain, for potatoes and turnips and other root vegetables. Bushel baskets for carrying goods to market. Tools and implements and rope and twine. Flat sharpening stones and stone-sharpened scythes. Rusting bits of one thing or another on the floor in the corner, waiting to be fixed or turned into something else altogether. Last fall's hay in the loft.

There, that's it, Livie thought. That's the whole entire world. Turn again, nothing more, nothing new. Just her brothers, brows shiny with sweat, coming in from the oat field to get a drink of water from the well. Just skinny chickens wandering across the farmyard, just out of reach of that Mean Dog, heading behind the cattle byre. What were those foolish chickens doing? She galloped off to see.

"Stop it, Livie! Don't chase the chickens," warned Guillaume, as he always did. He waved at her with the water-dipper that hung from a hook at the well. "It makes them flighty." Which made Livie stand still for just a moment and ask herself the question once more: what did Guillaume think could be wrong with a flighty chicken? A chicken that could fly could roost in the branches of trees. It wouldn't need to be put in the henhouse at night, right? She didn't know. *So ask him,* said The Voice In Her Head.

But when she asked her brothers this, they laughed at her.

"A flighty chicken won't lay, silly girl," Jean-Charles said, wiping the wet in his scruffy beard with his sleeve. "Everyone knows that!"

"How does everyone know that?" Livie asked, wanting to know the answer, and just possibly wanting to continue to pester her older brother.

"They just know," said Guillaume. "Now go away, Livie. You're in the way." Her brother threw a small clod of the dirt sticking to his boots at her. Then he squatted next to the well, puffing. He'd been plowing with his *araire*, pulling the plowing tool behind him as it worked like a dull knife blade against the dirt, slowly carving it open. It was Guillaume's turn this morning to pull at the araire with his strong forearms, while a tow-rope wrapped about his chest, digging his boots in with his toes to push himself forward, while Jean-Charles guided the blade of the tool from behind. Along with cows, the farm also had neither horses nor oxen to hitch to a real plow with wheels for pulling through their hilly field.

Livie frowned, partly because Guillaume was cross with her, but also because she felt bad about how hard they had to work in the field, mostly in equal measure. She didn't reply, but stood quietly and watched her brothers trudge back to work. She followed to the edge of the plowed field and stopped. They didn't fight about turns at the tow-rope, her two brothers. As twins they somehow just decided such things without saying much about it. As he picked up the plow, Guillaume wiped his face with the back of his hand, smearing dirt into his own matching scruffy beard. With a grunt, he leaned against the araire and it dug in and moved forward. In this terribly exhausting way, the soil was broken and turned to the sunshine, to be ready for planting crops.

From across the field Papa waved his hand. Livie waved happily back, until she saw that he wasn't smiling. He made his way over to her, while the brothers went back to their labors on the stubborn field.

"Leave your brothers alone!" Papa growled as he approached. "They'll never get today's work done if you keep bothering them. You're as annoying as...as those Calvinists! Stop being in the way!"

Livie drooped. She didn't mean to be in the way. She wasn't completely sure that she was at all in the way. Everyone else was grumpy because they were busy, and there was nothing for her to do. Nothing interesting. Nothing fun. Nothing that really made her feel like she was helping. Oh, but there was plenty of work, only it was boring and mostly lonely, and it wasn't important work. It was just the work that

Papa and her brothers didn't want to do. And who were the...*Cattleists*? Farmers who could more easily plow their fields? No wonder that made Papa grumpy. She needed to ask him about that one, when he wasn't working, or tired, or just grim.

"Go gather weeds for the chickens," Papa said, wiping his face with a small gray bit of rough cloth. "They're so hungry that they are squawking my ears off." Papa walked over to a bench under an oak and sat with a sigh. He was mending a shovel. He hunched over the work, carving a wet piece of rawhide he'd pulled from a wooden bucket, to cover where the shovel's wooden handle had cracked. With the sharp little blade on his knife he poked holes around the edge of the stretchy rawhide. Using the tip of the blade he worked a short bit of leather thong back and forth across the holes, like lacing a boot, then slid the rawhide down over the shovel's handle. With his fingertips just as rough as dry rawhide, Papa tugged the thong's tips tightly, tucking them through the lacing so that they wouldn't slip nor stick out from the shovel handle. He nodded his head at his handiwork. Even though she was risking being fussed at again, Livie leaned in to see. When it dried, the rawhide would shrink, tightening around the handle as strongly as the wood itself. A good fix. Papa looked up, and gave a little smile as if he was surprised to see her still there. He tapped Livie on the forehead with his hard finger, shaking his head. Then he poured the little bit of water still in the bucket on the ground and held the empty container out to her.

"Chickens," he reminded.

"Papa, what's a Cattleist?" she asked, in spite of herself. Tired, grim, Papa grinned anyhow and shook his head some more. Livie liked when Papa grinned. If he was having a good time with this, she would continue.

"You mean *Calvinist*. Calvinists live in town. They go to a church without priests."

"Is that bad?"

"Some people think it is, that's for sure," Papa said, as much to

10

himself as to her.

"Are we Calvinists?"

"No." Now, suddenly, she could hear Papa's voice beginning to change, the way it did when a frost dropped on new sprouting fields, or when it looked like rain on the drying haymow. What was Papa's problem with Calvinists? she wondered. It was probably not a good time, but were they good questions? She pushed ahead.

"What, then? What are we, Papa?"

"We are Church of Rome. Yes. But I am too busy to go into town on a Sunday and spend all day there, just to sit and pray." Ah, his contented voice returned. Then they were good questions. The rain didn't fall. Papa wiped his face again. "You, of course, are a heathen."

"Oh. Is that...good?" Livie asked softly. "I mean, to be a heathen?" Papa gave a snort, more-than-half-laugh and a little less than half I've-heard-enough-questions.

"Your Maman would say no. But with you, girl, there is no choice."

"Could we go to church sometime?"

"Oh...yes, sometime," Papa answered, as if he were daydreaming.

"And we could pray, then?" Livie was hopeful, not completely sure what praying was. Papa had explained it before, but mostly it sounded like talking with The Voice In Her Head, and she already did that a fair bit.

"For things we cannot have? A waste of time," Papa said. Everything bad was a waste of time, the worst thing Papa could imagine.

"Still, I'd like to try it, sometime," Livie said, wistfully. "Do you think?"

Papa looked at her, tapping his lip with a finger. He was thinking about something, but like he so often did, he wasn't saying what he was thinking. Instead he smiled a sad sort of smile and shook his head.

"Go, girl. You stand still like a statue, when you have things to do.

Go!"

"Yes, Papa," Livie said, and taking the bucket by the rope handle, she ran off. One thing she did know very well for all her questions and being underfoot was not to talk back.

OK. Time to collect weeds. Yes, weeds. Oh, Papa, she'd said before. Weeds? Why not just let the chickens go over to the weeds themselves? Let me herd them over. Why not? Because she already knew Papa's answer to that one. *Foolish child, if you teach those chickens to walk to the weeds themselves, then you teach them to walk past you to the oat field and the rye field. Do you think that birds can tell the difference? Do you even know the difference?*

She knew the difference, and she also knew full well that chickens could not tell the difference between weeds and oats and so once they discovered that the oats were there would eat all of it that they could stuff into their gizzards, and that was why she had to run up the hill to the top, past where the farm's crops were planted, above the trees that lined the lane and gave shade to the farmyard, to where the rocks stuck through the soil and only weeds would grow. It wouldn't do for chickens to roam around up here, she understood, not where all of the kites and kestrels could see them. So it was Livie's job to protect the oats and rye from the chickens and the chickens from the kestrels that eat chickens, if you are not careful. This was pretty important work, she knew full well.

Livie scuffed her wooden sabots in the dust of the lane, away from the low stone walls that edged the farmyard. Each clippity-clop step she took carried her up, up and away from the farm. Like her father and brothers, she wiped at her own brow with the sleeve of her old dress. Turning, she looked back. Papa's farm was far below now. She turned around, slowly. Here where she stood was the highest point of the highest hill around, and it was quiet and breezy and she was alone. No one else saw what she saw. It was so high that it was like flying. Out there above the bright-green leafed trees she saw a short-steeple of a church, pointing out of the leaves like a lone tall tree. Just beyond it, a curve of dark green. Beyond that, more trees, low hills fading away into the distance. Places she'd never been.

Livie turned to look at the wildflowers. She knew none of their names, only that each one was beautiful and mysterious and special. The pale white lace-flower, with its soft bed of tiny blooms atop a thin stalk, perfect for a bumblebee to rest on. She sniffed, her nose wrinkling at the odor. Wasn't its perfume bitter, though? *Not everything is meant for little girls*, said The Voice In Her Head. *This flower is meant for bumblebees.* That made sense, Livie decided. She sniffed each wildflower – the bright yellow sprays that looked like flames spreading in the fields of weeds. The tiny and delicate pale blue blooms hiding beneath the bent weeds at the edge of the cart lane. None of them had a pleasant scent. Indeed, these were not intended for the pleasure of little girls, but for the bees and wasps that landed on them, looking for something. She wondered what that something was.

Plucking the seed tops of white-lace and pale blue and the flame bloom, she filled her bucket halfway. On top of the seeds, she filled the bucket with the softest, newest green leaves of the grasses that sprouted in clumps near the lane. By mid-summer these plants would be crisp and brown and would make shushing noises in the breezes that touched and spun the dust up here on the hill's peak. Then they would be of no good for feeding chickens.

The one whose name she knew – thistle – grew up here, too, with purple heads like the crown of the king of France himself. She loved to see them blowing in the wind, royally waving at the crowds of other weeds. *Yes, yes, thank you, thank you all so much*, said The Voice. *You don't even know anything about the King.* Oh, but I can imagine, she thought. The tall flowers could look out over the countryside, above the roofs of Livie's house and the cattle-byre and the cold-barn where the potatoes and carrots and parsnips and other vegetables were stored, and down past Papa's sloping fields to the road which led to town. How much more could one ask?

How nice would they also be growing around the farm? Blooming around the stone foundation of the house, or next to Maman's vegetable garden. Livie could wake each summer morning to the buzzing of bumblebees.

Livie wondered if Maman also might love beautiful flowers growing in her garden. Perhaps she even knew the names for them. If not, then they could make up new names together. Livie giggled while she snapped off the stems of each flower, and placed them gently in her bucket so the blooms wouldn't be damaged. *You must have the roots to plant the flower* said The Voice. Of course, she thought. I'm so stupid. She'd watched Guillaume and Jean-Charles before as they worked in the tomato patch, cautiously weeding so that they wouldn't damage the plants or their branches or their tender flowers. She tugged on one of the lace plants and it broke. Sorry, little flower, she thought. She set the bloom down gently, as if it were a baby bird that had fallen from its nest. Livie picked a different one. Scrabbling at the dirt beneath the blooming plant, the next one came reluctantly with a clump around its roots. *Perfect.* She placed this one in her bucket. *Next!* It was more difficult with the yellow flame-flower, because its stem was fragile, but Livie was persistent. Even harder was the thorny thistle. Eventually, she filled her bucket with the beautiful blooms.

A movement in the corner of her eye made her turn. My goodness! Livie stared. A deer, grass drooping from its mouth, stood on the far side of the hill meadow looking at her. If deer could be amazed back, Livie thought, than this creature was so. Its red coat was as bright as dry clay. Short antlers, like spikes on its head. *He's probably wondering where yours are*, said The Voice. *Wants to have a fight with you, maybe.* Or maybe he wants me to stop picking his flowers, Livie decided. She held her breath, wondering if she could go closer to the deer. But after a long moment, something must have alarmed the creature, for it raised its tail and dashed away. Livie sighed to see it go.

She galloped down the hill, looking down at the path so that every clip-clop step in her *sabots* was sure, racing faster and faster until the breeze blew in her ears like a windstorm, the kind of storm that meant that summer was truly here, with clouds that seemed to reach fat gray fingers up to heaven, trying to pluck someone up like the hand of God. Like God's own hand. Looking up from her feet, she imagined Him lifting her up into the sky so that she might fly, out over the town. The world was larger than her farmyard, larger than this hill that they lived on. *Beautiful*, said the quiet, annoying little voice in her head. *Absolutely lovely. But you being up in the sky, Olivia, is like fish walking on the land. This is silly thinking, just like your brothers always say. And if you can't get more serious, you will always be a little girl to them, good only for picking weeds and staying out of the way.*

"What in the world do you have there?" asked Maman as she ran into the farmyard. "Weeds?"

"Flowers, Maman. I see them all the time on top of the hill. They're for you to have in a garden. I even got their roots, so that they can be planted." Livie set down her bucket and showed Maman how carefully she had gathered each flowering plant. She smiled widely. Maman frowned.

"Foolish child, these are weeds. You cannot have a garden of weeds." Maman shook her head slowly. "They will spread to other gardens, to the herbs and the tomatoes and potatoes. Their roots would choke the plants we need, drink their water. That is what weeds do."

Livie's smile wilted. She didn't know that.

"They are so beautiful; I thought that they were flowers."

Maman turned the thistle gingerly between her fingers, admiring its purple head. Then she pulled it off its stem and dropped it in the bucket.

"I wish that we might have flowers, but we cannot. We have only time for the things we must grow to make money to live. You're too young to understand that."

Livie was crestfallen. She picked up the bucket and walked to the byre to feed the chickens.

Chapter Two

Livie looked. Up and down the lane. Up the lane to the top of the hill which led to Purgatoire's farm. Down the lane which led, so she had always been told, all the way into Town. Although where *town* actually was could be clearly seen from the top of the hill, up where Livie picked chicken-weeds, town itself was mostly hidden by trees. There was a river down there, too; Livie could only just see how it curved close to the edge of town, and other hills beyond it. Not so far away, even. Some days, when the breeze was just right she thought she could sniff the fragrant kitchen-fire smoke from town. Town - what it looked like and who was there and how they sounded and acted and what they did - was actually a mystery and a wonder. When she thought about going to town it was something that both caused her to worry and yet called out to her. But the truth was that she knew nothing of it. Nothing!

Because Livie's family never went to town. Oh, it was a long walk down there and back, and a complete waste of an entire day, Papa would say every time Livie asked *could they go to town?*, or *why didn't they go to town?*, or even *isn't there anything we need in town, we haven't been there in such a long while?*

That last question wasn't even true. Livie had never been there, ever. However – and this was very, very important – going to town was one of those things that she would only mention and then must leave alone. She didn't want *town* to be something that Papa thought about whenever he was unhappy or frustrated with her. Perhaps someday he would change his mind, decide that he did need something in town, or that it was better for him to go to town to sell their goods, rather than letting Purgatoire take everything for him. And then, just maybe, he would take her with him. But not today, because Purgatoire was already on his way here.

Livie looked up again. She'd never seen it either, but their neighbor Purgatoire's farm was just up the lane and down the other side of the hill from the Bien farm. So close. And it had so much better soil than theirs. How many tired evenings after supper had Papa had said that he knew this was true? Often enough. Also, Purgatoire owned a large wagon and strong and healthy oxen for pulling his wagon. And the old man also had three men-for-hire who worked in his fields, while on the Bien farm Papa only had Jean-Charles and Guillaume, and thank goodness neither of them was for-hire, or Papa couldn't even have afforded them. Oh, my, that had been said at supper more than once. And not with a happy voice from Papa, either.

It was Papa who called the old man Purgatoire, often preceded with a growl or following a sneer. Apparently this was a joke of some sort that Livie didn't get, because Guillaume or Jean-Charles would usually chuckle when Papa said the old man's name. And although Papa didn't like him – not really – and Livie was pretty sure that neither did Guillaume or Jean-Charles, they were always polite to Purgatoire in person. My goodness, they called him *Monsieur*, as if he were a proper gentleman, and hurried to fetch baskets or get him a dipper of fresh water from the well. As for herself, Livie wasn't too sure.

Purgatoire was ugly and old, short in the legs, but with a long skinny neck and a bent-beak of a nose. His oddly-placed gray chin-whiskers made no sense, for they covered nothing completely nor well. And what had Maman said? "His hair," Maman said, "is always poking like dirty straw out from under his hat." And although his farm was successful – this Papa had said – the man wore strangely colored patches on his old coat. That made Maman stand with her hands on her hips when she said, "So why doesn't he get himself a new one?" Alright then, Livie had decided. He's messy, and ugly, and has patched clothing. What of it? She'd looked down at her own dress. I'm messy and patched, and probably ugly myself.

Maybe he's just a crazy old man, Livie thought. Just a crazy...but wait. Her ears perked. She heard the great creaking wheels with their iron tires even before she saw anything. Here Purgatoire came, over the top and down the gentle slope of the hill walking in front of his laboring oxen, holding traces leading back to their snouts as they pulled a wagon load of potatoes or perhaps carrots and turnips. The idea of it made her smile. She had to admit it was a pleasant change from things, and when he brought animals to sell, like chattering hens or squawking ducks, it was always a special event. And the beasts had collars made of leather, with bells attached, so that there was a cheerful clink-clank with every swinging step they took.

Livie scampered out to the lane to see him coming. She imagined it to be a carnival wagon; the creaking and clanging, the puffing breaths the oxen took, all music to her ears. What surprise would Purgatoire have this morning? She listened, and then she knew. Today the little old man's wagon was stacked with basket-crates of young piglets. Every bump on the road jostled them around in their cages, and the piglets let everyone know with their irritated squeals that this didn't make them happy. Purgatoire waved to her as she watched from the side of the road. As if on cue the baskets let out another piglet-chorus. Livie laughed and clapped her hands.

"And how are you this morning, maiden-of-the-mountain?" he

called to her.

Livie held a bit of her dress-hem and curtseyed.

"Everything goes well in your kingdom, I hope? No dragons or ogres, at least not so far as I can see." The old man held his hand up to his brow, as if he was blocking the glare of the morning's sun, even though his old hat shaded his eyes. He winked one eye at her and it wasn't a mean wink. Unlike almost everyone else, Purgatoire never ignored her.

"Here, Livie-bean," he said, mispronouncing her name for fun. He tossed her something he pulled from his coat pocket. She held out her apron to catch it. A radish, flipping towards her, brilliant pink-red, a small gift. Purgatoire led the oxen to the cattle-byre where Guillaume and Jean-Charles waited with baskets of tomatoes. Livie walked behind the wagon, nibbling on the bitter-sweet radish.

Papa came up behind her.

"So he's got piglets. How many, I wonder? Sounds like a good dozen, maybe more. Both of his sows must have thrown litters. Ah, someday..." Papa whispered, as much to himself as to Livie. He had been on the hill, walking the sloping field, when he'd heard Purgatoire's wagon rumbling on the road. "He's got enough piglets to sell. If we had piglets, I would feed them potato skins to make them grow big."

Livie grinned at the thought of little piglets running around for her to herd.

"We could smoke them into bacon," her father continued in a low voice. "How dear is bacon at market?" Her smile melted away. She hadn't thought of that. Pigs become bacon. Suddenly there was a clamor of barking and squealing of piglets. Papa clomped away from Livie without another word and she followed him over to Purgatoire's wagon. Her father dipped his head in a small bow when the little old man offered his good-morning. Guillaume came up from the cattle-byre where he had hushed the mean dog with no name. The piglets settled down again in their crates.

"It is a good thing to have such stout rope for your dog," said Purgatoire to Papa with a smile. "Else you would owe me for some piglets."

Papa grunted. Livie wondered whether her father wished that the dog was gone, or that it had indeed come off of the rope and given Purgatoire a run around the yard.

"Good tomatoes, Monsieur Bien," the ugly little farmer complimented Papa. "How very early to have such nice red fruit, eh?"

"The rain has held off," Papa said quietly, as if he didn't want to remark about the weather at all. One of the things he always said at supper was that to speak about the weather was to put a hex on it.

"And how are your boys?" Purgatoire looked at Jean-Charles and Guillaume. "You both are getting as strong as my oxen."

Livie's brothers scuffed their boots at the kind words.

"They work hard, when they work," said Papa, pointing abruptly at the baskets and the wagon. The boys began carefully loading the baskets of tomatoes behind the piglets. The little animals could smell the fresh-picked fruit and grunted now to be fed.

"It's a good thing we have good cages, or I would owe you for all of your tomatoes. They are hungry little creatures," the little man laughed at himself for turning around his previous jest.

"Yes, we couldn't have you owing me money," Papa said slowly. Purgatoire waggled his head in agreement. He held out his hand, then lowered it when Papa didn't shake it.

"They should all sell, Monsieur Bien. I am confident of that. On a good sunny market day? I could advance you now, minus my two-percent for transporting. If you would prefer, of course," he said.

Livie understood that this was a good thing, that Purgatoire would take the tomatoes to market, but pay Papa right now for all of them.

"I couldn't ask you to be so generous," Papa began softly. He took a deep breath, as if he was going to say something else, but the little man spoke.

"It is nothing. We are neighbors," Purgatoire said.

Livie could see the smile in the ugly man's eyes. It was not unkind. But Papa couldn't find a way to make himself happy.

"It is enough that you carry my goods to the market," he said. Papa's voice was harder now.

Purgatoire shrugged slightly, his smile still in place. He picked up the leather traces and the oxen shook their heads with a jangle of their neck-bells.

"Well then, Monsieur Bien, I am off to make our fortune. Monsieurs?" He bowed slightly to Jean-Charles and Guillaume. "And my dear maiden-of-the-mountain."

Livie giggled as the man bowed deeply towards her. Then with a small tug, Purgatoire got the oxen moving forward and the piglets squealed with the movement, causing Livie to giggle even more. The wagon rumbled down the hill road. Livie knew that down that hill the road would make a turn and head towards the town.

Livie's brothers must have known that Papa was now in a rotten mood, because they marched themselves back into the fields as soon as Purgatoire's wagon was out of sight. Livie stood still as her father opened and shut his big hands, making fists and releasing them. It was always so on market-day, she thought.

"If I had a damned wagon, I could take my own goods to market," Papa growled under his breath. "Why should I pay Purgatoire to take them for me? And why couldn't I have my own stall, selling tomatoes and cabbages and carrots and even herbs? There are people who cannot grow their own herbs. Why not sell them? But without a wagon, that little gnome Purgatoire must take them for me. I just know the old man sells my tomatoes to a shopkeeper who buys them in bulk. The lowest price he can get." He shook his head. He waved a hand at the empty down-hill road, as if he was disgusted with the slope of the road itself causing this situation. Then he looked at Livie.

"We can't grow piglets unless we can afford the sow. We can't afford the sow without getting a better price on our goods. We can't get a better price for goods until we have a wagon to take the goods to town. And then oxen? For crying out loud!"

"*Oui*, Papa. Yes, Papa. For crying out loud," Livie agreed. She lifted her fist to shake it at the empty road. But then, as if Papa was only just now seeing her for the first time, he frowned.

"That's enough, Livie. We can't wish for what we can't have. Go do your chores, *cherie*."

And with that surprising *cherie*, that "sweetie", Livie skipped off to weed Maman's herbs.

Maman grew her herbs close to the house, to protect them from the sun and the rain and the wind and everything else. Livie enjoyed hunkering down in among these plants, each one with its own heady perfume and memory. The rosemary, like a little Yuletide tree, smelled like Maman's best dress. Maman kept a sachet of rosemary in the dress, which was folded around it, and which resided in the chest in her parent's small bedroom. The dress was made of soft linen and dyed a beautiful blue, as blue as morning sky, as blue as the ocean must be. Livie had never seen the ocean before, but was absolutely sure that it was such a gorgeous blue.

"Is it far from here?" she had asked Maman, when once her mother had worn the dress to town, to the Fair. That was two years ago, and Maman had looked so lovely, so young, that Livie almost didn't recognize her. Her hair was down, too, and combed with the silver comb, the one that was so special because Papa had given it to Maman on their wedding night. She'd asked Maman if she would comb her hair with that silver comb, and Maman had shaken her head, just once. Not now, she said. When you're older, yes, but not now. The answer she received for so many things. When can I go to town with you? When can I comb my hair? When can I...?

Thyme, coriander, marjoram, fennel. Rosemary and savory. She rubbed her hand through the thyme, releasing a smell like a breeze carrying springtime itself. Nearby, leaves of spearmint, fresh and sharp. Livie pinched one off and nibbled at it, the taste so clean that it tickled her nose. Beneath the plant, an orange ladybug crawled on the

22

dirt. Livie put her hand down on the ground for the ladybug to climb on, but the tiny creature turned instead. *See, Olivia, your little hand is not a bridge, but a wall,* said The Voice In Her Head. *I suppose you think that we each need someone to treat poorly.*

"No!" Livie said, lifting her hand. "I'm sorry, little one. Go on your way." She began gently pulling out the new sprouting weeds beneath the herb plants. The early summer sun was warm on her shoulders and along with the mixed scents of herb it made her eyes heavy. After a while, she rested her head on her arm, and soon she slept.
******

"Asleep," someone squeaked.

"Yes. We must go around." A different squeak.

"But I don't want to go around," squeaked the first. "Over, perhaps. Or under."

"No, leave it alone. Go around."

"It's not an *it*. It's a girl. I mean, she's a girl." That was the first again.

"So you're so brave? You go ahead and say something to her."

"Pardon me. You're in my way, *mademoiselle*," squeaked the first. Livie opened her eyes. There, down the end of her nose. A mouse.

No, Olivia. Two mice, said The Voice. They stepped back as Livie inhaled sharply.

"So terribly sorry to bother, miss, but you see our house is over there," the first mouse squeaked, pointing with one tiny finger of tiny paw up and over Livie's shoulder. "And you're blocking the way, you understand. But I don't want to trouble you, of course." He gave her a little bow.

"Oh, my," Livie said, and the two mice jumped back, squealing, covering their tiny ears with their paws.

Too loud, The Voice said. *You have to speak quietly. No shouting here.*

"I'm sorry," Livie whispered. "I mean both for shouting, and for being in your way." She carefully sat up and dusted off her dress-front.

23

"Not at all," said the first mouse. He skittered past Livie, and made his way into the grass and towards the cattle-byre.

Livie frowned. *Well what do you think about that?* asked The Voice In Her Head. I don't quite know what to think, she thought in reply.

"Mice can't talk," she said aloud. The second mouse looked at her quizzically.

"'course we can. We're talking now, aren't we?" Its whiskers waggled in a friendly manner.

"But I know mice can't talk. I don't know how you are doing it now," said Livie.

"Well a great deal of sense that makes," the second mouse seemed to smile. Then it lowered its voice and said mockingly, "you can't talk, although you're talking, and I don't know how." The little creature sat up on its hind legs and covered its mouth with its paws as it loosed a peal of squeaking laughter.

Livie decided that it must be a girl mouse and smiled. She couldn't help herself. It didn't make much sense after all, but she knew so few girls – just Maman - that it was nice to meet another.

"Well, why don't you talk with us all of the time?" she asked.

"Who? You? Most of the time, you people aren't very polite," the second mouse held up her tiny accusing finger.

Livie's eyebrows rose and the little creature put its paws on its hips.

"First of all, you shouldn't show your teeth when you smile. That way you don't look like you're going to eat anyone."

"I didn't think of that," Livie whispered. She smiled carefully with her lips together.

"Well, there you are," said the second mouse. "And don't try to trap us, or sic the big dog on us. And we won't even talk about how we thank goodness that you don't have..." she paused dramatically. "...*un chat.*" A cat!

Livie thought about that, how she had often wished that she had a little kitty to be her companion, her playmate. Now she wasn't so sure. She liked this little mouse.

"Well, like I said, I didn't know," she said with a touch of petulance in her voice.

"There are certainly many things you don't know. Don't you go to school?"

"No," said the little girl. "Of course not."

"My goodness!" said the girl-mouse. "Even mice go to school. How else can one learn what food to eat and how to avoid being trapped? At school we are taught how to get away from the cat, and which herbs go with tomatoes and which with potatoes. We learn how the summer is warm and why the winter is cool. Which clouds mean a beautiful day, and when they mean rain is arriving soon. You should be learning things, too. How can you know anything until you go to school?"

"School is in town."

"Then I suppose it follows that you would need to go to town," the girl-mouse replied.

"But there is no school for girls. And even if there was, my family needs me...here."

The mouse stared at her for a moment as if contemplating such a story, then looked around.

"You have a pretty garden," she admired. "*Un belle jardin.*"

"Thank you," Livie said, although it was Maman's garden. This was indeed a polite mouse.

"Too bad there are no flowers in it, though," continued the mouse. She shook her head slowly. "Yes, yes. I believe that you should have lilies. The sun shines so fine here that lilies would do very well."

"Lilies," Livie repeated. She'd never heard of them. Were they pretty? Perhaps Maman would like to have them here, but just hadn't considered the idea. "How do you grow them? Are they dear?"

"I have no idea. I'm just a mouse." The girl mouse giggled again in peals of squeaks. "But you do have a nice garden," she said to Livie, and started to follow her friend towards the cattle-byre.

"Actually, it is my Maman's garden," said Livie, hesitantly. The little creature stopped.

"But you do the weeding?"

"Yes," said Livie.

"And you fetch the herbs when your mother asks?"

Livie thought about plucking sprigs of thyme for Maman's stew, or rosemary for her sachets. Yes, she did a fair bit of fetching.

"She sends me to get things when she needs them. And weeding is my chore."

"Well then you know about gardening; that is for certain. And it sounds to me like this is also your garden, *mademoiselle.* Of course, I don't know. That's just my opinion." And with that the second mouse ran off.

****

"Wake up, you lazy girl!" Maman shouted.

Chapter Three

Maman stood over her, frowning. "I sent you out here to do a task, and you take a nap? You are good for nothing!"

Livie jumped to her feet, but couldn't dodge her mother's hand, which had at the end of it a wooden spoon, dripping watery gravy. The spoon caught her on her backside and stung. She yelped, and took off towards the cattle-byre.

"Livie! Useless girl, lazy girl! Come back here right now!" That is what Maman shouted. Livie didn't come back, right now or otherwise, and knew immediately that this was trouble, but suddenly she had worse problems than thinking about what Maman would do if she didn't *come back right now*. In her haste to get away, she hadn't given thought to where she was going. And Livie had run smack into the mean, nameless dog that her brothers tied up down at the cattle-byre.

The big black dog didn't bark at Livie. Instead, it rumbled in its throat, like distant thunder. Livie skidded to a halt and stared, frozen in her tracks. The creature's teeth, long and yellow, peeked out from its jowls. Its eyes were dark and rheumy with old age. Still, it looked ferocious. And particularly, even snarlingly, hungry. Did dogs eat little girls? Livie supposed that they could if they wanted to, so probably they did. And could this really be the dog she had wanted to name? This was no pet dog at all, but a beast. No wonder her brothers had laughed at her.

"Oh, my. I'm so very sorry," she told the big black dog. Livie could smell the dog's sour breath and winced to be so close. She looked around without moving her head. The rope, she noticed, was tied around its neck, but it was slack on the ground, connected back to a pillar in the cattle-byre. When the dog decided to lunge for her, it would reach her with no trouble.

"I didn't mean to wake you," the girl said, in a squeaky whisper. She felt very...mouselike. She wanted to apologize to the dog, even explain that she had just been awakened herself, but was trying to hold her breath at the same time. "Papa always tells me not to run so much, because I will get into trouble. I should know better. And so here I am, bothering you." Still, she didn't move. The dog stopped growling. It tilted its head at her, curious. For some reason she was just as curious and she tilted her own as well.

"Wait, you're not so bad, are you? Certainly you don't really want to bite me." But the truth was that Livie wasn't certain about this at all. Indeed, she decided that it looked as if the big black dog was sizing her up for a meal. I could turn and run, she thought. But then he might leap at her while she turned. And she very much did not want to be eaten. Friendly, she decided. All I have to do is be friendly, and it will be friendly back to me. Livie slowly held out her open hand.

"Livie!" roared Guillaume. Her brother had chosen that moment to come from behind the cattle-byre. Livie startled, snatching her hand away, and the dog snapped at her, its yellow teeth just missing her fingers.

"*Non!* No!" Waving his hands wildly, her brother shouted at the big black dog, which turned to see the new commotion. Livie bolted, as the farmyard erupted into a roar of barking and yelling. There was no point in staying for her brother's scolding, or to see if Papa came, or Maman, to yell at her for her additional foolishness. She reached the lane in a flash, and continued on up the hill, her wooden shoes carrying her along, clomping toward the top where she knew things would be quieter, if not less trouble. She only stopped when she could no longer hear barking or shouting.

Sitting in the tall grass, her dress spread about her like a tablecloth, Livie sighed as she panted. Here at the top of the hill, there was only the slightest of breezes and it was very hot, and now she was thirsty. Her mouth felt full of dust, which it probably was, and her nose wanted to sneeze, but just wouldn't. Hungry as well, she nibbled on a blade of grass. It had that...green...taste of summer, not good but not unpleasant, either.

Blue-gray clouds scudded by overhead, chasing a scattering of starlings. She thought about the little mouse and what it had said. One should know if clouds mean a beautiful day, or if they mean that rain is coming. Why birds can fly and people cannot. She pulled the bit of grass from her lips. Why did it already taste like summer?

Livie wondered at these mysteries. Her head actually hurt a little at how could there be so many things she didn't know, and not knowing what must she do to learn them. She looked out over the countryside. If there was a school in town, could she actually go there? Or did she have to be a boy? That made no sense, because Jean-Charles and Guillaume did not go to school, but spent every day working the farm. But they were grown-ups, or nearly so. Had they gone to school when they were her age? Why had she never bothered to ask them about that?

She made a fist and shook it at...nothing. It's not much to ask to go to school, she decided. *Oh, but it is a lot to ask*, said The Voice In Her Head. *You are not the only one in your family. What about your Papa?* Yes, she agreed after thinking about it. Papa needs a wagon more than anything else, to bring everything to market himself. And what good is a wagon without oxen to pull it? Just like that, she realized that there was no point in ever bringing it up at supper, should she at some point wander back down the hill and suffer the punishment that was surely waiting for her.

Disappointed, Livie flopped back into the deep weeds and gazed at the sky. Blue and clouds. Blue again and then more clouds. Bigger clouds.

Not rain clouds, right? *Of course, rain clouds*, said The Voice. *I believe your day is about to get worse.* I don't see how, she thought. Maman's mad at me, as it seems she always is. If he wasn't already mad before, Papa is surely mad now, for the rain will spoil a perfect market day afternoon. And if it rains too much here, the tomatoes still on vines will not be so fine as they were before. At the very least, Guillaume is mad at me for bothering the big black dog. And the big black dog is hungry. It's probably angry with me now, too, for reasons only a dog can know.

When the first big droplet of rain hit her *plunk* on the nose, Livie stood. She looked off, down the hill. The town was hidden, behind a curtain. Rain? Yes. It was already raining in town. Oh, why couldn't she live in town? she asked herself. How nice it must be to live in a house with a comfortable fire-place and friendly neighbors to talk to. Having things to do that didn't always get one in trouble. Although what those things were, Livie couldn't imagine. Not chasing after weeds to feed the chickens, no. Maybe mending trousers and resewing buttons on shirts? Then again, Maman always reminded her to stay out of the candle-light while she worked on Papa's or Jean-Charles' buttons, replacing the *petit* wooden disks when they snapped in two from age. Or cooking! But Livie didn't do well stirring soup or working in the herb-garden either. Surely people in town didn't putter in herb-gardens like country-folk. She imagined that they had wonderful flower gardens, with different colored blooms as bright as a rainbow. How...fantastic, she thought, to have a flower garden.

As if her silent thoughts had somehow been heard, at that moment the afternoon sun peeked out from a crack in the clouds and threw a beam down over the town. Rainbow! Livie reached out her hand, the stripes of yellow, red and blue appeared to be the same height above the town as her hiding place on the hill. Weren't rainbows made of sparkling lights high in the sky, out of the reach of children? Didn't they blow away in the wind? Such was the story that Maman had told her, long ago when she was little and Maman still used to sit on her bed and tell her stories. Livie pushed the hair out of her eyes; the breeze that couldn't even cool her off a moment ago was making her chilly now. *Of course, Olivia, they are rain clouds*, The Voice repeated firmly. *And still they come, and you are here.* Then, reminding her of the growl of the big black dog, the clouds thundered together in the distance.

But Livie didn't go home, didn't get up and walk back down the hill. Instead, glancing about her, she looked for somewhere to get out of the weather. The weeds began to sway in the freshening wind. The sound they made was like someone shushing her, finger to their lips. Hush child! Be quiet, Livie, can't you?

There were no trees up here on the hilltop; none, that is, large enough for a young girl to hide beneath. Livie stood. I don't want to go home, she thought. Add this moment to everything else she had done wrong today: standing outside in a coming storm, confronting the big dog, sleeping in the herbs, asking too many questions. No punishment she could imagine would be awful enough. Her dress blew around her and whipped in the wind. At her feet, the purple thistles bowed their heads at her beneath the gusts.

Time to go, Maiden-of-the-Mountain. Where, she asked The Voice. *There. If you're not going home, go there.* Livie turned. On the far side of the hill, she saw it: in the meadow of weeds was a large rock jutting from the earth like a broken tooth. She had been over there before, walking among the weeds, but it had never revealed itself. Could it have just now pushed out of the ground? No. It was always there, but the weeds were flattened presently so that she might see. Go! said The Voice. Go now! She ran towards the rock, bounding over the lane and through the weeds. This was harder than she thought it might be. The storm had caught up with her, blowing her dress and hair every which way, pushing her as if it didn't want to let her get away. The deep rumble of thunder chased her, too, and the sun was gone now, the sky a not-night darkness.

Hard droplets of rain splashing against her face soon had her gasping. The little girl stole a look over her shoulder. No rainbow now, just the deep grays of clouds. Lightning crackled and she startled, almost falling in the deep weeds. She reached the rock, large enough for her to duck under, curling up beneath its overhang. She looked around. Just in time. The curtain of rain closed behind her.

Livie clutched her apron to her face, like a mask, to keep the spray of out of her eyes. Her dress became soaked as the wind whipped about her. The sandy dust around and beneath the rock blew into her hair and ears and against her hands and stung her skin. I must look a fright now, she thought. At least she wasn't scared much, not of mere rain and strong wind. Then lightning flashed, and she saw it through her clenched eyes and the apron's cloth. The crash of thunder rolled over her, causing her to jump and bang her head against the rock. Livie changed her mind. She decided that she *was* scared. What if this was only the beginning? For the wind seemed to grow even stronger, pulling, trying to pry her out from beneath the rock with invisible fingers. *This was not a good idea*, said The Voice In Her Head. *Not good at all.* I've had too many not-good ideas today, if you ask me, she replied. But I don't know what to do. Lightning flickered again, followed by a crackle and crash of thunder.

The storm? It's God, and it's because he's mad at you. Livie pondered that one. She imagined Him lifting her up like a dried thistle, carrying her through the sky. Or just tossing her. He could be mad at her, she supposed. Everyone else was.

So, get up and go, The Voice told her. *You can run home, right this moment.* No I can't, Livie thought. I was almost blown down by the wind before. If it wanted, the storm could blow me right off the hill-top.

Then, through all of the wind and rain and between the thunder's mighty rumbles, she heard something different, something which didn't belong in all the noise of a storm.

The deep clang of ox-bells.

Chapter Four

Livie couldn't see through the driving rain, but she trusted her hearing. Nothing else sounded like those bells, clanging from the collars on Purgatoire's oxen. Crawling out from beneath the overhang, she was immediately soaked by the driving rain. A boom of thunder! Ducking back under the rock, she thought to herself. I can't. The storm is too much. But she knew that she shouldn't wait. The market was closed. Purgatoire was going home, down the back side of the hill. Better hurry!

The wind did seem to try to toss her. Or else her feet became tangled in the rain-trampled grass. Either way, Livie fell as she ran, her *sabots* slipping from her feet. Water streamed from her hair into her face. Well, at least the mud is washing off, she thought. She found one shoe, slipping it back on, but the other eluded her. There it was, hidden beneath a sheaf of pressed-down grass. Once more, she heard the bells.

"Hello!" she called, but the wind carried her voice away from the lane. Arms up for some protection, Livie leaned into the wind. Her dress was wet and heavy, the wind trying to tug on it, to push her here and there, anywhere but the direction of the lane. She could barely keep her eyes open against the stinging rain. It was so dark and raining so hard now that Livie couldn't see at all.

"Who is out there?" someone shouted. "Stay away, thief!" The bells jangled again against the howling wind.

"But I'm not a thief," Livie called and she ran towards the voice, and the bells.

It was Purgatoire.

"My God!" The old man cried from his seat on the wagon. He was trying to make his way over the hill, heading back from Market. He yanked on the leads and the oxen lowed. Clambering down, the old man slipped on the wet ground and nearly fell himself. Then he bowed to her, water streaming off of his tri-corn. He shouted, "Mademoiselle Bien, may I ask what are you doing out in this storm?"

"Monsieur Purgatoire! The storm came too fast and I tried to hide. I was stuck under a rock. Over there." Livie pointed back across the meadow, but of course there was nothing to be seen in the gloom and downpour. She waited for the old man to begin yelling at her for being out in the storm in the first place. What in the world was she doing? Didn't she know better? But Purgatoire only shook his head. He snatched off his own patched overcoat, which was soaked through, and wrapped it around her.

"Up, girl. Get up on the wagon." The old man helped lift her up onto the bench and pulled himself up beside her.

"What in the name of the Lord were you doing under a rock?" he shouted, because the wind was whipping now, with an unearthly sound.

With the rumbling thunder occasionally interrupting her, Livie tried to explain about the herb garden and Maman catching her there and the big black dog wanting to eat her and of course her running up here to get away from everyone, and the storm approaching so swiftly that she'd hidden beneath the rock. She left out only the part about the two talking mice and their useful advice.

"My goodness, that's more like an adventure than a story. I'm surprised, however, that you left out the parts where you battled the ogres. I'm sure that was exciting as well." Lightning crackled overhead and thunder exploded. The old man flinched and Livie clenched her eyes shut.

"No ogres, Monsieur Purgatoire."

"Oh, well. We'll have to find them next time. Right now, we need to get you home."

Livie was wet and cold and hungry. She couldn't imagine feeling more uncomfortable and unhappy. Despite not wanting to cry, she felt her eyes brim with tears.

"I'm afraid that Papa and Maman will be so angry with me."

"Well, then," said Purgatoire, leaning close so that she could hear him. "Don't think about that right now. Let's just think about getting out of this weather. Right?" With one hand he swiped the water from his face.

"You just stay there under my coat. I will take you back to your family's house," Purgatoire shouted. "We'll get this wagon turned around." He gave the leads a tug and the oxen took faltering steps, rattling their bells and slowly starting the wagon down the lane.

Purgatoire whistled at the beasts, but the noise was swept away by the wind.

"We have a problem," he shouted to Livie. He pointed at the oxen. It wasn't possible to turn the wagon around, not on the thin little lane. What with the wind blowing so hard and the pelting rain and the lightning and thunder frightening the oxen; the boys, as he called them, didn't wish to turn around.

"It's a bit like steering a sailing ship, you know. Sometimes the wind won't let you do what you think you must. We'll let them take us how they want." Purgatoire told her that the best thing to do was to continue on to his farm and wait for the storm to blow over.

"But we have a bigger problem. I know your parents must be worried," the old man said, wiping his eyes with his soaking shirt. He reached over and pulled the collar of his coat up over Livie's neck and face. "Stay in there. We'll get you home as soon as we can."

Inside the wet overcoat, Livie shivered and sniffled. The coat smelled of sweat and smoke, and...piglets? Suddenly, however, she found that she didn't care. Didn't mind that it was stuffy being all wrapped up in soaking wool, because she also didn't feel the hard sting of the wind-blown rain, and the thunder rolling overhead was muffled by the rumbling wheels, and it was very good not to be scared of being all alone.

She remembered a storm when she was younger, lying in her bed in the upstairs room late at night when everyone else was already asleep. She couldn't sleep though, not with lightning glaring, leaving behind its glow in her closed eyes, and the following crashes of thunder making her jump, even though she knew they were coming. Suddenly her small window swung open from the wind's strength, as if a huge hand was just pushing it out of the way. Livie had huddled on the floor, wrapped in her quilt. The wind tore around the room, raising dust until it began to push rain before it, soaking her bed and her quilt and the floor and Livie. She was trapped there, wanting to call for Papa but at the same time worried that shouting for him would somehow make the noise of the storm even worse.

The old man tapped her gently on the top of the head. She burrowed out of the collar.

"Don't be afraid."

She shook her head before she realized that Purgatoire couldn't see her do it. He didn't seem to care about that, holding the leads, squinting through the rain at the oxen as they struggled to pull the wagon, and shouting to her.

"The boys know how to get themselves home, don't you worry. My big fellows want to get out of the storm as much as we do. We'll get them into their barn and let them have some dry hay, and we'll have some hot soup and wait for the storm to pass. It's a bad one, all right. *My God*, I've never seen lightning like this before."

Huddling on the bench, rocking from side to side with each bump in the lane and each gust of wind, Livie said nothing. She felt the wagon began to lean as the lane led downhill. In the flickering dark-ness, she could see trees, the beginnings of the woods. They rose around the wagon, their branches reaching out over them and waving with each gust of wind. She wondered where Purgatoire's farm was. Maybe he even owned the top of the hill, where she'd always thought Papa's farm began. She wanted to say something, but another gust of wind shook the branches and made them howl. Livie ducked her face back inside the old man's coat, closing her eyes. She'd never been this far from home before.

****

There was wood stacked in the big stone kitchen and it was dry. It didn't take long for Purgatoire to get the hearth fire roaring nicely. Soup, on the other hand, was going to take some time. There was nothing prepared, sitting cold in the pot.

"We can use rainwater to make the soup, how does that sound?" the old man laughed, pulling another coat over his wet shirt and trousers, instead of putting on dry things. He'd set Livie on a chair by the fire, still wrapped in the overcoat, and opened the door. Holding an iron pot under the eaves of the roof, it filled with water. "It's a slate roof, so we won't taste anything strange, unless one of those chickens of mine has been of a mind to lay an egg up there."

The thought of an egg rolling off the roof into their soup-water made Livie smile.

"We have a slate roof on the cattle-byre," she said. "But our house has thatch."

"Oh! Thatch is nice and warm," he replied.

The old man found a knife on a shelf and pulled potatoes out of a bin. He sliced them on the table, then turned the slices into small pieces, gingerly placing them in the soup pot he had hung over the fire.

He pulled his hands quickly back from the heat.

"Don't you have a wife, Monsieur Purgatoire?" Livie asked.

"What did you say?" the old man looked at her quizzically. Livie started, not knowing what she had said wrong. She shrugged, looking down at the stone hearth.

"No girl, it is alright. What did you call me?" he grinned. "Did you say 'Purgatoire'?"

"Oui, Monsieur. Yes, Sir," Livie replied.

"That is so funny, my dear. Purgatoire! Ha!" He threw back his head with a guffaw.

"What is so funny?" asked Livie.

"My name is Picoult, not Purgatoire."

Livie felt her face flushed hot. "I am so sorry, Monsieur...Monsieur Picoult."

"I'll bet that your Papa told you that one, didn't he?" Picoult asked with a tilt to his head. "Haw! Very good..." He was slicing carrots now, concentrating. Livie was still embarrassed, but her mouth was watering with hunger, too. She didn't want to make the old man mad, so she stifled a shrug. But he didn't seem to be mad. He was smiling while he worked. The smile was in his eyes, too, just like before.

"Purgatoire means the place near Hell. Funny, eh? Was he near Hell, or was I? I wonder. Well, your Papa always did think that I was the devil. It is alright. A good joke on me." He laughed again, then snorted and that made him laugh some more. It was an infectious laugh, and Livie giggled. Picoult wiped his eyes.

What a thing, she thought. We've been out in a storm, soaked to the skin and starving, and here we are laughing as if it is the best time ever. She even forgot her question. Instead she asked a different one.

"Do you go to church, Monsieur Picoult?" Her head also tilted.

Picoult smiled, but his eyes were serious.

"Why? What makes you ask that?"

"I'm not sure. Papa said that we are...that is, my family goes to... well, we belong to the Church of Rome. Oh, I don't know, because

I've never been to Rome, so perhaps that is why Papa says that I am a heathen. I don't exactly know what a heathen is."

Picoult leaned back as if he might laugh again, but instead took a deep breath.

"That is a lot of questions. First, let's get some food going."

"What are you making, Monsieur Picoult?" Livie asked.

"What do you mean? Haven't you made a peasant's soup before?"

Livie shook her head once. Maman had never really let her near the cooking fire. The food she served was a mystery of slicing and dicing and the herbs brought in from the garden.

"Well, then. It is high time for you to learn what makes things go together in a soup, eh?"

He beckoned Livie over to the thick wooden table where he was working. She left the coat on the chair and joined him. There he had an onion, some parsnips as thin as carrots, a clay pot, and a bowl with some leaves in it.

"We cut the onion up, but it won't taste good if we just drop it in the pot. Get the iron pan, please." Picoult pointed at a hook where an iron frying-pan hung. It was heavy and took two hands for Livie to carry it.

"I will do this part," he said, and with his knife he deftly cut the top and bottom off the onion and peeled back the dry brown skin. Chopping the white onion into pieces, he scooped something with his fingers from the clay jar and dropped it into the pan. Licking his fingers, he walked over to the hearth and set the pan down on the stones near the flame.

"Renderings. You know, bacon fat. Very tasty. We'll cook the onions a little and then add them to our broth." He pointed at the knife on the table.

"Can you chop the parsnips? Have you done that before? No? Be very careful. The knife is a sharp one." The old man turned his back.

Maman had never, never let Livie touch her knife. This one sat on the kitchen table like something wild and dangerous, a snake waiting to bite her. But Picoult hadn't told her not to touch it. Indeed, he actually wanted her to use it. She looked over at the old man, puttering around with the frying pan. See? He needed her to help him. Livie tentatively picked up the knife and set it down in front of her. No bites. Just be careful. She picked up a parsnip, pale and rigid, turning it over in her hand. She sniffed it, but it smelled only of the earth, and the freshness of spring. Holding it on the table she sliced the tip off, like she'd seen Maman do so many times. The knife was indeed very sharp. Taking her time, she cut the parsnip, moving her fingers back with each slice. Then she started the next, working until she had a pile of little parsnip disks.

"Is this right?" she asked shyly. Picoult turned and nodded with a smile.

"Bring them here," he said. With two hands she gathered them up. "Put them in with these onions." Livie carefully dropped the vegetables in the pan.

"See how the onions are turning brown?" Picoult said. "They are surrendering to the heat of the fire and giving up their sweetness,"

Livie, who had nibbled wild onions before and didn't much like their flavor, was skeptical that they could ever be sweet and tasty. She watched as Picoult jiggled the frying pan for a moment and then turned it around so the other side of the pan would heat. The onions were hissing and sizzling in the pan and soon the parsnips joined them and the room began to fill with the wonderful smell of food cooking. Picoult winced a little because the handle of the frying pan was getting hot. He motioned for Livie to fetch the knife, which he then used to stir the onions and parsnips.

Then, slipping the damp sleeve of his shirt over his hand, he lifted the hot frying pan and tipped the sizzling vegetables into the soup pot, letting the bacon fat drip in as well. The soup was bubbling, too. Livie leaned over to see, but then stood up and stepped back. Maman always scolded her for getting too near the cooking fire. She looked at Picoult, but he was already back at the table. He motioned her over.

"This is..."

"Thyme. I know thyme; it grows in Maman's herb garden. I weed there."

"Ah, then it is your herb garden as well." Picoult had taken the knife and was chopping the thyme into small aromatic bits.

"That is what the mice said also," Livie said, then popped her hand over her mouth for letting out her secret.

"Oh, they did, did they?" said Picoult without looking up or even a hint of a teasing smile. "Mice are smart that way, I think." He carried a small handful of thyme to the pot and brushed it off his hands into the soup.

"What about the carrots? Do you want me to cut them up?"

"Oh, no! Not yet. They are far too delicate. Carrots we save for going in later. That way they won't break down into the broth, but will be there for us to chew and to look pretty and orange." Ah, Livie thought. Of course, she hadn't known that.

"Now the broth can work for a while on its own," he said. "Go sit on your chair and get warm again." Picoult took the damp overcoat and hung it on a peg behind the kitchen door. Then he took a blanket from a chest and shoo'ed Livie back to her chair by the fire. He covered her legs with the blanket and she pulled it up to her chin. The fire was wonderfully warm. The kitchen smelled marvelous, better than anything she could have imagined in Maman's kitchen. It was sort of magical.

****

"Rain's passed," said one familiar squeak. Livie opened her eyes. It was gloomy-dark. She lay on her side, the coat about her shoulders. She was back in the wagon, lying on the bench, and she could see behind her into the wagon. At first there was nothing to see. Then she spied something small, moving with the rolling of the wagon. It was the little girl-mouse.

"Good evening," Livie whispered. The little mouse curtseyed, inasmuch as a mouse can even do such a thing. Livie smiled. "How did you get on this wagon?"

"How did you get on this wagon?" mocked the little girl-mouse cheekily. "I climbed on, of course. How did *you* get on?"

"I...I don't know," Livie started, then remembered. "Oh! Monsieur Picoult picked me up out of the storm."

"Who..." the little girl-mouse asked. "is Monsieur Picoult?"

"He's right there." Livie tried to sit up, but the wagon jounced and so she stayed put rather than risk rolling off the bench. "Driving the wagon."

"That's silly," said the little mouse. "My Pierrot is driving the wagon, of course." Livie turned her head, peeking over the collar of the damp coat. Her Pierrot? Aha! There indeed was the little boy-mouse, with a tiny, rather dented tri-corn hat, holding tiny traces out to the enormous oxen. He gave a toothy mouse smile.

"How do you do, *made-mouse-elle*?" he asked and tilted his head in a small bow.

Livie giggled at the boy-mouse's joke. "How do you do, Monsieur Pierrot?"

Pierrot tipped his hat to Livie.

"He can be very silly sometimes," said the girl-mouse.

"Ah, but he drives the wagon quite well."

"Oh, don't say that too loudly. He thinks so highly of himself that his head is quite swollen enough." The little girl-mouse shook her head.

"You know what? I'm hungry," Pierrot said. "I could use a little something to nibble on."

"When are you not hungry?" asked the little girl-mouse with a sly smile.

"Never," laughed Pierrot. "But something smells good."

"Oooh! Something does smell good," Livie said. She sniffed. Actually, something smelled delicious. But what was that? Something else, something she couldn't place. A sound. "Do you hear that?"

The little girl-mouse shrugged. The wagon bounced and she steadied herself by dropping on all-fours.

Livie wanted to turn her head, try and place the sound, but all she could do is move her eyes, which saw the bench she was lying on and the little girl-mouse and Pierrot the driver. The sound was as wonderful as the odor that she sniffed, but different, of course. Like nothing ever in her memory. And how very frustrating it was, not to be able to place what was going on around her. The little girl-mouse must have sensed this, because she had a look of mouse-concern on her tiny face.

"It's alright, dear. Not to worry. We're going past a farmhouse. Perhaps it's your own farmhouse. I can't see out of the wagon, myself."

Livie giggled. Of course a mouse couldn't see out of the wagon - that made sense. Unless you thought about the mouse driving the wagon, which made no sense at all.

"Where are we?" Livie asked Pierrot.

"In the wagon, of course," the tiny wagon-driver said with a mousy giggle.

Livie smiled again. She would have to remember to ask her questions more carefully.

"I mean, where are we going?"

"We're going home. That's where we're going. We're going home. We don't mind going back up the hill. You want to go home, don't you?" the little girl-mouse said softly, as the wagon rocked her against her shoulder. "You want to go home, don't you?
****

Livie slowly opened her eyes. Monsieur Picoult stood over her. He was gently shaking her shoulder.

"Well, hello again. Now then, are you awake? It's time to eat, get some warm food in your belly," he said. "The rain has stopped, I think, and soon the boys won't mind going back up the hill. You want to go home, don't you?"

Livie sniffed, and her mouth watered. That same smell - wonderful! The soup must be done. But then she recalled that something else, that thing she had heard. Her ears perked up. Nothing unusual.

What was that sound? Her heart seemed to skip a beat. It had been more beautiful than anything she'd ever heard before, more than the song of birds or the whisper of wind through pine needles. She didn't really have the words to explain.

Chapter Five

Picoult pointed a bony finger at the cupboard.

"We will need bowls. They're right there, if you would." Livie opened the door and saw all of the dishes. She inhaled sharply. Carefully picking up a bowl, she stared. It was beautiful, creamy white with paintings of pale blue flowers on them. He couldn't mean for them to eat from one of these. It looked so fragile that she wanted to place it back down for fear it might break just by her holding it.

"These were my wife's dishes," he said, watching her.

"Oh, then we mustn't use them," Livie said softly. She wondered where Monsieur Picoult's wife was. He hadn't answered the question.

"No, girl. It is alright, they won't break. They're made of something called porcelain. All the way from China, if you can believe it."

"Where's China?" Livie asked. She'd not heard the word before. Perhaps it was the name of the town at the bottom of the hill. Her brothers had told her was called *Annonay*, but they might indeed have been teasing her about it. She asked Picoult if this was so. Now

Picoult stared, with a smile on his face, then the smile fading. He shook his head.

"Yes, Annonay is the town at the foot of the hill, by the *Riviere Deume*. But you don't know where China is?"

"I've never heard of China. Is it in France?" Livie tilted her head, frowning with embarrassment.

"No, it's not in France," Picoult said gently and without smiling. "It is a land far across the oceans. Have you ever been to the ocean?"

"No, monsieur," Livie replied. "I've not even been to town." The truth was, she'd never been off of the hill where her family's farm was, as far as she knew. Perhaps when she was a baby? But Papa had no wagon, so she couldn't imagine how it might have happened. Could Maman have carried her? Was the ocean far?

"I know nothing," she said, her voice low.

"Surely that is not true. Everyone knows something."

Livie thought hard about it.

"I can count."

"Well, then, there you go. Counting is good. And some day soon you will go to Annonay as well. I guess it is like any place. The houses are close together. The market is always busy. There are many people who shop there. There is a friend of mine who sells fish. When you meet him he will try to give you a kiss on both cheeks, but he smells, so tell him no." Picoult laughed. "Some day you may have your own shop, and you can count the money that people spend on your vegetables. Other farmers will buy them from you, too. People come into the market from all around, from farms like your father's, servants who work in kitchens and do the cooking, fishermen who cast nets on the Deume or who take their little boats on the wide and slow Rhone for eel and carp and bullheads and those fresh-water mullet that jump right into your boat, if you wave a torch above them at night."

Livie assumed that all of those words were names of things. Fish?

"I've never seen the river, either. I can see where it is, though, from the top of the hill. Some day I would like to do more even than that," Livie said. "I want to know what is beyond the town, beyond the next town. I want to know about France and...and China."

She half expected Monsieur Picoult to laugh at her, but he didn't. He didn't even smile, but nodded with a serious look in his eyes.

"So much to learn about, eh?" Picoult said softly, dishing her some soup from the pot with a long-handled wooden ladle. It was thickened now, and steaming. She carefully carried it to the table and sat on a stool that Picoult had set there. Her dress was dry, or at least dry enough that she felt warm in Picoult's kitchen.

"Get yourself a spoon, mademoiselle," Picoult pointed again to the cupboard. Livie fetched two; marvelous silver spoons. She'd never eaten with silver spoons before - at home her spoon was wooden.

"They're fashioned of pewter. Don't put yours in the soup quite yet, or the handle will bend from the heat. Blow to cool it a little bit." Then he winked at her and she smiled to see it, his funny, ugly, friend- ly face. Livie blew on the soup, but her stomach was gurgling with hunger and she almost wanted to dip in with her fingers to get some into her mouth. It looked and smelled amazing. And it was almost as thick as the mud in a plowed field after a rain. So very different from Maman's slim broth.

"I added some pepper, of course," Picoult said, sitting across from her with his own bowl full in front of him. "I am fond of pepper, aren't you?"

Livie nodded, although she rarely had pepper in anything. Pepper is so dear, Maman often told her. As dear as salt, and you must use twice as much.

"Pepper comes from half the world away. A land called India."

"India," Livie repeated. So far away that it was just a word to her. "Like China? Do people from there bring the pepper here?"

"Oh, no, I shouldn't think so. Ships from France go to China and India. The king sends them. Do you know about our king? King Louis?" The old man blew gently at his bowl of soup. Livie was astonished at herself. She hadn't even known that the king of France was named Louis. *There is an awful lot to learn*, muttered The Voice.

"I'll bet you don't know what else they have there. In India." His smile was mischievous, and it made Livie smile. And to believe that she had once thought Picoult to be an ugly old man! She shook her head, for she had no idea what was in India.

"There are animals so large and strange, that you can hardly imagine such things. They are called Elephants. Larger even than the boys. They are creatures so strange that their ears and noses and even their teeth don't fit them, but hang and dangle from their heads."

Elephants, Livie thought. With ears and noses and teeth that don't fit. She tried to picture it in her mind, but couldn't. India was half the world away. How large was the world? She would never see an elephant; that was for certain. She sighed, and her sigh turned into a deep sniff of the soup.

"I've put in a surprise," Picoult said, pursing his lips thoughtfully. "Taste!"

What other surprise could be put into soup? Livie wondered. This already had more things in it than Maman ever put in her soup. Of course Livie had had turnip soup before, and potato soup and on the rarest of occasions carrot and potato soup, but never carrot and potato and parsnip soup. Picoult picked up his spoon and dipped into his bowl. Livie took her own spoon and scooped. She almost spilt it into her lap, she was so impatient.

"Oh!" she exclaimed when she tasted the soup.

"Did you burn yourself, little one? I'm sorry. I told you that it was very hot," Picoult scolded, but with a twinkle in his eye.

"Oh, *non*. No. It's just that it's..." but Livie could think of no words for it. She felt a shiver come over her, but she was no longer cold. Sitting here, tasting this soup, was more than marvelous. It was like all of the senses of summertime placed gently in her bowl. She smiled and the soup almost leaked out from between her teeth. Picoult laughed, and she held her hand to her mouth so that she wouldn't spill a drop.

"*Bien!* Good, eh?" he said.

"Oh, monsieur! Better than I would ever have thought. Better than good," Livie frowned to think of what she meant. "Like all of the wildflowers on top of the hill. They all belong there, to make it look so fine. So all of the things in this soup are here to make it taste...wonderful." She scooped another spoonful and put it in her mouth.

Picoult sat up straight. He rubbed the stubble on his chin.

"I've never heard such a compliment, little one. You move me to tears. It is only a peasant's soup, but when you say your words you make it quite the feast."

"It's that I wouldn't have thought that these same things that Maman uses in her soup would taste like this."

"Now, you know that I added something to the soup that your Maman might not place there every time." He lifted a spoonful from his own bowl. There was a tiny piece of chicken in it. Livie recognized it immediately. So, that's what made it taste so wonderful. But how different from home! She explained to the old man that on the most rare of days, Papa would take one of the chickens and hack off its head so that Maman could roast it for a special meal, a holiday like Easter. Then she would take the bones and skin and fat and put them in a pot of water to make a chicken broth. Even those soups, however were not like this. Not richly thick with vegetables and savory with herbs. Instead, however, they were made for when one of the family took ill with a fever or some other ailment. Maman would season the broth with vinegar to preserve it and then seal it tightly in a jar with paraffin. Livie had tasted it, too, during the winter when her chest ached from coughing and her nose was so stuffed that she couldn't breathe through it. The soup was hot and awful-sour flavored, only vaguely tasting of chicken. Not like this soup at all, made to warm you up and stop your hunger after being out on a cold, wet night.

"I've never had anything like this before," she told Picoult honestly. He nodded.

"Well, you know what? I didn't even know that there were flowers on top of the hill. I go to market all of the time, and never noticed. Imagine that," Picoult said.

Livie frowned.

"Not really flowers, monsieur. Wildflowers. Maman says that they are weeds, and not to be brought into the farmyard."

The old man nodded.

"Weeds will take all of the soil to themselves, if you let them. Their roots will strangle the roots of your potatoes and carrots and squash. That is how weeds survive."

"They are pretty, though," Livie said.

"Yes, I am sure. And as such it is a small payment for taking food from your mouth, isn't it?" Picoult tapped his spoon on the edge of his bowl and it rang a perfect note.

"Are they truly beautiful?" he asked.

"Yes."

They began to eat, quietly now, so that their food would not get cold. Then Picoult took her bowl and filled it once more from the pot, and his own. Her eyes opened wide - she'd never had a second helping before. What was the right thing to do? She didn't know, so she apologized, which made Picoult laugh again, and which made her laugh again, too. Then they each worked on their soup again, blowing on it, smelling anew the steaming herbs and dipping mouthful after mouthful until their bellies groaned from being so full.

Livie grinned. She couldn't remember ever having so much that she couldn't eat anymore. She felt like giggling.

Picoult rested his spoon atop his bowl, balancing it from one edge to another.

"This was my wife's favorite meal. Chicken soup. She made it often."

Livie looked at the old man, who seemed to be staring into his empty bowl. She remembered her earlier unanswered question, but said nothing.

"She took care of our chickens, and she loved them and hated them at the same time. 'Oh they give me a pain in the neck,' she would often say, 'but not like the one I plan to give them.'" Picoult made a motion with his hands like wringing a chicken's neck.

"But then she would go outside in the snow to make sure that they had food. She had a good heart. I thought it was also a strong one. You see, she died giving birth to my son. He died too, soon afterward. I don't know why. It seemed that he was healthy and strong. But perhaps he didn't want to be here without her." The old man's voice was different now, whispery and hoarse.

"Oh, monsieur, I am sorry for your sadness." The polite words just came to Livie, naturally, as if someone was speaking quietly into her ear, although she had never known anyone who had died, or anyone who knew anyone who had died.

"Thank you, *cherie*. It happened so long ago, probably even before you were born. But I can still see her face, hear her voice. And when I cook this soup, I can also smell her cooking. You know, I like to think of them both being in heaven, together, taking care of one another. Maybe they even look down on me from time to time, to make sure that I'm alright."

"Surely they do, monsieur," Livie said.

"It is not so nice being alone. I have no brothers or sisters here, so I have to hire people to work on my farm, like your brothers work with your father. It is not as nice as it might have been, had things turned out differently. Having family is important, I think. Don't you agree?"

Livie puzzled over that, trying to find an answer. Her brothers weren't always nice to her, and they sometimes picked on her, and often they smelled. But she'd never thought about what it would be like if Jean-Charles or Guillaume weren't around. How lonely it must be for Monsieur Picoult.

"And my wife liked to play," Picoult said, standing. "She even taught me a little bit. I'm not very fine, but I know a couple of tunes."

Livie's was puzzled.

"Are you fond of music? Come and see," Picoult said and went into the living room.

In one corner of the room was a wooden box. Or something which looked like a wooden box, but not quite. There was a small three-legged stool in front of it.

"Come," he repeated, sitting at the wooden stool, as if he might shell peas. He lifted his hands to the odd wooden box.

The sound that resulted was the same one she had heard while dozing in the chair in front of the fire.

Sometimes, very rarely, Maman hummed softly to herself. When she did, it was when she thought no one was nearby to listen. Livie liked hearing Maman's singing, because it meant that Maman was happy. But it was nothing that Livie would call beautiful. Nothing at all like this.

"Do you like this song?" he asked. It was dim in the room, only lit by the light of the kitchen. Livie couldn't have explained what was happening. Picoult moved his fingers and the box made sound. He was pressing down on small dark and light pieces of wood that stuck into the box. Somehow...it caused such beautiful sounds.

She opened her mouth to speak, but could only stand, breathing as quietly as she was able. What was there to say? Of course she liked this song. She loved it. The sounds washed over her like warm water, like a soft breeze. Like the aroma of chicken soup. Only, she thought, it wasn't noises, because they came together as he moved his arms and hands and fingers, so that what he was doing was not many things but one thing and the different sounds became one sound, together. And without even asking the question, Livie knew what *music* was. Wonderful.

"This was hers. It's called a *virginal*," Picoult said while he pressed his fingers in different places on the box. "I am told it is like a tall harpsichord. Italian, you understand."

Livie didn't understand, but just listened to what the old man was doing. He made the sound grow in intensity, so that it filled her mind, with shapes and pictures. Then Picoult leaned forward, and began moving his fingers faster, and when he did so the sound changed; everything changed so that the color Livie saw in her mind changed along with it. She felt a heaviness in her chest, and this became a lump in her throat, as if the sound coming from the wooden box caused her to have a feeling in the same way that the sound of wind in the winter could make her know the sense of cold even while she sat next to the kitchen fire. Livie met it there with her own hand, trying to hold back a sigh. Then, in a moment where she could recognize that it was suddenly appropriate to do so, Picoult stopped his fingers and the sound stopped as well, except that it continued in her mind and the sensation that she was having continued in her heart. She only reluctantly dared to continue breathing. She felt suddenly lonely for home. Such loneliness surprised her.

"It will be dawn soon. I should think that the boys are now ready for the return trip, don't you?" said Picoult, as if he was hearing Livie's thoughts spoken aloud. "And I'll wager the rain has stopped."

Chapter Six

Livie and the old man slogged across the muddy farmyard. She shook her head. Apparently, while the soup cooked and Livie slept by the fire, Picoult had gone back out in the night, removed the oxen from their yoke and put them away in the barn. Now, a few hardy crickets chirped, but the storm was reduced to the sound of dripping from the farmhouse roof into rain barrels. Even the thunder was gone. It was still dark outside, but with a candle-lantern they made their way to the large stone-and-wood building. Picoult heaved the great wooden door open; it was well-balanced and swung easily on its hinges. He hung the lantern from a hook on the wall, behind which was a tin reflector. The room was immediately brighter. Livie saw the boys, they shared a large stall. The oxen were munching on hay and the barn smelled warm and comfortable in that way that a place full of contented animals will, and did not seem at all gloomy by flickering candle-light.

"Come, boys. Come," called Picoult. "We have to get this young lady home, don't we?" As if it understood, one of the oxen lowed soft-ly, a strange sound to Livie's ears; something like the wind moaning. She giggled and moaned back at the creature, which made Picoult guf-faw and slap his knee with his hand, and then the ox lowed again, caus-ing them both to laugh until Picoult began coughing and had to lean on the hay to catch his breath.

"I think that you and he will be good friends. Do you know what you said to him?"

Livie shook her head.

"Me either, and I've had oxen since I was a boy. You would think I might have learned to speak their language after all this time." Picoult snorted a laugh.

He lifted the great wooden yoke with a grunt and hung it by an iron hook from a rope that dangled from the barn's ceiling. Livie could see that the rope was just the right height, and the yoke was spe-cially curved and smooth beneath, for resting on the creatures' shoul-ders as comfortably as it could. With a short rope draped around the animal's neck, Picoult led the boys one by one to the yoke, and patted each one on the nose while he buckled the leather hasp beneath their necks.

"If oxen are still tired, they'll let you know. They won't even both-er to take on the yoke," Picoult observed. "But the boys are strong, and they've been eating their suppers, same as us. And I think they know that you have to get home safely."

"Thank you," Livie curtseyed to the oxen, which caused Picoult to burble with more laughter.

"Do you think that you could lead them out to the wagon?" asked the old man. "I will get the lantern."

"I don't know how," she gulped. She wondered if she was sup-posed to lead them by the rings through their noses, as she had seen Picoult do on market-day. That would be very strange.

Picoult pointed at the lead still looped around the one creature's neck. He lifted the candle-lantern off of its hook.

"Balderdash. Sure you do. Just pick up that rope and give him a little tug. If they aren't willing to come, they won't. But I think they're rested and ready. They like working. Give the lead a tug, and he'll come along, and the other will follow. Well, not exactly follow; they're attached by the yoke side-by-side. But you only have to get one of them coming with you and the other will join. It's easy." And he walked out the barn doorway.

Livie gingerly picked up the oxen's lead. *Never done anything like this before*, said The Voice In Her Head. She gave the lead a small tug, and the ox took a step forward, the other stepping out almost at the same moment. They huffed at her through their noses, and she could smell their sweet hay-breath. *If they don't want to move, they won't.*

"Come boys. Come," she said softly and walked slowly towards the door. The oxen followed her, their huge hooves clomping on the ground. The neck-bells clanked softly. My goodness. She felt like laughing out loud.

Picoult was at the wagon, readying it for the oxen. The wagon tongue was pointing straight up, and harnesses and traces were draped over the wagon's bench. The lantern hung from an iron hook next to the bench.

"You see? They like you. Your slightest touch is their command to follow."

Livie was grinning. She felt like she might walk all the way home, just leading her two charges.

"Do they have names?" she asked.

Picoult took the lead from her hand and maneuvered the two oxen in front of the wagon and beneath the wagon's tongue. The heavy leather harnesses went on next, buckled and tied. Then the old man carefully lowered the tongue and attached it to the yoke and harnesses.

"Names, eh?" he said, frowning thoughtfully in the dim candle-light. "Well, the one with the lead is George."

"*Salut*, George," Livie said to the ox.

"Ah, but he's not always the one with the lead."

Livie didn't understand.

"You mean that George isn't always the leader?"

"No. I'm saying that George is always the leader. But I don't always put the same boy as lead. But it's easier just to call the leader George, I guess." Picoult shrugged.

"Oh, that's not nice," Livie scolded the old man in spite of herself. "Everyone deserves a proper name. One that's theirs to keep. My brothers won't name the big black dog that watches our farm. I don't know why. I've asked them many times. They think that it's all one big joke."

Picoult looked at her for a long time. He bowed.

"You are right. It's not funny, and I was wrong." He scratched his chin. "From now on, this one on lead will always be George. The other one will be..."

"Louis," said Livie.

Picoult laughed, holding his old tri-corn hat in his hand and whacking it against his leg.

"Very nice! Very nice! After our own great and glorious king. Long live Louis! Hail George, the sovereign of England. The two kings!" He bowed deeply, sweeping his hat on the ground.

Livie was amazed. Before tonight she hadn't even known that Louis was the name of France's king. Nor had she known England's king's name.

"Louis and George," she whispered. But where in the world was England anyway? Was it a neighbor of France's, as she, Livie, was a neighbor of Monsieur Picoult? Perhaps it was just over the next hill, or many days' journey away. I am going to learn. I know so little, she thought.

"Up you go," said Picoult, and he lifted Livie up onto the bench. Then with a heave he pulled himself up as well, and took the traces in hand. "We're off."

Livie looked behind her in the wagon's bed. Empty, but for a few rain-wet baskets. Papa's, which Picoult hadn't been able to return yet. She looked up in the sky, it was almost clear now. Even with the lantern light, she could see the fantastic array of stars overhead, as if she might reach up and grab one and pull it down to help light their way. But what if instead they were very far away? How large was the world she lived in? How many stars in the sky? Suddenly, Livie knew in her heart that she wanted to find out *everything*.

Riding in the wagon back up the hill was as jouncy as it had been going down, but Livie didn't mind at all. She was dry, full of soup and knew where she was. Indeed she was excited to be going home, and trusted her new friends George and Louis to get her there safely by starlight. Looking over at Monsieur Picoult, she wondered how he lived all by himself, without a wife or child, but was not an unhappy man. Would he be different if his wife was still alive? Would he be happier with a son working the farm by his side, helping him lead Louis and George to market? She suspected it to be true.

Through the woods the wagon rolled, shadows wriggling inside dark holes, thrown by the swinging candle-lantern. But except for the crunch of hooves and wheels, it was quiet. All of the creatures of the night had been blown away or sent into hiding by the rain storm.

On the hilltop, the oxen slowed to a stop.

"Ah, my boys, you have your habits," Picoult said.

"What is that?" Livie asked.

"On days when we go to market. This is their first resting spot," said Picoult softly. "They know that it's a long downhill slope from this place, and will be harder yet for them to hold the wagon back than it is to pull it."

Again, it was beautiful here on top of the hill.

"Look over there," Picoult pointed. Livie followed the direction of his hand. Although the sun wasn't up yet, the sky over the town was beginning to change from black with the glowing specks of stars to a deep and dark blue. She could only just make out the shadowy shapes of the roofs of the buildings in Annonay. Not a light trickled up from town. Everyone was still asleep.

"The east," the old man continued. "is where the sun rises. And there is the steep and rocky *Riviere* Deume. She is our river and she spills down to the Rhone, which is slow and mighty, like an ox, and if you are floating on her she will carry you all the way to the sea, as all rivers must eventually do. Do you see it - down there near town? The west is how the sun sets." He pointed with his thumb behind them.

"West," Livie interrupted softly. "I've never seen the west at all, then."

"Surely you have. You have been to my farm, which is in the west from your papa's farm."

"Does the sun set near your farm?"

Picoult hmmph'd a slight laugh, then cleared his throat.

"Oh, my, no. The world is larger by far than that."

Livie's eyes widened. How much larger could it be?

"What else is there?" she asked

Picoult scratched his scruffy beard again, as he seemed to do whenever he was thinking or about to grin.

"Well, I don't know everywhere, but beyond this hill, to the west past my farm and other farms is *le Chateau du Comte*. Where the Count lives. He is a cousin to the King and he has a fabulous palace."

"What is a Count? Does he live by himself?" Livie asked.

"I shouldn't think so, because he is very powerful and one of King Louis's many cousins, so people want to live with him and work in his gardens and take care of his beautiful horses and..."

"His cows and oxen?"

Picoult nodded. "Oh, yes. And chickens. And geese."

"What does he do?"

"I don't know. I expect he spends most of his time in Paris, where all of the counts and dukes and their duchesses live, to be near the King."

"Why does he have a palace near here, then?" Livie asked.

"He rules most of *Ardeche*," Picoult said with a shrug.

Ah, Livie thought. *What "Ah?"* asked The Voice. *You don't know...* True, she replied in her mind.

"Where is Ardeche?" she now inquired most fearlessly.

Picoult didn't smile or giggle or laugh aloud at her.

"That is a good question. Ardeche is the land all around our town, Annonay. We are in Ardeche." He pointed out, towards everything. "This all, is Ardeche."

Ah, Livie thought again with a nod. This time there was nothing from The Voice.

"Yes, a terribly busy man, the Count. And to the north, beyond the Count's palace are other farms and other towns like ours and more palaces and then beyond all of them is the city of Paris. And the palace of Versailles, where King Louis lives. Then to the west again, on and on, to the ocean. My dear, the world is very large."

Livie nodded. *See? How many more things you now know*, whispered The Voice.

"I've not been to town. Papa almost never goes. I never even thought of it as being ours," she said.

"Well, now. We feed the people in Annonay and Ardeche. With our potatoes and turnips and tomatoes. And our piglets, right?"

"Yes!" That was so.

"Then I imagine that it is our town as much as anyone's," Picoult said with satisfaction. "Even the Count would agree with that." He touched the traces and the big oxen turned to the side a little bit, so that they might munch on some of the weeds at the side of the lane.

"I wonder if we wait here, we'll see the first morning fires lit in town. As the night's stars go out?" Picoult said, leaning back on the bench.

"Who puts the stars out?" Livie asked.

"Another good question! One have not given it much thought, more's the pity. Do you think perhaps that it is the same people that put them on at night? Perhaps God's angels." Picoult leaned back and took off his tri-corn so that it wouldn't fall from his head. He looked at the pre-dawn sky.

Livie scrunched her brow in thought, looked up at the stars herself.

"Monsieur, are you a Calvinist?" she blurted.

"Ha! Do you see how you are becoming a student, maiden-of-the-mountain? Remember, there is no question you shouldn't ask, if you might learn something from the answer." He looked over at the young girl. Livie looked back at her friend, who was no longer ugly or even particularly old looking to her. His mouth twisted to one side as he thought about his answer.

"Do you know what I think? That there is too much that makes us different already. Some of us are farmers, and others are kings. Soldiers and peasants, women and men, rich and poor. Our beliefs, the differences in wealth or birth or age, don't matter to God. I'm not sure what He wants, he keeps that a mystery from you and me, but I think he wants us to try harder to be kind to each other. And how we see Him shouldn't be one more thing to possibly push us apart, no?"

Livie didn't completely understand what Picoult meant, but decided it didn't matter. She looked around.

"This is the spot where I found you." Even in the dark she could see that the meadow had been mashed down by the driving rain and fierce wind. Then she noticed. "Oh, where are they?"

"What, cherie? What can you see?"

Livie pointed out at the meadow. She was crestfallen.

"All of my flowers are gone!"

Indeed, the storm's wind had blown away the lace blooms, the golden flames, even the hearty purple blooms of the thistles.

Picoult tsk'd with his tongue. "It is a shame. And I never bothered to look at them. Unforgiveable! Well, we'll have to put them back."

"No, monsieur. You don't understand. They grew here on their own."

"Then God will replace them, as he does each spring. This must be a wildflower place, if wildflowers grew here."

But Livie wasn't convinced. Picoult patted her on the shoulder.

"I like flowers, too. So did my wife. Lilies were her favorite. Dark red and purple like a stormy sky. Yellow as bright as the sun. And white as pale as a cloud. She kept them in her garden."

"I've never seen a lily," she said. "I only know the wild flowers."

"Which ones do you know?" he asked.

"Oh, monsieur, I don't know that they are called," Livie said, shyly.

Picoult hmmph'd.

"Well, now. How would you like it if you weren't called by your own name? Just like George and Louis. I will tell you, though. A lily is a beautiful thing. Each bloom is a perfection of its own, as if God attended especially to it. Delicate, yes, but also strong. Beautiful because it is, and because it doesn't last. I planted them on her grave, so that they bloom every summer," Picoult said quietly.

Livie thought about that, and about Picoult's wife, and why he and his wife had never had children. *But how can you ask such a personal question, Olivia?* said The Voice. You cannot, she thought. It would be like bringing weeds into a garden. And so they sat without saying anything else, while one by one the stars winked out and the sky turned from black to purple to the first light of dawn.

She heard it. Distant shouting. Someone calling.

"Do you hear that?" Picoult asked, turning an ear towards the sound.

"Yes."

Someone was shouting her name. Livie! *Olivia!*

Chapter Seven

They rolled slowly downhill. The boys, George and Louis, dug their hooves into the mud to hold the heavy wagon back rather than pulling it. Livie saw Papa on the lane first - the rising sun set the sky blue just enough to see shadows and shapes - and that was Papa's shape, barrel-chested and arms firmly on hips. There was still calling for her; Maman somewhere up their lane, probably near the house. Her brothers were out in the fields, shouting her name.

"She's here!" Papa yelled, like the lowing of an ox. "I've found her!" Which was only partly so - she didn't think she'd been lost anyway and if she had, she'd found herself. With Monsieur Picoult's help, of course.

The boys stopped in front of Papa. It was light enough now to see her father's frown, creasing his forehead deeply.

"Come down," he rumbled softly. "Go to the house." Livie felt a lump in her belly that had been warm and comfortable now go cold. Picoult held out his hand and she lowered herself from the bench to the muddy lane.

"I'm sorry, Papa," she said. She was, and she wasn't, both in equal measure.

"Go to the house," he repeated. Livie turned and walked down the lane. She could hear Papa speaking quietly with Monsieur Picoult, but not what he was saying. She peeked over her shoulder. The old man stood holding his tri-corn hat, while Papa growled like the big black dog. Livie wished that she could go back and make Papa stop. For a moment she even wished that Picoult was her Papa. Oh, she thought with regret. I didn't even have a chance to thank him.

****

Livie squatted on a stool in the kitchen. Maman was at the table, wringing her hands. Her eyes were red and swollen and Livie could tell that she had been crying for a long time. She'd already stood once, waved an angry finger at Livie, and stomped from the kitchen, only to return with eyes even more swollen. But Maman had yet to say a word. Instead, she stirred the pot over the morning fire. Guillaume and Jean-Charles stood accusingly over Livie, shaking their heads, explaining how frightened the family had been with her lost in the storm all night.

"Selfish little girl!" Guillaume muttered, his mouth full of hot mush.

"You can't imagine how Maman worried about you," growled Jean-Charles, before leaning over his own breakfast.

And that was true enough. Livie couldn't imagine it. Maman worried about her? She'd told Livie how under foot she was. Always it was, "Get out! Get out!" Well, now Livie had *been* out. And why hadn't anyone come to get her when she was up on the hilltop? That was what Livie wanted to ask. But she said nothing.

There were no tears in her own eyes, however. She couldn't make herself cry. How many times had she been stung by a wasp, or stubbed a toe against one of the stools around the table? Or when Maman tried to untangle her hair with the rough old wooden comb, it was as easy to make the tears flow as easy as water spilt from a well-bucket. But last night and today, something had changed inside her. Livie was tired, so sleepy, but she wasn't sad at all. Rather it had been a very long night and she'd been wet and cold and frightened and then warm and dry and full of food. The cat-naps she'd caught hadn't been enough rest, of that she was certain. So she rubbed her eyes red with the heels of her hands so that Maman wouldn't wonder what was wrong with her, and perhaps swat her with the wooden spoon to remove all doubt.

Oh, so you're the grown-up now, The Voice In Her Head mocked. *You are wiser than your Maman?* No, Livie wasn't sure of that. But she was certain that there were things she did want to know, and Maman wasn't going to give her answers to her questions. She sat silently, waiting for the real storm.

After Picoult left for his farm, slowly leading the boys and the empty wagon back up the hill, Papa had walked slowly down the lane, carrying the empty baskets and the few coins the vegetables had earned at market. At first, Livie was relieved, thinking that he had decided to go out into the field and to let Maman handle her punishment. Oh, but she would not be so lucky! Apparently he was just getting himself ready to rain on her like last night's storm. While Maman wept, Papa stomped into the house as loudly as one of the oxen, bashing into the door, swinging his head around as if it had horns and might hook something in anger. Her brothers tried to casually slip out. She heard the kitchen door open again, then shut softly. They didn't get away cleanly, though. Papa pulled the kitchen door open again.

"Yes! Get to work, you lazy louts!" Papa roared after them, and slammed the door for emphasis. Then he became quiet. Turning, Papa rubbed his hands together as if they were cold and he was trying to get the blood circulating. Livie winced to think of the spanking that was coming, but he didn't raise his hand to her. Then her father surprised her by sitting on a stool with a sigh. She dropped her eyes, confused.

"I don't think I've ever been so angry," Papa growled convincingly through clenched teeth. "I cannot begin to guess what you were think-ing."

Livie couldn't think of a thing to say.

Her father stood and began stalking back and forth like the mean dog with no name, grumbling to himself about what a foolish daugh-ter he had and how he might, just might, be sending her to a convent, whatever that might be. What manner of child would just wander off in a storm?

Livie sat on the stool. She had no answer for him.

Olivia, do you think that this might be because Papa's right? asked The Voice. *Because you really don't think?* No, she thought. Because he wouldn't understand. Papa can't imagine the world outside the farm. He just doesn't know how I feel. Where has Papa ever been, except out to the farmyard, or to the edges of the field of rye? He doesn't know where the ocean is, he's never seen it. He doesn't miss flowers he's never seen. He has no friends.

"At least Purgatoire had sense enough to bring you home," Papa said. "Not that *that* isn't embarrassing enough."

"His name is *Monsieur Picoult!*" Livie blurted. "And he was nice to me. He saved me from the storm. He fed me soup."

Papa's eyebrows scrunched in confusion.

"A storm which you shouldn't even have been out in to begin with," Maman whined, her face shiny with tears.

"Soup?" Papa asked.

"See? You don't understand," Livie said without looking at her mother. "Yes, he fed me soup."

"What was he doing making soup out in the storm? I always thought he was mad." Papa shook his head.

"No, Papa. Not in the storm. On his farm. In the kitchen. His wife is dead." Livie tried to explain but suddenly Maman was talking too loudly.

"What was she doing? Running away? Is that it? That is it! She was running away." Maman waved her hand at Papa, who shook his head some more.

"Don't you see what it is that you do to your mother?" Papa added.

"Monsieur Picoult. He fed you soup. Isn't that nice," said Maman.

"I helped make the soup. I cut the turnips. There was chicken in the soup, even. It was his wife's recipe," Livie knew that she was talking too much, and that it wasn't helping. Maman wasn't interested in what she was saying and it was probably making things worse, but she had started and couldn't stop herself.

"Oh. Monsieur Picoult puts chicken in the soup for his wife?"

"No. His wife is dead. She loved flowers. Lilies! Purple and yellow and...and white." Now Livie started to cry. *Why now?*" asked The Voice. I don't know, she thought.

"She died when his son was born, but his son died, too," Livie wept.

Papa gave a small shrug. Livie looked at him. His eyes were dark, distant.

"Oh," Maman said softly.

"Why don't you know that? That's awful! Monsieur Picoult is our neighbor," Livie accused her mother. She sobbed uncontrollably, holding her apron to her face.

Maman stood up and walked into the front room again; waving one hand in confused dismissal, and wiping her tears on the hem of her own apron with the other.

"Do you see?" Papa asked again, letting Livie cry.

"*Oui*, Papa. Yes, Papa," Livie said, in the way she always did, but not really the same, because it was all different now. "You knew that. About Monsieur Picoult's wife?"

"Of course," Papa said.

"But you never said anything about it to Maman," she said quietly.

"No, I didn't."

And nothing else was said about it. Livie sat in one chair and Papa in the other. Surely her punishment wasn't to be so...painless. Maman came back in, her lips pressed grimly together in a thin line, her eyes dry. She waved everyone out of the kitchen. Livie and Papa went into the front room and stood quietly, listening to Maman stir at the kitchen hearth fire with the iron poker and adjust the iron pot. Then Papa grumbled that Jean-Charles and Guillaume were probably lazing about in the rye field, which had suffered under the torrential rains of the night before. He jammed his hat down on his head, pointing Livie upstairs. She was sent to her bedroom - Papa pointing upstairs and Livie going up without another word.

That was all then: just her going, and then sitting beneath the window in her room, which streamed in the morning light and reflected tiny motes of dust like sparkling gems. She cried some more before she was quiet, her breath hiccupping from the weeping, and then even that stopped. Finally, sitting on the floor on the bit of rough-woven cloth that lay beneath her bed, Livie curled her legs beneath her and thought.

She felt like a pot of soup boiling over. Her thoughts poured out like the rain of the previous night. The storm, being terrified in the middle of the rain and thunder, all alone. Monsieur Picoult! All this time we have a neighbor we don't even know. My goodness! We live above a town we never visit, by a river we've never seen that leads to a world we've never heard of. We choose to be alone, and to know nothing and no one. We choose to not put chicken in our soup! Livie smiled at that one, leaning back, her memory of the wonderful taste as clear as the bright sunshine out of her window. We are the problem - not Monsieur Picoult, or his oxen and wagon, or the weather and the price of tomatoes, or the Calvinists in town.

· But I don't want to be like that anymore, Livie told herself. I have new friends. And a neighbor! I want to visit Monsieur Picoult. I want to talk about the world. I wish to go to town, and to, to... see beyond this hillside. I want to plant flowers! Why didn't she? Her family!

She could think of nothing about them that was pleasant. Nothing likeable. Was there anything she could do with them?

Well, you can try to stay out of trouble, grumbled The Voice, which apparently even now was choosing to never say anything nice and never, it seemed, to shut up when Livie wanted it to. She sat up. *You could give that a try. But you just go looking for it.* I don't. Not really. But I know what you mean, she thought. I don't try to get in trouble, but sometimes trouble finds me... *Trouble sent you running up the hill?* asked The Voice. *Kept you from going home when the storm was approaching? Please.*

And I suppose I could try not letting trouble find me, couldn't I? Livie was amazed at where her thinking had taken her. I could try and see how well that works. Just for a while.

Chapter Eight

Whenever she thought about it, Livie felt the disappointment of not seeing her new friends. Loneliness was a strange, dull hurt in her stomach; a feeling much like hunger. But she discovered that after a while she didn't think about it all of the time, because potatoes needed to be dug, baskets carried to the cellar in the cattle byre. Meals were eaten, nights followed days.

Summer was almost over. The nights were cooler, more often than not. Papa and her brothers had already mown the rye, and stacked it to dry in tall, mounded sheaves. They looked up at the sky a lot, watching the clouds, hoping it wouldn't rain and ruin their crop. Livie was assigned the task of gleaning, gathering loose stalks missed by her brothers - carrying handfuls of rye like bland dried flowers and setting them on the drying piles of grain. It was boring work, and bending over was tiring, but Papa did not scold her for being slow, and perhaps because of this she didn't daydream like she used to, but stuck to the task, row after tedious row.

Each bit of rye is important to the family, Papa remarked at every supper through the harvest. We can't leave food on the ground for the mice. Winter is coming soon enough and winters are always hard. And he always followed with this refrain: that it had been a good growing season – they'd been lucky and God had blessed them, so far.

"Even the smallest handful of grain..." he said directly to Livie, who nodded.

"*Oui*, Papa. Yes, Papa." She knew how that sentence ended. No waste.

He nodded back at her. Well, she decided, if he wasn't exactly cheerful he seemed strangely contented.

Her brothers were somehow different, too. At first, they had ignored her even more than they had before the storm, if that was possible. So Livie ignored them back. She could do just as well without them, anyhow. *Don't go looking for trouble*, The Voice reminded her. No, no. I'll do my work, they can do theirs.

And then, when one morning the big mean black dog finally snapped his frayed old rope and came tearing out into the field where she was weeding, Livie didn't scream and run. Although she was afraid, Livie stood as still as one of the stalks of rye. The beast came galloping towards her, its husky bark like thunder. It ran a circle around her, barking and growling. Livie shut her eyes. She could feel the bits of dirt that the big black dog's claws kicked up against her arms and legs. Over the noise she could hear Guillaume shouting "Livie! No!" from the far side of the field, as if something here was her fault. She peeked, saw Guillaume running towards them, and squeezed her eyes shut again. If the dog wanted to attack, now was its opportunity. *After all, what can you do?* asked The Voice. *Your brother is too far away.* What indeed, she thought. I can continue to do nothing. Or... Livie opened her eyes. The big black dog now stood in front of her, menacingly shifting from side to side, its fur looking greasy and breath stinking as sourly as a night-jar. It seemed to wriggle in anticipation, Livie thought, of what she could only guess. Eating her. She also saw Jean-

72

Charles come jogging from the root field, where he'd been weeding potatoes with an iron rake. He carried the implement over his shoulder. What's he plan to do with that? Is it for me or this dog? Livie asked herself. I'm tired of this. Tired of being afraid of this dog.

Something had to be done. Livie took a deep breath. Bending her legs she leapt at the big black dog, screaming at the top of her lungs.

****

"I've no idea what has come over you, Livie," Guillaume said, weaving the two broken pieces of rope together. "Biting the dog? Did you lose your mind?"

"The dog wanted to bite me," she said matter-of-factly. "And so I bit him first."

"You don't bite dogs." Her other brother shook his head. He stifled a smile, but Livie could tell he wasn't really mad at her.

"And I think that this dog, this nameless dog, won't decide to bite me again, either." She spat on the ground again. The dog's ear had tasted nasty.

"I shouldn't think so, little sister. You've given him a good nick on the ear. He'll remember that."

Guillaume and Jean-Charles laughed when Livie started calling the big black dog Nick. And so, now when Livie went out to the cattle-byre, the beast lay flat on its belly until she passed, not cowering, but no longer threatening her, either. Livie decided that she and Nick respected each other.

It was Maman who'd changed the most over the summer. She seemed to not want to go back to her old rarely affectionate and often grumpy self. Livie knew that she'd hurt her mother's feelings by telling her about Monsieur Picoult's wonderful soup. *And by getting lost in the storm*, The Voice reminded her. But mostly the soup. Well, alright then. It would take time to mend the wounds between them. I'll just do my work, she told herself. Maman will see.

And, apparently and quite suddenly, Maman did see. She left

Livie alone to do her tasks without asking twice, and to complete them without further nagging. She didn't fuss at Livie about washing her face or hands – and Livie did it without asking. Livie helped as well, staying out from under foot in the kitchen when Maman was cooking. Ripe tomatoes were picked from the vines before they fell into the dirt. She duly weeded the herb garden.

Of this Livie was fairly certain: had gardening and washing and staying out of trouble been absolutely everything, and the only things that happened on the farm, everyone would have noticed the new Livie, and perhaps treated her differently. But things don't always turn out the way they seem they might, and absolutely everything is awfully hard to control. And on Livie's family's farm, something else would change things first.

That something else began on the first of the late summer market days. Livie heard the wagon, the clank of bells. Oh! George and Louis! she thought. And my friend, Monsieur Picoult, coming down the hillside lane. I wonder what they are taking to town? Let's go see! One moment she was stripping sun dried beans from their vines running up long ash-wood poles; the next, she dropped those bean-pods that were in her hand near the basket, and started to gallop off towards the sound. Livie skidded to a stop in the dirt. *No, Olivia*, said The Voice In Her Head. *You have a job to do – it is to finish harvesting the beans. Papa and your brothers will ready our goods for market.* But I want to see my friend, Livie thought. I want to talk with him, and hear him call me the maiden-of-the-mountain. Only for a few moments, then I will get back to work. *But good girls don't stop working when they feel like it*, whispered The Voice. *They keep at their tasks until they are complete.* Yes, she thought. They do. She picked up the discarded beans, put them in the basket. She almost stomped her *sabot* in frustration, but didn't. She felt like crying.

Pluck. Pluck. She pulled the bean-pods from the sturdy vines. Sweat rolled down her cheeks like cool tears. After a while, the bells rang again, and she knew that Monsieur Picoult's wagon was going on

74

its way, off to town to the market, with Papa's early potatoes and the midsummer carrots. No one had called her to come see the visitor, her friend.

She shook her head. Don't be silly. Go! Running as quick as she was able to the front of the farmyard, she slowed as she saw Monsieur Picoult already down the hill, too far away to catch and say hello. Too far away to shout hello. Now Livie did stamp her *sabot* in the dust, once, and turned to go back to her work.

Maman brought food outside to a small table under the shade of an oak tree near the fields, and Papa and Guillaume and Jean-Charles put down their tools and walked over.

"Livie, lunch!" Papa called. Livie brought her basket of beans with her to give to Maman. The beans would be stored in the cold cellar for their winter soups. They would have bean soup so often that Papa would growl by springtime that he never wanted to eat it again in his lifetime. Of course, by the following autumn he would have it for lunch and supper, day after day.

Livie sat on the rough wood bench in the shade of the oak. Maman had brought a small loaf of bread, and wooden bowls for soup. Papa sat next to her. Guillaume and Jean-Charles sprawled on the shady grass. The pot was small, just for carrying, and there was no odor from it, because it was cool. Last night's soup: turnips and bitter-greens. Livie said nothing, didn't make a face, because the soup might be the same old thing, but having the bread was special. It was a rye-loaf, crusty on the outside and sort-of sweet and chewy on the inside, even though it was made of rye flour. Maman handed her a torn-off bit of the bread, which Livie dipped in the soup and chewed. The broth was cold and thin. The bread, though, was good and filling. By dipping and chewing, she drank the broth of the soup. Then, with a small bit of crust left, she used it as a scoop to eat the soft turnips and limp-cooked greens, which tasted both familiar and vile. But her jaw ached with so much wonderful chewing.

"You didn't come and see your friend?" Papa asked softly, his mouth full of bread. He nudged Livie gently with his elbow. She shook her head without looking him in the eye. I was busy, she said softly. In fact, she wondered if Monsieur Picoult was hurt that she didn't go to see him.

"Too bad," Papa said. "Old Purgatoire asked about you." Livie nodded and shrugged. She didn't correct Papa. She knew that he was not unhappy that she hadn't come running when the wagon came down the lane. Maman waved her wooden spoon.

"Leave her alone, Papa. She was working hard with the pole-beans."

"I know, I know," Papa said, waving a bit of bread crust. "Well, then. He brought you something."

"What?" she asked, trying hard to not sound too interested. "Something for me?"

"Yes, it's up in a basket by the door."

"May I go see? I'll bring the beans to the kitchen, Maman," Livie said.

"Yes. That's a good girl." Maman looked at her oddly, but Livie just took the basket of beans and walked to the house.

Maman and Papa are *jealous* of Monsieur Picoult? Livie decided as she brought the basket into the kitchen. *Of course,* said The Voice. *What's not to be jealous of? He has piglets and a wagon, and oxen. He puts chicken in his soup, and brings you gifts. If you were permitted to, you would talk about him all day and into the night. So what does your father do? He works scraping in the dirt. He must ask Monsieur Picoult to carry his goods to market for him, s'il vous plaît.*

Is that all? Livie asked.

Your Papa is also jealous because Monsieur Picoult saved you from the storm.

Livie set the beans down in the kitchen and went into the front room. There, by the door, was a small wooden basket. She peered into it. It seemed to be full of dirty rocks. What a strange thing to give someone as s gift.

Not rocks, foolish girl, said The Voice. *These are bulbs. Don't you remember? Flower bulbs.*

She picked one up. Yes, they felt different from rocks, lighter. She turned it over in her hand. It was irregularly shaped, and dried dirt clung to crevasses in the thing. Flowers grow from these. She was amazed. Then it came to her.

"Like turnips. This is the root of the flower, then."

But what was she to do with it? She set it gently back down in the basket, like something fragile. There were more in there than she knew how to count. Her mind raced. These were real flowers. Monsieur Picoult had brought her flowers. Lilies. They must be lilies. She felt her face flush. How beautiful these must be. The colors of the sky, and clouds and summer sunsets. Livie turned in a circle, ready to gallop out of the house and tell everyone that she had flowers, and afraid to say anything for fear that they wouldn't care. No. She put her hands on her hips. She would *behave*.

She wanted to plant them immediately. Should they be planted immediately? Everything had a proper season for planting, she knew that. Who would know this? Monsieur Picoult, but I cannot ask him. Papa? Papa knew everything about planting. How would he feel about planting flowers? Livie shook her head. Her brothers would not be able to keep quiet if she asked them. Surely they already knew about the gift, and that she would eventually have to ask someone for a place to plant them, or how to plant them. But everyone was changing towards her, treating her differently because she was behaving now, and working hard. She frowned in thought. No. My family is changing because I behave; that is so. But everything has changed because they think that I behave for Monsieur Picoult. I think that is what Maman and Papa and even Jean-Charles and Guillaume think. They are jealous of Monsieur Picoult, or rather of her friendship with Monsieur Picoult. So she couldn't ask her brothers.

Only Maman would know how to plant lilies, and would give her an answer without any problems. Maman would be happy to tell her, if, she asked in the right way, at the right time. She went back outside to help Maman clean up lunch.

"What was in the basket?" Jean-Charles asked at supper. Livie looked up from her soup. Her brothers were looking at her. *Olivia, they know what is in the basket*, said The Voice, *as well as they know what is in tonight's soup.* Probably even better, Livie thought.

"Flower bulbs, I think," she said softly. "I'm not sure."

"Yes, root bulbs," Papa grumbled as he ate a spoonful of soup. But it was not his normal grumble, but a thoughtful grumble. He wiped his chin with a sleeve. "Lilies I think. Or perhaps irises. Not those Dutch tulips, though. Yes, lilies." He took another spoonful of soup, which dribbled on his chin again.

"What are you going to do with them?" Guillaume asked Papa. Surprised, Livie looked from her brother to her father. Papa shrugged.

"They're not my lilies," he grumbled again. Everyone looked at Maman now.

Maman pretended to be irritated that everyone was looking at her for an answer.

"Why are you fools looking at me? They're not my lilies, either. I have no idea what should be done with them. Who would give such a gift?" Maman got up to tend the fire, muttering about how foolish her family was.

Suddenly it was the wrong time to ask Maman anything. Even though everything was changing, Livie couldn't talk with her about flowers. She was certain her brothers and Papa had spoiled the moment, sensed this deeply in her belly, which almost wriggled with worry that Maman would tell her to toss the bulbs out – that they would be like the weed-flowers, that there was nowhere good to plant them, no time to care for them on a busy farm. Or was it that the gift had been from Monsieur Picoult to Livie, and that made Maman jealous all over again? Oh, please ask me what I want to do with them, she begged silently, lifting her wooden spoon full of soup and blowing on it before sipping it, although it was quite cool enough. She kept eating, not looking at Maman or her brothers or Papa.

"Well then," Papa grumbled once more. "Nothing need be done about it." Livie felt her heart sink.

"Not right now, anyway," he continued. "Bulbs are planted in the late Fall." Livie looked up. Papa was looking at her, His lips pursed, hidden behind his whiskers. He was not smiling. But then he did something she couldn't remember him ever doing before. He gave her a wink.

Chapter Nine

Livie supposed that she liked autumn better than any other season. The air was cool, with playful breezes in the morning that chased the chickens around the yard. The leaves of the big oak at the edge of the rye field had changed to orange and red to replace the summer sunsets.

She gathered acorns into her apron, shivering; her shift-dress was worn thin. It was also too short now and her stockings were torn at the knees and heels.

"My goodness, you look like a waif without a home," Maman tut-tutted. Livie's mother sat on the bench beneath the oak tree, her face hidden by the brim of her straw hat, a woven basket in her lap. She was using a horseshoe nail to crack open the acorns and pick out the meats, which she dropped into a wooden bowl beside her on the bench. The acorn meats, Livie knew, would be dried and then ground to make rough flour.

"I will need to get some cloth to sew you a new dress and you will mend your own stockings. Your apron..." Maman looked up from her work, shaking her head. "I don't know."

Livie lifted her apron; it was stained with so many different colors that she couldn't say what had caused which mark on the dull gray cloth.

"You will have to keep your apron, for a while. It is...serviceable." Maman lifted her face and rolled her eyes. Livie saw her but said nothing.

"Thank you, Maman. I don't know how to mend stockings," Livie said.

"No, but I will show you how, *cherie*. Tonight."

Cherie! Livie looked at her mother. Maman's eyes were deep set, the skin crinkled at the corners, almost bruised looking. Maman's tired eyes. Silently, they continued to work.

They were tired eyes, for Maman woke this morning like she woke every morning, before the dawn. She started the fire at the kitchen hearth from last night's coals buried under the ashes she'd carefully banked last night. After the fire caught, more difficult on rainy days with damp logs, she'd climbed the stairs and shook Livie's feet to wake her.

"Up, child. New day," Maman had said flatly. Always the same words. Livie could have said them for her.

Before – that is, before the storm – Livie might have sighed and rolled over and pretended to still be asleep, or sick, even. Maman would have had to tramp back up the stairs to get her a second time, grumpy for the wasted time and effort. The day's mood would be changed. Every word from Maman's mouth until the sun went down would be clipped short with her.

Now before Maman was out the door, Livie rose and put on her too-small dress and stained apron, and slid on her *sabots*. Carefully and quietly she descended the stairs, so as not to wake Papa and her brothers. Maman had already pulled a fresh bucket of water from the well, poured it into the pot, pulled another, rinsed her face and hands, and then carried the full pot to the fire to begin boiling the water for breakfast. Livie, too, rinsed her own face from the bucket, leaving the remaining frigid water to warm a bit in the air for Papa and her brothers.

In the kitchen, Maman placed a double handful of whatever cereal was available - barley or oats or rye - added a pinch of precious salt, and a dollop of sorghum molasses into the boiling water. This roiled and cooked over the morning fire until the grain burst open and the sweet thick smell of the steaming molasses filled the kitchen.

This is what woke the men. Livie listened as they moaned and groaned - no doubt stretching sore arms and legs - and their tramping around upstairs causing the floorboards to creak as if the house, too, was waking up under protest.

One by one they stomped noisily downstairs and made their way outside to the well, where they scrubbed themselves awake in the still-cold wash-water and dried with an old gray towel that Livie carried to them.

Pouring four bowls of the breakfast mush - setting three on the table for the men and handing one to Livie - Maman retreated to the cattle-byre to gather the makings for lunch and supper, potatoes or turnips or rutabagas, onions, tight heads of green or red cabbage. With her wooden spoon, Livie ate her mush, chewing on the heat-softened grain; the chewy barley, sweet oats, the bitter-sour rye. She sipped the salty molasses-water, listening to her father and brothers slurp down their own bowls. They talked through their chewing, about what field they would work in, what needed turning, or harvesting, or storing in the cattle-byre. Was it getting warm or cool too fast? Too slow? Would rain delay harvesting the hayfield? Probably so, probably so. Was there straw that needed raking for the potato cellar? At that, eyes turned to Livie, almost frightening her because she didn't know that they even considered her there, part of the conversation. Papa's eyebrows went up in silent question, and she nodded in understanding that this would be one of her morning's tasks.

Presently, Maman returned, her apron full, just as the men were heading out. No words were spoken here, no affectionate good mornings shared, no breakfast thank-yous beyond a nod. Hats were pulled down over still-sleepy eyes, as Papa and Livie's brothers tramped out into the breaking dawn. Maman dumped her wares onto the kitchen table among the abandoned breakfast bowls and dirty spoons. Livie looked at the small pile of potatoes, bruised, and the limpest of turnips and carrots. She stood with her hands by her side. The vegetables barely looked like food.

Maman took her knife and wiped it on her apron. She took a carrot and chopped it into disks, then carefully placed every piece in the pot of water. But the carrots go in last, Livie thought of Monsieur Picoult's words. They are the most delicate.

The turnip went next. There was a small spot of rot on it, which Maman cut out and tossed onto the fire, where it sizzled and smoked. The other bits joined the soup.

Maman glanced up now. Livie looked down at her *sabots*, feeling embarrassed at having been caught watching.

"What is it, girl?" Maman asked.

"Nothing," Livie whispered.

"Tell me. It's alright to tell me," Maman said. Livie wanted to hug her mother, but didn't. She couldn't remember when she had last hugged Maman. She had been very young, to be sure.

"Monsieur Picoult let me help make his soup."

"Is that so?" Maman said, without looking up from the table. "Well it's about time, then. Do you think you can cut these potatoes?" Maman lifted her eyes now to meet Livie's. The girl nodded and held out her hand.

"It's not a very sharp knife, so you'll have to be more careful," Maman said.

Livie frowned. That didn't make sense. A sharper knife would be more dangerous, true?

"A dull knife you have to push harder to make slice, so be careful."

Maman took her long-handled wooden spoon and stirred the pot.

"Salt?"

"No salt today. No pepper either. Not for lunch-soup, *cherie*," Maman said.

Livie carefully carried the sliced potatoes to Maman, who placed them carefully into the hot water.

"It will fill them up," said Maman. "But I am sorry that it doesn't taste better. But at least we eat every day. Some do not, you know."

Livie had never thought of that. Did any people in Annonay live on turnip soup? Or was their fare better? Or could it be worse? Was their anything worse than bitter, sour turnip soup? She couldn't imagine it. And she just wanted something to taste good, for a change. That was how it had felt, at Picoult's. A wondrous change.

"The food we eat. The vegetables. Why are they always the worst?" Livie asked. She expected Maman to snap at her, but her mother just looked sadly tired.

"The best is for selling, child." No complaints. "We never eat the best." Just the truth about things. *Ah, so that is why Picoult gave you his tasty soup*, griped The Voice. *It was not his everyday supper, but something special just for you, Olivia. Don't you see?*

I think I do see, Livie thought. But I don't know why.

****

Acorn meats were bitter, but Livie nibbled one anyway. She was hungry and it wasn't lunch time yet. Maman was chewing on one, too.

"Not good," Livie offered.

"No, not very," Maman replied without taking her eyes off of her work. She swallowed the bit in her mouth and took another. "But if we mix it with oat or barley flour, or even the rye, we can make almost twice as much bread. And it's not so bitter, then. Your Papa doesn't mind an acorn loaf."

Livie looked at her mother. Her chest felt full watching Maman's busy hands leaning over the bowl of nut-meats, broken shells fallen at her feet. Maman knew how to keep the family from going without in winter. The food was not tasty, perhaps, but they were never hungry.

Livie walked out to the edge of the shade, where the oak had dropped its mast of acorns. She knelt on the ground, sweeping the hulls together in a pile, picking through them. This was something she was familiar with, knowing which nuts were the ones Maman would want for grinding, and which were too small, too sour even for them to eat. She gathered the best into her apron, stood and dumped them into Maman's basket, then looked out into the sunny field where Papa was working

"Do you love Papa?"

Maman glanced up, a puzzled look in her eyes.

"Love?"

"Yes, Maman."

"Papa is strong," Maman said.

"Yes, Maman. That's true," said Livie. Her father had arms like the branches of the oak tree they were beneath. Many times she had watched Papa while moved rocks from the fields her brothers plowed, stacking them on the walls that already framed the fields.

"Papa works hard," Maman said.

"*Yes,* Maman," said Livie once again. Surely, no one worked harder than Papa. She squinted out at the field beyond the oak tree. Papa was gathering straw from the rye field this morning. It was hard work, to bend and slash at the harvested rye stubble with a sickle, laying each handful of light-brown onto the ground, to dry for one more day and then gather it all back up to be put into the cattle-byre for drying and threshing. Papa would come in this evening, his back as bent as the sickle he was swinging, Livie knew.

"And he is patient," said Maman. Her mother waved her hand in front of her face, as if brushing away flies.

Livie frowned. Patient? *That means he doesn't get angry easily,* said The Voice. I know what it means, Livie thought. But is Papa quick to anger? she asked herself. She supposed not. Not on a sunny day like today, far on the other side of the rye field. His frown and gruff voice was very far away today.

But do you love him, she thought. I wonder. Maman's eyes were hidden again by the brim of her hat. She hadn't said yes, or no.

"Come. Too many questions, child. Let us get this done," Maman said softly. She looked up. "We have something else to do this morning and then we still must get their lunch to them." She pointed at the field where the men worked.

"What is it?" Livie asked. But with a strange, sly smile, her mother went back to her work, her nimble fingers digging with the horseshoe nail to break more of the acorns that Livie had dumped from her apron into the basket.

Maman softly hummed a tune. What was this all about? Livie tried to remember a time when her mother had seemed so...cheerful. It was like listening to the breeze blow through the leaves. Then Maman finally stood.

"Come, we will put these out to dry." She carried the bowl on her hip and walked back towards the house, Livie following, carrying the basket.

They couldn't leave the nutmeats outside, because squirrels would steal them to feast on. Maman spread them on the kitchen table. At the hearth, she nudged the logs in the fireplace. Flames flickered to life, to warm the room some, and help the acorns dry.

"Let's go," she said. "It's time. Go and get your basket." What basket? she thought. Oh! Livie's eyes went wide. The lily basket!

Her mother tilted her head.

"Don't you want to plant them? How else do you think they will grow?"

Yes, yes! thought Livie. She nodded.

Maman went out the front door onto the lane. Livie scampered behind her, her little basket-gift over her arm.

Chapter Ten

Walking up the hill behind Maman, Livie grinned, then bit her tongue to make her silly smile go away because Maman might look over her shoulder and see it. Sometimes, she realized, just when you think you are beginning to understand how things work, and how people handle how things work, that's when everything wants to change. Spring. Summer. Autumn and Winter. Steadily tramp the seasons, like climbing a hill. Up rolls the sun, down falls the rain, leaves grow, leaves fall, criss-cross travels the moon, hither and thither blows the wind. Though you don't always understand the rules. still you may see how dry and wet, hot and cold, blustery and calm...well, everything *is*.

I'm beginning to know, she thought. Actually know things. *But are you surprised that this is not so with people?* asked The Voice. *You can never be sure with people, and if you think that you are, you'd better be ready to look again.* I know, I know, she sang aloud to The Voice. Suddenly aware that she was singing, Livie stopped, smiled at Maman who'd turned to look, then shrugged and swung her arms as she walked. She shook her head at herself, then looked down just to make sure that her feet were on the ground. Yes, still kicking up dust, still clomping up the hill. Livie couldn't risk saying another word. Oh, my! They were going out to plant the bulbs. Her lilies. It would be just like having *un belle jardin*, her very own pretty garden.

Maman's wooden *sabots* kicking up little puffs of dust in the lane, making her seem, from Livie's vantage, to be a woman just taking a morning stroll, not going anywhere in particular. *How would you know that? When*, asked The Voice, *have you ever seen a woman taking a stroll?* True enough, she thought. Never, as far back as she could remember. But it must have happened, else why would I think of it? *Because you are sometimes – just sometimes – a silly girl.* Yes, Livie admitted, but not today. Not now, I'm not. The sun bore down, and she wiped the sweat off of her brow, leaving a dark patch on the arm of her dress. I don't care! With a skip, she ran to catch up with Maman.

She set the basket down on the lane. The grass was dry and brown, and the breeze that blew through it made a shushing noise, like someone afraid that a baby might overhear too-loud talking. The autumn sky was a deep blue, marked by only a handful of small clouds. Maman nodded her head.

"Pretty," Maman said. "A very pretty place."

"Oh, Maman, I wish..." Livie bit her tongue again. She wished that there were still some of the wildflowers for her mother to see. So that she would know how they looked. But of course Maman had said that they were weeds.

"What do you wish?" Maman asked. Her hands were on her hips, turning slowly, taking it all in.

"When I was here before, there were lace flowers and yellow ones like the flames in a hearth when it is burning down at night."

"Where?" Maman asked. Livie pointed. Her face flushed, and there was a lump in her throat. See, she told The Voice. Maman *is* interested. And see? There, by the side of the lane, a broken head of thistle, most of its purple bloom gone, just sun-dried threads remaining. Maman saw it and gently shook the thistle's head, to shake loose the last seeds. She looked over at Livie and smiled.

"Let's get to work," Maman said softly. Wading into the grass as if it were the water of a shallow pond, she moved off of the road.

Maman worked without talking, without explaining, and Livie did what she did. Together, they pulled out handfuls of the brown grass, snapping and twisting it down to stubble, piling the grass outside a small circle that Maman was making. Then, Maman scratched at the stubble with the rough tips of her fingers until she had bared some of the grass roots. Pinching them in her fists she pulled them out, baring more tough roots, and pulling those out as well. She grunted with the effort of each tug, and wiped her own brow on a sleeve. Livie knelt across from her mother and scratched at the stubble. It was hot work, but the breeze was good, and they were steadily clearing a space in the dirt to plant her flowers, and so Livie couldn't help but smile. In a while they had made a small clearing in the weeds down to the bare dirt, big enough for both of them to kneel in. Then Maman scratched at the bare dirt, digging in it with her tough fingertips. Livie did the same, her fingers aching.

"Look at this," Maman said softly. She held up a clump from the basket. The thing had a shape difficult to describe – not round, not like an egg or a nut from a tree. "This is the root of the flower. Ugly, but containing beauty inside it. It holds the life, and allows it to be reborn each spring. Like our Lord Jesus, it dies and rises again." Maman took her other hand and touched her forehead, crossing herself. Livie copied her. Then Maman pointed at a spot on the thing.

"See here? Find the stump of the old root on one side and the base of the stem on the other, then plant it as it was taken from the ground." Maman scooped a small hole in the loose dirt they had cleared of grass, and placed the bulb in, the withered stem of the bulb facing up. She cupped her hand and scooped the dirt into the hole, covering the bulb.

"Now you try," Maman said. "Show me." Livie picked a bulb

from the basket.

"Good. Where is the stem? Can you see the difference between stem and root?"

Livie turned it over in her hands. There. That was the old stem, and that the bit of root-hair hanging down. She patiently scooped her own hole.

"Good," Maman said. "They should be far enough apart from each other so that they don't steal each other's water. And not quite so deep. You want them in the ground before winter, and to feel the cold without freezing, but not to have to struggle so much in the spring. Right?"

Livie nodded, imagining the stalk of the plant trying to push through the cold earth next spring, reaching up and seeing the sunshine, feeling the breeze on the hilltop. She scratched another hole in the dry dirt, tossing aside the old weed-roots, and picking another bulb. This side goes up, she thought, and placed it gently into the hole. One by one, they planted each bulb, each future flower.

Maman sat back on the dry, flattened grass and sighed. There was dirt on her cheek and forehead, and a dark lock of hair had slipped from her kerchief that she wore beneath her straw sunhat. Livie sat up, too, and grinned at her mother. Every bulb was planted.

"You have dirt on your face, Maman."

"As do you, cherie. But this is going to be beautiful. Perhaps even as beautiful as your wildflowers, don't you think?"

Even more so, Livie thought. Yes, yes, although I've never seen a lily, I believe that it shall be more beautiful.

"I'm thirsty." Maman waved her hand toward the lane. "Go and bring us some water from the well, will you? Mind you, not a whole bucket but a half, so that it is not too heavy to carry but enough for us to drink."

"Do we need to water these?" Livie pointed at their garden.

"No, we will let the next rain water them."

"But what if it doesn't rain all autumn?" Livie asked.

"Of course it will." Maman shook her head and looked up at the startlingly blue sky. "Not today, perhaps, but in its own time. Go, Livie, and get us water. I'm parched and cannot wait for rain."

Livie set off down the lane at a trot. Her fingers were tired from scraping at the roots and dirt. Hurry, hurry, she told herself. Before Maman decides she's had enough of this for the morning.

It wasn't a particularly slippery place or too steep, and the pebble wasn't notable at all except that it was round, or rather somewhat round, as pebbles will often be. But it was what it was and where it was, a round pebble on a dusty hillside lane, and the wooden sole of Livie's left sabot landed on it just so, and it rolled some more, and Livie slipped. Her feet went up in the air, and her shoes flew off and she fell flat on her back with a thud and a hmmph! of air rushing out of her as she hit the ground. Ouch, said The Voice. That hurt. Not too much, Livie thought. She caught a first big breath and coughed and gagged as she tried to take a second breath because she had also kicked up a cloud of dust. This is what I get for running. Yes, scolded The Voice. How many times has Papa told you? More than even you can count. Hush, she thought. With her eyes closed, she rubbed the back of her head. It hadn't hit the road so much as it had a clump of dried weed, there like a pillow by the side of the lane. And her backside wasn't too sore either, considering. Now, if she could only just find her shoes. Livie opened her eyes, and gasped.

She must have bumped her head harder than she thought. Something so beautiful, and so very much like a flower, only nothing at all like a flower. At least no flower that Livie had ever seen before. A flower of her dreams.

Floating in the sky, the thing moved slowly, as if it was pushed by a breeze, the way an oak leaf falling from its branch might drift along. Or a chicken feather, drifting around the farmyard in ways that for some reason a chicken itself could not. Livie watched, still lying on the ground where she had fallen.

Was it an angel? She'd always imagined that angels would look like people, like someone so beautiful that to look right at them it would hurt your heart, but perhaps this was not actually the way of things. This angel looked more like the night-moon, round but not exactly round. A moon with some part of it missing, as the moon sometimes had. And it was coming closer. Oh, I hope it is an angel, she thought.

Then...what was that? Her ears perked up. There! Thunder in the otherwise clear blue sky. Livie frowned, but did not take her eyes off of the floating angel. The thunder grew louder, like a fast-coming storm. She shivered. Not again, she thought. She wasn't sure she could handle being caught out in another rainstorm. But the sky; there was no sign of rain in it. This thunder even sounded different. Was this angel coming for her, in heavenly anger for something she had done? A shout rang out. Look out! The rumbling of thunder approached.

Get up, Olivia. Get away from the storm, said The Voice. But she couldn't move. The angel was calling out to her. Look out!

In a flurry of noise and dust, something passed over her head and she threw up her hands to cover her face and screamed. Whatever was passing over her screamed as well. Livie squeezed her eyes tightly shut again. The thunder abruptly stopped. She was caught in a battle between an oncoming angel and the arriving devil!

"In the name of all that's holy, what are you doing lying in the road?" asked a man's voice. "Are you hurt?"

"No, I'm fine. Leave me alone, devil," Livie grunted, answering the voice honestly in spite of herself, choking on dust, and still lying on the ground.

"Crazy child! Have you lost your mind?"

Livie shook her head, eyes closed. She didn't feel like having a conversation with the devil, that was for sure.

"Well, then, get up out of the road. There! It's coming down right here," said the man's voice, the devil.

Yes, Livie thought. That's what you get, devil. That angel comes for you. She wasn't at all sure that this was how things went between such creatures, as she had never been to church and Papa only rarely spoke of the things of God. Livie had, however, seen ants fight each other, and small birds chase away the lone crow. It made sense to her – conflict was a natural event.

"You are very foolish to be lying in the road, little girl, and yet wise to know the peculiarities of the atmosphere, so that you could predict where my balloon would alight." Then the rumble again. Even with her eyes closed tightly, Livie could now tell that it wasn't at all thunder, but hooves, like those of Monsieur Picoult's boys. What is a balloon? Oh, please, hurry here, angel. If there is to be a battle, well, this would be one to see, she imagined, although she wasn't at all sure she wanted to lay eyes on a devil - turned out in red with hooves and horns and an impish smile. On the other hand, she was curious. She tried to open her eyes through the dust, but they stung painfully.

"Ah, I am sorry about the dirt. Take my handkerchief and wipe them, please," said the devil, and she felt a soft cloth pass by her hands, and reached for it. What in the world? Devils never helped people, never handed a cloth to clean with. She wiped her face, and sniffed deeply. Oh, my, the bit of cloth smelled wonderful, like many different flowers all in a bunch.

Cautiously, Livie peeked. And found that she was almost disappointed. It was only a man, there, sitting on a horse. *Yes, but what a horse*, said The Voice. Quite true, she thought. Not a farm-dray, which Livie had seen once or twice before, leading a small cart up the lane to, she assumed, Monsieur Picoult's farm, and for which Papa had occasionally expressed envy. This, on the other hand, was a marvelously beautiful kind of horse, all black with long, smooth legs that looked perfectly created for the very kind of jumping that it must have just done, over the top of her as she'd lain on the ground. Mounted on the charger was a young man with a strange white face and an old man's white hair, an ornamented tri-corn hat and the fanciest clothes that Livie had ever seen. Trousers more blue than the sky itself. A high-collared jacket of a different shade of blue and a different cloth - not faded, but made to look that way, which he wore unbuttoned. Beneath the jacket, a golden vest and a smock so white it defied dirt to land on it. Livie had never seen such colors in clothing. They were almost as pretty as flowers. Who wears clothing like this to work? Or to ride a horse? Maybe this was the devil, after all, sent to tempt people like her. But he was looking up in the air and smiling, and it didn't seem to her a smile of defiance or challenge. Just a happy smile. And ignoring her altogether. Alright, then, Livie thought. Not a devil at all, so far as she was able to judge such things.

"And now here it comes. Can you favor me by holding my horse's reins, young miss?" asked the young man, looking directly at her, not ignoring her at all. "You're not afraid of him, are you? You don't need to be."

Livie imagined that the horse wasn't so hard to handle as the boys on their yoke and took the animal's reins from the man. The young man lighted from the horse and looked up. Livie followed his gaze, and saw the most amazing thing.

So, the angel wasn't an angel at all, but something else altogether. It was nearly directly above the two of them, and floating gently down towards the hilltop. Closer, it was light brown, with strange markings on the sides. Not a person, not a box, but more round in shape. Hollow, as far as Livie could tell. What held it up, suspended in the air?

"I call it a *balloon*. It's a bag of paper, you see," the young man said, spinning on his heels as he watched it overhead. "That's how it flies. Light enough, I suppose. But if I want something larger, I'm going to have to come up with better paste." He seemed to be talking to himself as much as to her. Livie stood to watch the descent of the thing. She stepped on another pebble and yelped.

"Where are my shoes?" Then she remembered that they had flown off of her feet when she fell.

"You own shoes?" asked the young man, still looking up at his fly-

94

ing device.

Livie frowned, thinking about how she must look in threadbare dress and torn stockings.

"Of course I own shoes. Don't you own shoes?"

The young man didn't even turn around to look at her. He seemed too...*busy* with his balloon to be making insults, so perhaps he hadn't meant it to be so.

"Why would you want something larger?" she asked.

"Because this balloon is too small to carry anything. It can only lift its own weight. There they are, *mademoiselle*." The man looked around and pointed at the side of the road, in the brown grass. Her *sabots* had landed one next to the other, as if dropped there on purpose. Wasn't that lucky? He strode purposefully over and picked them up, handing them back to her.

"*Merci*, Monsieur. Thank you, sir," Livie said, slipping her shoes on and giving a small curtsey, with the reins of the charger still in her hand.

"Oh, let me take those, unless you don't mind it for a moment more. Here comes the balloon."

The flying thing was coming down a bit faster now. Heading for the top of the hill. The top of the hill where Maman sat resting in the grass.

A scream pierced the late morning air. A loud scream that sounded a great deal like Maman.

Chapter Eleven

The young man clomped swiftly up the hill, without Livie and without his beautiful horse. Another scream. Oh! That was Maman for sure, Livie thought, screaming so piercingly that surely even Papa down the hill must have heard it. She looked down the lane toward the farm and hoped not.

"Come, *cherie*," Livie whispered to the charger and started leading the horse up the rest of the hill. The big animal followed her obediently.

The angel balloon had landed in the brown weeds near Livie's garden, crumpling just a bit like the hollow thing that it was. Maman was lying on the ground, and the young man was kneeling beside her, his fancy hat in hand.

Livie didn't know what to do first, go to the balloon, or Maman, or to just keep holding onto the charger's reins.

"Oh, my, I believe that she has fainted," the young man said with a shrug.

"That is my Maman," Livie said.

"You all fall down a lot," said the man, who seemed not to know what to do next. "Do you think that you might tie off Apollo there? Just loop the reins around a branch, if you would. I don't think your mother wants to wake up and see me, do you?"

Livie wrapped the reins around a small scrubby bush and patted the horse on the shoulder. Apollo, she thought. A nice name. Then she galloped through the weeds to where Maman lay on the ground.

"She was thirsty," Livie offered. "I was supposed to be bringing her water from our well. Perhaps that is that why she fainted?"

The young man shook his head. Every white hair on his head was in place, perfect. Wait, she thought. It wasn't his own hair.

"No, I think she was frightened by the balloon, that's all."

"She must have thought that the balloon was an angel," Livie replied. After all, that was what she thought, so perhaps Maman thought so, too?

"I am sorry, I have no water with me now," the young man reported, as if he might typically have carried some along for any other ride. She looked at him closely. He was not so handsome as she might have imagined such a well-dressed gentleman to be, if she thought about what gentlemen looked like at all. His skin was deathly pale, but oddly reddened about his cheeks and nose, and his eyes bulged somewhat. His lips were thin, and so red that they made his mouth look like a raw gash. And what was his hair about, anyway? As white as a grandfather's. But Livie had learned not to think about someone's appearance as being who they are. *And quite as strange as it looks, his smile seems real*, said The Voice.

"I must go get some water," Livie said. But she couldn't ask the man to stay here, a stranger.

"No, I will go. Your farm down the hill, yes? The one I just passed?" Livie nodded.

At that moment, a breeze chose to stir the weeds, cool and strong. Once more, Livie could smell the young man's perfume; somewhat like flowers, and also a bit like his horse. The gust lifted the crumpled balloon again.

'Oh, no!" cried the young man. "It will tear!"

Maman opened her eyes, saw the young man with the white hair and squawked, like one of the hens when Nick the mean black dog chased it across the yard.

"Maman, Maman! No!" Livie said. "It's, me, Livie! I'm right here, it's alright. I'm right here!"

"Oh, child, what happened? In the sky! I saw this thing!" She swung hear head back and forth looking for what she had seen.

"I know, Maman, I saw it too. It is this gentleman's...balloon." Livie looked at the young man kneeling on the ground with them. He tipped his head towards Maman, then groaned aloud as the balloon began to tumble before another gust of wind. Maman stared at the gentleman as if he was the reason she had fainted in the first place.

"Excuse me, please," he bowed again to Maman, whose eyes were wide with confusion. Then the young man stood and started running across the meadow after the balloon.

Livie leapt up, too, and chased after the big paper bag, which was tumbling across the dry brown weeds. It was heading towards the trees that marked the edge of the meadow and the beginning of the slope down towards Monsieur Picoult's farm, and would surely tear to shreds if it caught on the low branches poking out in all directions. She passed the gentleman, who stumbled and fell in the thick weeds, rolling head over heels. Once more Livie's *sabots* kicked off and, barefoot, she ran as fast as she was able, her hair flying out behind her. But there seemed no way she would catch up with it.

But the wind is a tricky thing. It twists and turns and seems to change out of spite. Just when the crumpling balloon was nearing the trees, the breeze chose that moment to change direction. The balloon rolled and bounced along the meadow's edge, and Livie pursued it.

"My goodness! We must run! Faster!" shouted the young man behind her. He was on his feet again, chasing after them. Livie had no idea what she would do if she caught the elusive thing. *Jump on it,* offered The Voice.

There! She could just reach out, but it was tossed up and out of reach by a not-so-playful gust of wind. *Jump on it,* The Voice barked again. So Livie did.

It crushed beneath her, with a sound like tearing cloth. I've ruined it, she thought. But, no. It wasn't there. Somehow it had blown out from beneath her, the tearing sound the bag's scraping across the weeds and up into the air again. Livie scrambled to her feet, as the thing rolled away again as if with a purpose: to escape the gentleman and her.

But it was not escaping with a hole torn in its side, like a gaping wound. *Oh, Olivia. You damaged it. I think that you will be in trouble for this one,* said The Voice. She looked back at the young man, running behind her but with less enthusiasm. He was gasping for breath, but did not look angry with her, or the thing itself. She put on another burst of speed and jumped again, arms out. With her eyes closed tight, the breath knocked out of her and she heard the snapping of twigs. She gasped as warm, smoky air washed over her. Oh no, she thought, we've hit the trees.

****

"My young friend, I must thank you very much. That was nicely done," said the young man, stooped over and leaning hands on knees. He was wiping his own face now. The handkerchief swabbed off the sweat and most of the white of his skin, which was apparently just stuff that he wore and not its real color. Without it he was no more handsome, but at least less strange-looking to her. And in his own fall he had lost the false white hair, a wig. Beneath it, his own hair was short and brown.

Smiling, Livie sat on the balloon, flattening more of it beneath her to the ground. Another gust of wind pulled and pushed at it. She decided that the breeze just didn't want to let the thing go. The torn bit flapped. There were broken parts as well - the snapping-twig sound she'd heard had been the frame of the balloon, made of light, thin strips of wood, giving way.

"It's damaged, Monsieur. I'm so sorry."

"Not at all. You did marvelously," the young man said. He folded his legs under him and sat on the dry weeds.

"But I think I heard something break."

"They are wooden ribs," he explained. "Like those in our chests, for holding air." He inhaled and thumped his chest with his thumb.

"The ribs can be replaced with fresh ones. And the skin can be patched. So you see, the damages are nothing that we cannot fix, with a little bit of paper and some paste."

She looked at the thing, crumpled, and could see that it was something more than just paper, wood and paste. It was intended to be beautiful. There was a design on the paper, a picture of something, but it was too wrinkled beneath her to tell just what. *He must enjoy the color blue,* said The Voice. It looks like a flower, Livie thought. A fanciful kind of flower. A lily, perhaps.

Livie started with a jerk. Lilies. Maman! She almost jumped to her feet, but realized that if she had, she would have torn brand new holes in the balloon.

"What is it," the young man asked, seeing the alarm on her face.

"My mother is still lying over on the ground, Monsieur," she said softly.

Now it was he who looked horrified. The young man leapt up and ran as quickly as he could to the other side of the meadow. Livie watched as he ran. He was ungainly for a young man, first slipping then crashing to the ground once more as he pulled up short so that he wouldn't startle Maman again.

She sat on the balloon. Looked down at the thing - which seemed no more now than a large bit of fancy trash, then up in the sky. A bird winged overhead, so high that it was just a black shape above her. Before today she might not have given thought to something like this. Why did some things fly and others not? Was this just a matter of air and feathers? Because if that was so then why couldn't the hens in the farmyard get off the ground beyond their squawking, dusty scampering away from Nick the dog? Was the wind part of the mystery – blowing leaves and snow and dust and birds high enough into the sky that they couldn't fall – and leaving people and rocks and potatoes and horses heavy on the ground? The young man must know this – after all, he had made this paper thing fly.

Livie's eyes went wide now. She pushed her hair out of her face. Here they came - Maman walking across the meadow, holding the arm of the young man. Livie smiled shyly, Maman looked torn between two emotions, complete embarrassment and almost-comfortable, as if the young gentleman had spoken to her, offered her his arm, patted her on the hand again and again to reassure her that there was nothing wrong, and that indeed something perfectly normal had happened when she'd withered to the ground in a faint.

"Are you alright, Maman?"

"Yes, the big paper bag frightened me at first," Maman said, shaking her head and holding her arms across her chest, protectively. She didn't notice that her hands were still brown with dirt from gardening. Then, still exhausted, Maman sat on the bag next to Livie as if it were a blanket. The young man didn't say anything, but crouched on the weeds again where he had been.

"Me too, Maman," Livie replied. "It scared me, too." She didn't tell her mother about how she had been thinking that the thing was an angel, though.

"I would like to thank you, my young friend," the young man added with a smile for Livie. "Without you, my balloon would still be rolling just out of my reach, yes? You saved my experiment."

"What will you do with it now," Livie asked. In spite of his earlier explanation, the contraption looked so very badly damaged.

"Who are you, sir?" Maman asked. "What do you do besides making flying things?"

The gentleman bowed now, deeply from the waist. Without his

hat and wig and face-paint, he looked both thoughtful and friendly. He also looked exhausted.

"Allow me to introduce myself. I am Joseph-Michel Montgolfier. Please call me Joseph."

With a huff, he sat again on the ground.

****

The Montgolfier family, Joseph explained, owned a paper factory in town which he now ran in partnership with his brother, Jacques-Etienne. But Joseph and his brother didn't always get along, particularly in business, and in social situations. Etienne had taken charge in the business, and liked to attend parties, which were called *les affaires* in Annonay, so that he could develop business relationships. Joseph, on the other hand, didn't mind attending the occasional *affaire*, but preferred to use his free time working on what his brother mockingly called his flying devices.

"And it's not that Etienne doesn't think that they are important discoveries - he does. My brother even understands the scientific method. However, he thinks I spend too much time on it. Do you know what I mean?" Livie shook her head and shrugged, expecting Joseph to roll his eyes and make a face, the way her own brothers did when she seemed simple and foolish. But Joseph sat up and talked to her. With his hands waving about excitedly like birds in front of him, he explained to her his love of science.

"Men of science believe that there is not just an explanation for everything, but that everything is reasonable and can be deduced. We must make assumptions - they are called hypotheses - and test our assumptions all the while carefully controlling the changing variables. Then we analyze our results. We can and must learn from our mistakes."

Livie nodded at that one. She surely knew about mistakes. Joseph smiled at her.

"Oh! And of course you have heard of the great Lavoisier? Antoine Lavoisier?"

In spite of her adventure, and being thirsty, Maman was listening as well. She shook her head politely at the young man. It appeared that she enjoyed listening to him talk. Joseph leaned back on one arm and waved the other around in front of him excitedly, as if his ideas were mosquitoes buzzing about his face that he could point to, one after another. Then he closed his eyes as he described how he had watched ashes lifting and floating above a fire. This, he had thought originally, was wind created by the flames.

"I kept looking, wondering if there was a way to harness that wind," he continued. "Night after night, I found myself staring into the fire, every fire, from the cooking coals in the kitchen to the candle-light next to my bed at night. Then one night it came to me that I was totally incorrect!"

Livie grinned. She'd never seen someone so happy about being wrong. For her to not know something, or to be mistaken, was a moment of despair. How interesting this was, to know that being wrong wasn't always bad.

"What I realized was that this so-called wind from the fire was actually just lighter air. The fire made it lighter, and carried the ashes up in the lighter air. And while I may not be able to harness it, but I might be able to capture the lighter air." Joseph sat up, cupping his hands as if scooping water from a bucket. He slowly opened his fingers and folded his hands together.

"Ah, but it is not enough to think of answers to the mighty questions of our age," he said softly. "You have to put on what the great Lavoisier calls the 'practical demonstrations.' So I took a large square of taffeta cloth and stretched it over a frame made of thin wooden slats. Like a box, you see."

Livie frowned. She did not really understand what Joseph meant by lighter air, and had no idea what taffeta was, but didn't want to interrupt. But Joseph saw her face and stopped.

"What is it, my young friend? Do I go too fast?"

Livie felt her face flush with embarrassment. *I know nothing*, she thought. She asked the question anyway.

"What is taffeta?"

"Light and thin cloth. Shiny, too. I will show it to you sometime. It is used in girl's dresses. To make my balloon, I will need the cloth for a hundred dresses. Maybe more." She grinned at the thought of a hundred dresses. The gentleman nodded excitedly. Montgolfier spoke as if not knowing something was the most natural thing in the world. As if everyone should ask questions, particularly if they didn't know, because to leave without learning was...wrong. And there was no sense of teasing in his voice, as if she should know what cloth is in girl's dresses anymore than understanding the lightness of hot air. He rambled on. Livie held on those words while he spoke. *I will show it to you sometime.*

Joseph described how he made his small box and lit a small pile of paper beneath it. To his delight, the fragile box had lifted off of the floor and drifted up to the ceiling.

"It was amazing. My first worry was that the heat from the fire would catch the box, but it did not. Instead, of course, it crashed into the chandelier and one of the candles tipped and burned a hole in the cloth. That must have let out the lighter air, because it fell back to the floor, and the wooden slats snapped and collapsed. Not unlike our balloon here." Joseph pointed at the crumpled sack upon which Livie and Maman sat. He made a great pretence of frowning at the thing and gave a tsk-tsk sound.

But Montgolfier further explained that following this experiment he himself had walked around lighter than air. He believed that it had been a terrific success, even though Etienne reminded him that in fact the balloon had fallen and broken, and there was no proof of lighter air, and he hadn't followed the proper scientific *method according to the great Lavoisier,* which was unfortunately true - he hadn't weighed the box, or the box full of the lighter air, or the paper bits he had burned. And Etienne enjoyed reminding him that he, Joseph, was not yet the great Lavoisier!

"Which is true, eh? Still, I think that this is the great age of science, going on right now. We are all living in it, you and I." Joseph clambered to his feet, and held out a hand for Maman. He pulled her up.

"Even you, Madame," he said with a smile, and Maman blushed. "Yes, even you live in this scientific time. And although you are afraid of large flying paper bags, at least you are aware that they are not monsters, or the ancient pagan gods returning, ready to throw down pails of fire and bolts of lightning. That is what I heard shouted in Annonay this day, as my invention took to the sky and loosed its tether. Can you believe it? There were actually shouts of 'save me, God, from the dragon!' What madness is a person's ignorance." The young man looked up in the sky and then down, scuffing the toe of his boot in the weeds.

"But I am guilty as well of such ignorance, I suppose. My brother Etienne tells me, 'your mistakes are just mistakes. You're not learning anything from them'." Montgolfier shrugged. "He is correct. I am not so interested in lighter air than I am in what it can do. So I made this balloon myself, and flew it myself. I used our factory's paper, too, because the taffeta is so very dear, and Etienne won't let me spend money on it. Well, there we are, then. As we can all see, the paper balloon flew quite well."

Livie remained perched on the balloon so that it wouldn't blow away again, although the breeze had subsided. Joseph crossed his arms, thinking, as if he was coming up with a plan. He grinned.

"You know? I do ride his horse, however, and he doesn't know that I do it. Apollo is a fine animal." He looked over his shoulder across the meadow. Then he looked at Livie and nodded.

"Could you help me roll up this balloon? I can carry it down the hill, if you will ride Apollo."

"Oh, Monsieur, I've never..." Livie started, her eyes wide. Joseph waved his hands at her to interrupt.

"No, no. He is easy to ride. He knows exactly what he's doing."

105

Joseph looked at Maman. "As gentle as the youngest spring lamb."

They rolled up the balloon, although the wooden slats poked through some spots, and it was a small enough package for Joseph to hold with two hands.

"I am quite thirsty," Joseph said. "Do you think that we might have some of that water, now?"

"Yes, Monsieur." Maman strode off across the meadow. Livie ran ahead to the horse. Joseph looked at her and at Apollo, then adjusted the leather bits of the sitting place on the horse's back. Then he took the reins from her and showed her how to put her foot in the stirrup and pull herself up into the saddle. Livie stood there, not sure how to climb up wearing her already too-short dress. Joseph must have realized her concern. He wove his fingers together and made a basket of his hands, Livie stepped in, and he carefully lifted her up onto the sitting place. Apollo stood as still as stone, and then, with Livie aboard, led the parade down to the farm. Livie patted the enormous beast on the neck. And she would have been as happy as she'd ever been before in her life, if she wasn't aware that lunchtime for her brothers and Papa had come and gone long before.

Chapter Twelve

Oh, my! Once again Papa was grumpily waiting – for Livie, for Maman, for his lunch, for some sort of explanation. He stalked about the farmyard in his big boots with his arms crossed, snorting gruffly and mumbling under his breath. Guillaume was grouchy as well, following Papa's footsteps, but Jean-Charles had managed to find himself a bowl and was spooning cold soup into his mouth while sitting on the bench outside the kitchen door.

But Papa said nothing when he saw Livie on horseback, followed by Maman and Joseph-Michel Montgolfier, who had found his wig and his tri-corn hat and looked from a short distance to be a real gentleman, although up close he was quite disheveled and carrying something in his arms that looked like a bale of...well, no one could quite tell. On seeing Joseph, Papa did stop stalking and snorting like a frustrated ox, but still stood there with his arms crossed.

It was Maman who stepped forward and shyly introduced Papa to Monsieur Montgolfier, and then Livie's brothers to the young man,

who seemed only a year or two older than they, but in his polite greet-
ings was so much more a gentleman than just his fancy clothes.
Montgolfier carefully set his bundle of balloon remains on the ground
in the yard and apologized for keeping Livie and Maman from their
work. He told Papa about the balloon crashing up on the hill, which
puzzled the farmer just enough that he couldn't help but be amused
by the whole thing.

Then everyone was bowing and bowing again, and Livie smiled,
although part of her wondered why they were so friendly with
Monsieur Montgolfier but not with Monsieur Picoult. That was puz-
zling, unless it was as simple and obvious a matter as clothing. Livie
thought of Picoult in his floppy old hat and looked at Montgolfier in
his tricorn trimmed with white braid and those incredible colors of
blue in his clothes in his pantaloons and vest. Perhaps it was just like
that: everyone cared more about what other folks looked like than
what they did, or had to say, or how they treated each other. And how
wrong was that?

Livie didn't want to stop riding Apollo, but Guillaume helped her
down and they led the horse over to the well and pulled a bucket of
water for him to drink. She patted the horse while it slurped noisily.

"Papa used to have a horse, you know," her brother said quietly,
that no one else might hear. "Back before you were born. Not like this
fellow, but a good strong plowhorse. He sold it when there was a bad
year and he couldn't afford the taxes."

Livie looked at her brother. That was why her brothers did all of
the plowing, pulling the *araire* through the hard dirt in the fields.

"What are taxes?" she asked.

Jean-Charles rolled his eyes and shook his head.

"Never mind. It's just that Papa sold the horse. He had to because
there wasn't enough money to pay those he owed. Like how he sold
the cows."

Now Livie's eyes were as wide as bowls.

"Papa had cows?"

"Of course it wasn't so many. But they were good milk cows. That was a different year when he sold them to pay the taxes." Jean-Charles spoke in a whisper. "He used to say he got the better of the deal, because it was only a matter of time before one cow or another broke its leg falling in a gopher hole."

"What's a gopher?"

"Like a big rat with no tail," Jean-Charles replied. "They dig tunnels in the ground."

"My goodness," Livie said to herself, though her brother heard her. Did they have gophers on their farm? She couldn't remember ever seeing one. He gave a small shrug.

"Well then, that is how it goes sometimes."

"How long ago was this? I don't remember that we ever had cows."

"Yes. It was about ten years ago that he sold them."

'Oh,' she said. Ten years ago was when she was born. *You were the reason Papa sold the cows, Olivia,* said The Voice, accusingly. Yes, well, I know that now, she thought.

Lunch was fetched by Maman; it was cold and, Livie thought, not very good. But Montgolfier took his wooden bowl and sat on the bench where Jean-Charles had been sitting, and ate, talking between mouthfuls as if it were a feast and he as comfortable as he could be. He even complimented Maman on her soup, which had her blushing as red as a May sunburn, and kept her scurrying around getting fresh well water to wash it down.

Livie took her bowl and sat cross-legged on the ground. She was suddenly surprised at how hungry she was, even for Maman's soup. What an exciting morning it had been. And just now Joseph was trying to explain to Papa and Guillaume about the balloon and his experiments, but they didn't understand much and didn't ask any questions, so the young gentleman was probably confused as to what exactly it was that they didn't understand. Then, without any warning Papa got up and said that it was time to get back to work and he made a face at Guillaume and Guillaume made a face at Jean-Charles. The brothers set their bowls on the ground and Papa gruffly thanked Montgolfier, although Livie wasn't sure for what - for visiting or for rescuing Maman from the balloon and bringing them home, or perhaps for entertaining everyone at lunch. Livie was saddened, because she thought that Joseph would take Papa's rudeness as an excuse to leave. But the young man nodded with his mouth full, smiling at the farmers, and didn't seem at all troubled that Papa had to go back to work.

Papa and Livie's brothers bowed once again, mumbling their confusion. And with his soup spoon hanging from his mouth, Joseph held out his hand, and Papa hesitantly shook it, his eyebrows raised at this odd young gentleman who was making himself at home in their farmyard. Then, shrugging at each other, Livie's brothers and father clomped back out into the afternoon sun. Joseph kept his seat and took another mouthful, just as comfortable as he could be. Livie enjoyed the quiet for a while. Maman stood, curtseyed, picked up the bowls on the ground, and carried them into the kitchen. Livie could hear her in there - she was quietly humming a tune, something she never did. Well, Livie thought. Perhaps this visitor was a sorcerer. Then Joseph looked at her.

"I would like to ask you a question, if I may. What were you doing up there on the hilltop? Were you waiting in the road for a horse to come and run you over?" Montgolfier winked at her.

Livie grinned. "Oh, no," she replied. "I was planting flowers and fell down. That is, Maman and I were planting flowers and then I was running to get Maman some water because she was thirsty and I saw the balloon, and my shoes fell off and I fell down because I thought the balloon was an angel." She stopped, blushing, for all of the words spilling from her mouth.

Joseph didn't seem to notice. *He is very polite*, said The Voice. *Yes, indeed.*

"What sort of flowers did you plant?"

"Lilies," she said.

"Oh, how fine! In what colors?"

Livie frowned. She had no idea. She shook her head.

"They were a gift from Monsieur Picoult. He is a friend of mine. He lives on the farm. The farm to the west of ours. I only saw their bulbs."

"That is a fine gift. And I suspect it shall be the nicest of surprises when they bloom, eh?" Joseph said, scratching his neck under his rumpled white wig. He grimaced and took the thing off, dropping it next to him on the bench. He glanced around the farmyard thoughtfully.

"You thought the balloon was an angel?"

"Well, I've...never seen an angel," Livie said.

"Nor have I, nor have I," murmured Joseph.

Again they sat quietly.

"How did your balloon come all the way up here?" she asked in a soft voice. "Didn't you know that it was so windy?"

Joseph grinned, his teeth shining and straight. He didn't seem at all concerned to be asked such a bold question by a young girl.

"Well, it wasn't quite so windy in town. And if I had known, I wouldn't have run my experiment today, eh?"

"Didn't you look at the tall trees? The ones near the steeple of the church? To see if the leaves were waving from the wind? Or how the clouds were moving in the sky?" Such a thing just occurred to Livie. Many times she had looked down from the hilltop towards town, at the church poking out from the tall trees. That was the way she might have checked, if it were up to her.

Montgolfier laughed, leaning back on the bench, slapping his knee.

"You see? That is exactly the kind of thinking I need to have. Good scientific reasoning. Not me. Instead I let the balloon go up, let go of its tether, and hoped for the best. Now, you have taught me something, my young friend. I should have had you there when I launched. Do you know where I was?"

"No," Livie said, frowning slightly. She didn't want Joseph to know that she had never, ever, been into town. That she was but a farm girl, and had always been one. She thought, That is all I am, a farm girl. I've never been anywhere, but to the top of the hill and back. Even when I went to Picoult's farm, it was in the dark and during a storm. I've never actually seen it in the daylight. For all I know, everyone in town has mouse-whiskers and wings!

"I was in the churchyard. It was the best, most flat space I could find around the paper factory, not in the middle of a street. You might imagine me ridiculous to be worried that someone would run the balloon over with a wagon, or poke it with a stick. But no one even bothered to come and watch. It was...fascinating how un-fascinated people can be." Montgolfier shook his head in amazement.

"Yes, Monsieur," Livie agreed, although she had no idea at all how "people" were. Indeed, how many people did she even know before, outside her own family? One? And now, two? Silly girl, she thought to herself before The Voice could say it. Of course, Joseph wasn't paying attention to her thoughts and continued.

"Anyhow, my young friend, I lit the paper scraps and covered them with the mouth of the balloon. Oh! I didn't tell you that I was worried that the balloon would come too close to the burning scraps and singe itself, did I? Yes? Well, all in the name of science, eh? Since then I've learned to be careful and let the flames burn down some before covering them. The hot, air filled the balloon. I could tell this because it was also very smoky inside."

Montgolfier waved his spoon in front of his face as if pushing away the smoke. Then he leaned towards Livie. "And, of course, one might have deduced that it was the smoke itself that was lighter than air, but I also felt the hot air when there was no smoke, and have held cool smoke in a balloon just as heavy as ever. Anyhow the hot air filled the balloon. It leapt out to the end of its tether like a hound on a lead. I released the rope and it lifted straightaway and with spirit and I was properly pleased, as I always am when things go well. I thought it would go up a bit and then come right back down. But above the churchyard it rose. One of priests came stomping out of the church – I don't remember his name – waving excitedly at me. At first I thought that he was shouting with me for the balloon's successful launch. He ran over to me, scolding me for standing in the churchyard. Well, you see, it is also a cemetery and he was shouting at me because I was walking on the graves. Ah so, such are the sacrifices in the name of science, I always say. Then the priest looked up, and he fell over backwards. I think that he also thought it was an angel ascending over him. He fell back on one of the graves and tipped a gravestone, so I made my exit. I'd thought the balloon might catch on a steeple, but it didn't. It started drifting west, and if you can believe it I hadn't even thought of having a ride prepared. That was why I had to grab Apollo. Etienne had left him tied, saddled and ready. Can you picture me galloping on foot down the street from the church to get a horse? I'm certain that I was hilarious to behold. And can you also imagine that still no one other than the priest paid me or the balloon the slightest notice? I think that all of Ardeche is quite mad. Excepting, of course, you and me, my young friend." Montgolfier shook his head, and Livie grinned at her friend's story. Lighter than air!

The young man took another spoonful of soup and smacked his lips, setting the bowl and spoon down on the bench. He pressed his hands to his knees, as if reaching a decision.

"Oh, but my brother is right, though. Taffeta is expensive. But if I want a bigger balloon that will not tear so easily, then I will have to use it, I think."

"You won't repair this balloon?" Livie asked.

Montgolfier shook his head slowly.

"No, I suppose not. But I thank you once again for helping me catch it, so that I could at least think about it. All in the name of science! And I am glad that you got to see my balloon fly. And I'm sorry that I fussed at you for lying in the road. I already knew that when the

hot air cooled that the balloon would come down again, so I should-
n't have been so testy. But I didn't know the whole story. Etienne
would say that I failed the scientific method again, not asking enough
questions before making a judgment. Ah, well."

"So you want to make a bigger balloon even than this?" Livie
asked. She stood and looked at the pile of paper and sticks that had
been the balloon, the angel.

"Certainly! It should be bigger. Ever so much bigger, if I am ever
going to fly with it."

Livie whirled to face Joseph. That hadn't occurred to her at all.
Her surprise showed clearly on her face, because the young man
leaned back and laughed.

"It's a good idea, isn't it? Doesn't everyone want to fly? Wouldn't
you like to?"

Livie's head spun. Would she? More than anything she'd ever
done. *That's not so,* said The Voice. *Tell him the truth. You'd be afraid.*
No I wouldn't, she told her voice. Yes I would, but I'd do it, anyway.

"Well, I'm going to make it. The taffeta balloon," Joseph said.
"And you will have to come to town and see me launch it."

Livie dropped her eyes. Her hair draped across her face, covering
her timidity.

"I would like that very much," she murmured.

"Good, then," said Joseph as if he didn't mind, or even notice, her
shyness. He stood and plopped his wig down on his head, slightly side-
ways so that his *culotte,* the wig's pony-tail, hung over his ear instead of
down the back of his neck. Then he pressed his tri-corn down over the
wig, and a strange sight it made. Livie couldn't help but wonder what
made people wear what they did. Like this smart and funny man, both
handsome and not so at the same time. She shook her head, but again
he didn't notice, or if he did, he didn't mind.

"You must come when I am close to launching my next balloon,
yes?" he asked her.

"How will I know when you are close?" Livie asked, surprised at

114

her own boldness.

Joseph rubbed his chin.

"We stop making paper for a while in the winter. It is too cold for drying it. So when we start again in the spring, you will know that I am back at work. You will be able to smell the paper, right? It will smell as sour as a wet dog."

Nick the Mean Dog never let himself get wet, Livie thought. Or anyone close enough to smell him if he did. She told Joseph this, and he laughed.

"I promise, you'll know what I mean. Surely you've smelled it before?"

Livie gave a shy shrug. She wasn't sure the smell reached all the way up here from town.

"Well, never mind, then. I will send for you when I am close to launching, eh?" said Joseph.

"Thank you, Monsieur," Livie said, with a curtsey.

"Not at all. It is I who thank you. My helper. And you must call me Joseph, of course." The young man pressed his hands together behind his back and made his way around the yard to the lane, where Apollo was standing, reins tied loosely to a small shrub. Apollo had nibbled most of the leaves on the shrub and Joseph tsk-tsk'd and turned to Livie with a shrug.

"It is alright. He was right to be hungry, too," Livie said. She pushed her hair out of her eyes and looked up at Joseph as he climbed up into the saddle.

"*Au revoir, mon ami.* Good day, my friend," Joseph bowed from his high perch. He pulled on the reins and Apollo seemed to bow as well. Then Joseph turned the horse and it clip-clopped up the lane.

"Monsieur? Joseph! Did you..." Livie started.

Joseph looked over his shoulder, his eyes raised in question.

"Did I what?"

She smiled. "Did you really like my mother's soup?"

He grinned back, each of his straight white teeth showing bright-

115

ly.

"Well of course I did. It is like science. I eat when I am hungry. I enjoy eating when I am hungry. I was very hungry, so it was very good. You will thank her again for me?"

Livie nodded in wonderment. Then Apollo cantered away.

Chapter Thirteen

What a young person will tell you, is that *time* is no steady measure. For them, the sun races across the sky on a fine afternoon, but a
day might drag along with pointless sloth when there is nothing happening of worth. Time might even stand stone frozen cold when one
is waiting for a promise to be fulfilled, for a long awaited invitation to
arrive. If you try to explain to them the truth, however, that passing
time is constant and sound; in their youth they will nod and even perhaps smile politely so that you don't feel that you've wasted your time
attempting to enlighten them. But inside, in the privacy of their heart,
they will feel a deep sorrow for you for not knowing the truth: that
waiting is sometimes the misery of forever, and now is often but a bliss-
ful instant.

The beginning-of-winter moon rose bright and yellow gold until it
reached that place in the sky where its light could fully glow through
the small window in Livie's room. From her bed, she watched shadows tossed on the wall, flickering, shifting and making shapes. They

wriggled and transformed, and through the cracks in the window-frame Livie also felt the breeze that had shaken the last old leaves still hanging faithfully onto the tree's smallest branches. She tucked herself deeply beneath her blankets. The chimney's heat from the kitchen fireplace downstairs – which had often made her room uncomfortably warm in the summer – kept it just warm enough now. She loved the summertime, but winter, too, had its own special beauty. Just a week ago, snow had fallen and it was beautiful, a sparkling white sheet covering the ground and draping the branches of the oak tree and the thatched slope of the cattle-byre. Clear jewel icicles pointed down from the roof. She'd cracked one off and sucked on it, tasting the ice melting into water in her mouth, as strange a sensation as it had been the first time she'd done it, many years ago. *What a shame that there is no ice for cooling well water to drink in the summer*, The Voice In Her Head said, and this time Livie had to agree.

But this winter she'd also been disappointed. It had already been three months since she'd seen the balloon, planted the lilies, talked and had lunch with Joseph. It had been so many months since she'd been in the storm and had soup with Monsieur Picoult. In the end, she decided, nothing in her life had really changed. Her hair was still long and in her face most of the time. Her dress was still old, although it had a couple of new patches made from old cloth. Her knees had scabs, one old, one new. Her life was...like her mattress, when the old straw crushed too flat for sleeping on was replaced with fresh. Despite its newness it was still just straw; jabbing and poking at her if she rolled over too much, still rustling under her weight. So things might appear to change; seasons changing from cold to warm, leaves on trees turning from green to brown to white, even the shape of the moon, but then the old always returned. That was the way it had been her whole life.

And she had to further admit that while she'd been excited before, prancing around the farm with winged feet, she'd talked herself somewhat out of the happiness she had felt. Monsieur Picoult hadn't visited. Montgolfier hadn't sent word about his next balloon. Livie wasn't sure what she had imagined would happen. For the gentlemen to come traipsing through the snow to see her? Ah, well, she thought.

Mostly, she was just bored. There wasn't much to do inside in the wintertime, and Papa and her brothers were also crowded inside, talking, repairing things, sharpening tools, sitting, grumping, telling her to *hush*. And if there wasn't much work for them to do outside, there wasn't much for her to do in the wintertime, either. And it was just *cold*. Too cold even to play outside except for the moments when she was so completely in Maman's way that her mother finally shoo'd her outside for a chore or two, wrapped in a blanket and scarf, to go pick up sticks for the kitchen fire, to throw chaff to the chickens huddling in the cattle-byre, to run around until her teeth chattered, *something*.

So today, after doing Mama's tasks for her, and balking at the idea of returning inside to the warm but crowded and grumpy house, Livie decided that although she was cold, she was less cold than she thought. She would take a walk up the hill, instead. She'd never been up there in wintertime. Pulling the blanket over her head like a shawl and pushing her icy feet as far into the *sabots* as they would go, she began slogging through the snow to the end of the lane.

Climbing the road she felt anew the wonder of discovery. Rising from the distant town were spires of smoke, from chimneys and kitchen fires hidden by distance. See there? Smoke rises, she thought. *Of course it does*, said The Voice. I've always known it, but never thought about it. Her own breath, puffing white like a cloud, rose above her head. Lighter than air.

She reached the top of the hill. How different it all looked, buried beneath the snow. Not everything, of course. The sky was desperately blue. To the west, along the lane, she looked for smoke, coming from Monsieur Picoult's farmhouse. Was that it, that wisp of something in the distance? Maybe. Oh, and her pretty little garden, *le petit belle jardin*. Where was it? Her heart jumped to think of it. She spun around on her getting-cold feet. It should be right over here.

She could see immediately that something was wrong. The snow had been scuffed away. Someone had been digging in the dirt. Where the bulbs had been carefully, lovingly planted there was torn and frozen dirt. Her first thought was that this was a terrible prank played on her by her brothers. Around and around in her head went the refrain: it's ruined, it's ruined, ruined. Why would they do such a thing? She tried to wipe the tears running cold down her cheeks. Then she saw the marks in the snow. Hoofprints.

****

Pictures drew themselves on her wall, painted by the moonlight through the window. Livie thought she saw the balloon on the wall, the shadow of the balloon. Then, in her imagination, it flew away on the next breeze. Replacing it were the summertime thistles waving by the side of the road. Apollo, as dark as night, running, his tail stretched out behind him. Beautiful, she thought. But she couldn't keep that picture in her mind from changing, altering into the slight, shy red-brown shape of a deer, pawing at the snow and dirt, digging up her bulbs and eating them. She rubbed her aching eyes, but there were no more tears. I hate him, she thought, even though she knew it wasn't true. The deer had only been hungry, and she'd been hungry enough before so she knew what it was like. But her garden. She sniffled.

"Ahem." Someone spoke.

She turned and was surprised to see in the gloom a mouse on the chair next to her bed. *Oh, if Maman sees, there will be shouting and a broom-chase,* said The Voice.

"Good evening," the mouse said. Livie could tell that it was the little girl mouse. It stood on its hind legs and gave a little curtsey.

"Good evening to you," Livie smiled. If the little girl mouse was a dream, then it was a nice dream.

"It's quite cold out tonight," the girl-mouse said matter-of-factly.

"The wind, yes?" Livie replied.

"Too chilly to stay outside."

120

"I should think so. Don't let Maman see you, though."

"Of course," said the girl-mouse. She turned around on the chair and sat quietly. They both watched the shadow pictures on the wall for a while.

"There's the black-dog," said the girl-mouse, pointing with her tiny paws at a peculiar shadow.

"I see it," Livie said. "His name is Nick, you know."

"Nick or not, I believe that he wants to eat me," the girl mouse said. "If you don't mind, I don't think I'll call him over by name."

Livie smiled again at the little girl-mouse.

"Yes, well. I believe that he wants to eat me, too."

"Really?"

"No," Livie said. "He doesn't eat people. I don't think..."

"Speaking of thinking, do you think that you are going to town?" asked the mouse, changing the subject.

"I don't know," Livie said wistfully. "Probably not."

"If you do go to town, perhaps you could take me with you," said the little girl-mouse. She brushed the fur of her cheek casually. "It has been such a long while since I was in town."

Livie leaned back in surprise. Even the mouse had been to town. "But I don't even know your name."

"How rude!" the little girl-mouse said, covering her mouth. Livie opened her eyes wide.

"No, I mean of me!" said the little girl mouse, tittering in a peal of laughter. "I should have told you my name long ago. I am so sorry. It's Beatrice."

"How do you do, Beatrice. I like your name. Mine is Olivia...Livie."

"My pleasure, Livie, I'm sure," said Beatrice.

"You know that I've never gone to town before, right?" Livie asked shyly. Beatrice nodded. "What makes you think that I'm ever going to go?"

"I think you will. Probably very soon. I just know it."

"I don't know, little one. No one has sent word since before all the leaves fell. I think they've all forgotten."

"Oh, no," said Beatrice, waving a dismissive paw. "They haven't forgotten you. It's just that everything takes it's time. That's the way everything works. In its own time."

Livie blinked at this smart mouse.

"Why do you want me to take you to town?"

"I have relations there. You know? Brothers, sisters, cousins. I would like to visit with them."

"Yes. Of course. I understand."

"Then I can go with you?" Beatrice clapped her tiny paws together and doing a little dance. "I won't take any room, and I won't eat your lunch, I promise."

Livie smiled a third time. "*Oui.* Yes you can go with me. If I ever go to town, you can go, too."
****

Maman woke her. The light through the window still seemed to be moonlight, but Maman smelled like breakfast fire and warm porridge.

"Wake up, *cherie.*" Maman sat on her bed and placed a hand on her shoulder. "Something has happened."

Livie opened her sleep-heavy eyes as wide as they could go. Then she felt a weigh in the pit of her stomach. How did Maman find out about the garden and the bulbs? She hadn't told her yet. But Maman just sat there quietly. This was quite curious. She couldn't remember Maman ever sitting with her on the bed, much less waking her up so gently. It had to be something else.

"What is it?"

Maman coughed quietly and looked down at her feet.

"Something has happened. Something has happened with your Monsieur Picoult," Maman murmured.

A chill rolled over Livie as strongly as if she had been standing outside in this cold winter morning. *Oh, no,* said The Voice In Her Head.

122

This is bad. Livie shook her head to hush The Voice. She tried to pull up her blanket, to feel warm, to cover her face so that she couldn't see Maman, so Maman couldn't see her. She wanted Maman to leave, not to be sitting on her bed as if Livie might sit up and give her a hug, or that Maman might lean over and give her one back. She didn't want to know whatever this was.

"One of the hands from his farm came this morning. He said that Monsieur Picoult asked for you. He is not well. The farmhand wants you to come with him, back to the old man's farm."

"No," Livie whispered. Oh, God, she thought.

"You don't have to if you don't want to," Maman said. "He's downstairs with Papa and your brothers. He brought the wagon for you to ride in."

Livie didn't close her eyes or turn over, or pull the blanket over her head. Instead she slowly got up and pulled on her old dress and tied her stained apron, pulled up her stockings and slipped on her sabots. She pushed the hair out of her eyes and put on the hat she rarely wore. Then she walked downstairs with Maman. She curtseyed to the man from Picoult's farm, who led her outside.

The oxen – the boys, Louis and George – were yoked to the wagon. Livie patted each of them gently on their noses and whispered *bonjour* – good morning, although it didn't feel like a good mornng. She pulled the wool shawl that Maman had given her to wear more closely around her and walking around to the wagon, made to pull herself up to the bench. Strong hands lifted her up. It was her brother Guillaume, who then climbed up after her. On the other side, the farmhand climbed up and took the reins and clicked his tongue. With a jolt, the boys began tugging the wagon and they rolled along the lane and up the hill.

Frost rimed the broken stalks of weeds alongside the lane and the boys puffed each breath they took like smoke from their nostrils. Livie looked over at her little garden, but it was now only an empty spot in the meadow, the bare dirt gray with frost. Nothing was growing.

Nothing would ever grow there, now. She slouched on the wagon bench, shivering in the cold.

"It's too early," Guillaume said softly. She looked over at her brother in surprise. He was staring straight ahead. "Bulbs like that won't break through the surface until spring. It has to do with sunlight as much as warmth, you know."

"Deer," Livie replied. A tear rolled down her cheek.

Guillaume reached over and tapped the farmhand on the shoulder.

"Hold, up, eh?" The farmhand clicked his tongue and gave the traces a pull and the boys slowed to a stop.

She bit her tongue so that she would stop crying. She explained to Guillaume what she had seen. Her brother listened without interrupting. She hadn't known that her brothers were even aware that she'd planted the bulbs, much less that they cared anything about them. Guillaume hopped down from the wagon. His boots crunched in the frosty ground as he walked over to *le petit belle jardin.*

"Ah, it still looks good," he said after a moment. "There are a few holes where rabbits and deer have dug them out. I suppose they'll do that, if they get hungry enough."

"How do you keep them away?" she asked.

Guillaume grinned. "Turn your head, Livie," he told her. She did what she was told, looking over at the farmhand, who was watching past her, curiously.

She heard a sound, and the farmhand grunted and smirked.

"Don't you look, little sister," her brother said gruffly.

Then Guillaume trotted back to the wagon, buttoning his trousers, and pulled himself aboard.

The ground around the garden was steaming, like the boys' breaths from their exhales. The steam rose, lighter than air.

"What did you do?" she asked.

"I'm freezing! But don't tell Maman." Guillaume poked her in the ribs. "No deer will come near it now."

124

Livie smiled, the cold morning falling away from her. *How many girls have brothers who will pee out in the winter cold for them?* asked The Voice. *Not too many, I'll guess.*

Smoke rose from the chimney of Picoult's house. The farmhand pulled the wagon up and Livie and Guillaume climbed down. The farmhand clicked his tongue again and the boys pulled away, toward their barn. Livie looked at Guillaume, who shrugged.

"A good sturdy house," he said admiringly. For the first time, Livie could see the tall stone walls and slate roof.

"Yes. Did you know that Monsieur Picoult has a wooden box that makes sounds?"

Guillaume looked at her crookedly.

"A box? What kind of sounds?"

"So beautiful. I can't remember what it is called. He presses it with his fingers and it makes music."

"Ah." Her brother shrugged again.

The farmhand was gone, into the barn with the oxen. It seemed strange to be standing there, alone, like uninvited guests. Guillaume peered in a window but it was frosted over.

Livie stepped up to the kitchen door and knocked. They waited, but no one answered. It was cold and Guillaume tucked his hands under his arms. Livie turned the handle on the door and opened it. No one was in the kitchen, but the fire was warm with banked coals. They stepped inside quickly and closed the door behind them, so that they wouldn't let the heat out. The room was draped in gloom, with just the small window and fireplace providing light.

"Hello?" Livie called. *This is very curious,* said The Voice.

They listened, but there was no sound but the quiet crackle from the fireplace. Then a sound from the other room. A cough. Livie led the way.

A lamp sat on top of the sound-making box, and it flickered, making an inconstant light. Still, Livie was surprised by what she saw. Monsieur Picoult lay on a small bed in the living room, covered with blankets and his head propped on pillows. His closed eyes were rimmed with black, and his hair lay every which way, like the weeds on top of a wind-blown hill. Livie wasn't sure she could hear him breathing, and the room was musty, as if no one had lived there for many months. She covered her mouth with her hand. My goodness, she thought. Oh, God. Was he...?

He was not. Picoult opened his eyes and his thin lips turned up in a slight smile.

"My good young friend. Maiden-of-the-mountain. I wasn't certain that you would come. I do believe that I have missed you very much."

Livie entered the living room. Her brother backed away into the kitchen. She pulled the stool from the sound-box over next to Picoult's bed. She sat by him.

"I hadn't heard from you in so long," she said.

"I am very sorry. I was sick, and then I thought that I was getting better, but instead I ended up like this." He lifted his hand: it seemed to be just skin stretched tightly over bones. "Tell me. How go things with you? Did you get my package? And is that your brother with you?"

She called Guillaume, who bowed to the old man from the kitchen doorway. Then Livie told Picoult all of her stories. about planting the lilies with Maman and how she was nearly run down by Montgolfier's horse and how she helped rescue the balloon and how she and Joseph had also become friends. She told him about the deer in her garden, and how Guillaume had protected the garden just this day. And Picoult laughed; a paper-thin whisper of a laugh that caused him to cough until he wheezed when he breathed and closed his eyes with his hands on his chest. When he opened his eyes again, he looked at her without speaking. He reached out and patted her head.

"I was hoping that you might do something for me." he said. "Do you think that you can remember? The soup? My wife's soup? Do you remember how it was made?"

126

Livie could recall each aspect of the lovely soup as if she were just now tasting it. She nodded.

"Make some, please," Picoult whispered. His eyes closed again, too tired to stay open when he spoke. "I'm so hungry for it. Have my man – his name is Gaston – fetch a chicken and clean it. Everything else is in the kitchen, or he can find it for you. Will you do this for me?"

"Of course," Livie replied and stood. She walked past Guillaume into the kitchen.

The fire was stoked, and Livie sent Guillaume to break the ice on the well and fetch fresh water. When the farmhand came in, his name was Gaston, she sent him back out to slaughter a chicken. The vegetables and herbs she sliced and crushed herself, and soon the pot was bubbling over the kitchen fire. She returned to the living room with the house beginning to fill with the perfume of cooking soup. Picoult was asleep now, but there was a rumble in his chest and throat like distant thunder and his breath was uneven. Livie sat on the stool, gently cradling the old man's bony hand.

Guillaume stood in the doorway to the kitchen, crunching the brim of his hat between his hands.

"The soup smells good," he said.

"I know," said Livie.

"I didn't know you knew how to cook." Her brother pulled thoughtfully on his whiskers.

"Monsieur Picoult showed me how. This is his wife's soup."

"He's quite sick."

"I know," said Livie. "His hand feels hot."

"I'm not so sick as all that," rumbled the old man. Picoult opened his eyes. "I just wanted some company and some soup."

"Oh, Monsieur," Livie started. *He's lying*, said The Voice. Hush, she thought.

"And there was no way your Papa was going to let you come to my house for lunch unless there was a good reason. That's why I sent

Gaston to fetch you."

"You look ill, Monsieur," said Guillaume.

"Oh, I'm not doing well, but I've nothing you can catch today. I'm old and that's how it goes. We all catch that in our own time," Picoult replied. He winked at Livie and squeezed her hand with his and smiled. "Now, go check the soup which smells so good. I'm hungry and it is time to eat."

Guillaume called Gaston in from the barn, and the two men brought chairs into the living room so that Picoult wouldn't have to be moved beyond propping him up with extra pillows. Then Livie served the soup in the same china bowls that she had used back on the night of the storm. She softly scolded the two younger men to be careful with them, as they had been brought from the other side of the world. And she warned everyone not to put the pewter spoons in the soup too soon, so that the handles wouldn't melt. Then everyone ate, chewing the tasty chicken, slurping the marvelous broth, and smiling at how wonderful it tasted.

"Well done, well *done*, my young friend," Picoult told Livie. "My wife couldn't have done any better."

Livie felt her face blush, although no one could see it by the weak candlelight of the living room. Picoult turned to Guillaume.

"On one of the shelves in the kitchen there should be a loaf of bread, not too old for us to eat, I think. See if I'm not mistaken, will you?" Guillaume looked at Gaston and Livie, and then got up to go to the kitchen. There was a short loaf there, and he brought it out and Picoult motioned for him to break it and pass it around. Livie took the heel and sniffed the wonderful bread smell of it and dipped it in her soup and everyone dipped and chewed and mopped up the broth with bread, the spoons tinkling softly around the china bowls' edges. Then they were done and sat quietly. Livie looked at the old man. His eyes were sunken deep and glowed with fever. She waited for him to rest from eating. Finally he placed his free hand on her arm.

"I have missed you, Olivia Bien."

She startled at hearing her whole name. The old man continued. "This meal wasn't the only reason I wanted you to visit, you know." He handed his bowl to Gaston who carried it to the kitchen.

"I don't have any people, you know," Picoult said softly and Livie nodded. "Oh, there's faithful Gaston, and the other hands that plow and plant and take care of the farm. But I've no family. All gone. You're the first person I've wanted to have as my friend for a long while." He patted her hand with his.

Then he turned to Guillaume again.

"Can you help me, young man? Over to the keyboard?" He pointed to the sound-making box. Livie pushed the stool over, and Guillaume steadied the old man as he got out of bed. Picoult sat on the stool and opened the box and suddenly the same sounds that Livie had heard before sprang from it, beautiful and soothing and lively as new grass waving and summertime birds and changing leaves and everything that winter was not. A lump caught in her throat and she thought that she might weep, or that her very heart might stop beating. She looked at her brother and his eyes were wide with wonder.

"*Good, good,*" the old man said when his fingers stopped moving and the sound ceased with it. No one else spoke. Picoult turned to Livie.

"I want you to take the boys home with you." Picoult smiled, his eyes closed.

"Oh, Monsieur, I cannot." Livie shook her head.

"Sure you can. Remember? You know how, just like I showed you. I want you to have them, and the wagon."

"Oh!" she cried.

"You will need the wagon, and both of your brothers' help, you see."

Livie looked at him quizzically.

"I want you to have the *virginal*." He touched the sound-box with his hand one more time. "Oh, I know you cannot play it yet, but you can learn, can't you? You learned how to make soup, and drive a wagon. And how to plant lilies. And how to make friends. True?"

Livie was weeping. She knew what her friend was doing. Her heart suddenly ached.

"Don't let anything pass you by, maiden of the mountain. Don't let others decide what you will do, eh? You can learn and you can go places and do things. I give you the oxen and the wagon to get you started," the old man whispered.

"What will you do without the wagon? How will you get to market? You cannot, Monsieur Picoult. It is too much."

The old man explained that Gaston would get another wagon for taking goods to the market. And for bringing her hay to store in the cattle-byre for them. She shouldn't worry about that at all. And there were always more oxen, although none quite so bold and strong as Louis and George.

"Just remember that they're for carrying you places," he said. Don't let them eat up all the hay for nothing."

"Yes, Monsieur. And I will take care of them. I promise." She held his hand for a while longer, then Guillaume touched her on the shoulder and they went out to the barn.

Chapter Fourteen

"Sometimes, I'm afraid that they're going to step on me," said Beatrice, the little girl mouse. "They're not very careful where they trod."

"Or where they...go," said Pietro, with his mousy-giggle. Livie frowned at the boy-mouse, her brow furrowed.

"They are gentle, though," Beatrice continued, giving Pietro a look that made him hush.

Livie was shoveling out the cattle-byre. Papa had given her an old mended shovel and a basket for gathering the smelly manure and old straw and told her to pile it behind the wall of the building. Livie was surprised. He didn't even mind the extra work tossing down rye straw and sweet hay from the hayloft for them to eat. They ate a lot of hay, and made a lot of manure.

"The manure is good," Papa told her, grudgingly. "For dressing on your Maman's vegetables. Everything will grow better."

And while Livie was pleased that Papa said such things, for her it was different. She just wanted to be able to work by herself, near the oxen, to hear them breathing, to talk to them about things. Mostly it was just...nice...to be able to be in the byre, where it was warmer and the big animals made everything seem alive.

As she was thinking this, George shifted his feet and bumped against the boards of his stall. He huffed and startled the two little mice, which skittered away through a crack where the stone wall met the floor.

"It's alright, everyone," Livie said soothingly, and patted the big ox on his rump. She hung the shovel from an old nail in the byre wall and picked up the basket of manure, pursing her lips against the stink.

"Worth the effort for good tomatoes, eh?" said Jean-Charles as he passed her walking through the yard, heading out to the fields. "Soon it will be warm enough to plant. I love spring, don't you, little sister?"

Livie nodded solemnly as she tipped the full basket into the heap, not wanting to open her mouth at that moment. She did love spring, but just not as much as she once had. She wasn't in the mood for running around full-tilt in the farmyard, chasing chickens or taunting Nick the Mean Dog. She no longer wandered about, daydreaming and looking at the sky.

****

Monsieur Picoult died only a few days after she visited. It turned out that he was truly as sick as he seemed to be. And because a blanket of snow had fallen again, no word was immediately sent about it from his farm. Days later, his man Gaston finally came with the news. Livie was angry; had she known, she could have gone one more time. She would have hitched the oxen to the wagon and gone over the hill. The farmhand stood in the Bien's living room with his hat crunched in his hand, head bowed. He haltingly explained that it had been Monsieur Picoult's wishes that she not be there when he was too sick. That was why, when there was the one day that he was able to get up from his bed, he'd had Gaston fetch her, so that they might have one more meal together.

"He knew that he didn't have long, miss," Gaston said softly, not looking at her.

Livie looked at the man, then at Maman and Papa.

"This is not good. It is not right. I should go and...something. Right?"

"No," Papa said slowly. "You already paid your respects when you visited before."

"I should say goodbye to him." Livie's eyes stung with fresh tears.

"No," Maman told her. "He's already been buried."

"I have to go," Livie wept, rubbing her eyes and wiping her hair from her face. "He is my friend. I have to say goodbye to him."

Maman sat in a chair. "Oh, Livie, child, I'm so sorry. You did already, both of you. He was saying goodbye to you. He gave you those things important to him. He trusted that you would understand." Maman's own eyes were wet with tears.

Livie finally nodded, so that Maman wouldn't cry for her pain. But she wasn't sure that she did understand. It was very difficult. She'd only had Monsieur Picoult as her friend for a short while.

"When someone has almost no friends, to lose one is more terrible, isn't it?" she asked.

"No, *cherie*. Not more terrible. Each loss is as terrible as it can be," said Maman.

Livie went into the living room and sat on the stool in front of the virginal. She hadn't laid a finger on the box that made music, the *instrument*, since she had brought it home with the oxen and the wagon. What good was it having something that could make such beautiful sound if she was not the one who could produce it? Picoult should have given it to someone who can make music, she thought. It seemed a shame to have it here. He told me to learn how, but I don't even know where to begiin. I don't know the simplest song.
****

But then, as they always do, one day followed another. And although Livie couldn't imagine it getting warmer again, yet it did.

New growth in the fields and in the dark, bent branches of the trees seemed quite impossible, yet began sprouting nonetheless. Livie didn't know how it was that he knew - perhaps he smelled it in the spring breeze - but one morning Papa declared that there would be no more frosts and that it was safe to sow the most fragile plants. Livie worked with Maman to take the precious tomato seeds, dried and saved from the previous fall's harvest, and place them carefully in the soil at one end of Maman's garden. At the other end, they sowed squash seeds. Together they positioned the small eyes of potatoes in soft, manicured dirt in the middle, and the tips of turnip, parsnip and carrot tubers. Dry, wrinkled beans were set in manured rows along the garden's far edge.

As Maman and she planted, birds twittered in the heights of the oak tree, scolding each other while flying to the thatch roof of the farmhouse and back again, carrying away loose bits of roof-straw. Livie wondered where they went during the worst cold of winter, and how they knew to return. Smart birds, she decided. The fields and gardens ready, everyone caught themselves looking up at the sky for clouds, for the first spring showers. And, of course, those first spring showers fell, with cool drops that disturbed the dust in the farmyard, and chased the scurrying chickens into the dry safety of the cattle-byre.

On the day of her birthday, Livie carried the bucket up the hill to fetch food for those chickens. Some things hadn't changed, she thought. No one said anything to her about her day. She hadn't expected them to. Alright, then, she was still the chicken-feeder. She shivered a little in the hilltop breezes.

The tips of the weeds were mostly brown and winter broken, but pushing out to the middle of the meadow, Livie found the dried heads of some old blooms. There were the crowns of thistles, their once-beautiful purple now dried and shriveled. These crumbled in her hands as she pulled them for the bucket, and the breezes caught the smallest bits and scattered them over the meadow. *What the birds don't find*, said The Voice In Her Head, *will grow. That's how it works.* Livie smiled. It is good to be part of making things grow, even a small part. Little by little, Livie filled her bucket with seed pods and dry grass heads. When she looked closely could she see the beginnings of the new meadow, green shoots pushing up to find the spring sun and new buds on the branches of thorn-bushes. She waded through the weeds to the plot where the lily bulbs had been planted.

But her her tiny garden was still bare, hoof-scarred dirt, marked with a broken leaf or two that had been blown by the winter wind. Everything about it seemed ruined. If there were any bulbs left, then why hadn't they sprouted? Perhaps she and Maman had done something wrong. Was the hilltop too cold, too exposed a place to plant real flowers? Had every bulb been eaten? She didn't know. Disappointment pressed down on her shoulders.

Livie gazed down the hill towards Annonay. Because the trees above town were still bare of leaves she could just see the outlines of roofs and the steeple of the church. Was that the church where Joseph-Michel Montgolfier had launched his balloon? Where he would launch his next one? She could imagine it, the great curves of cloth, cloth for making dresses, hundreds of them, rising into the sky, dancing up into the afternoon sky. The promise of it all, to be able to fly, to go somewhere, anywhere.

She turned again, to look over the meadow. To the west, beyond the meadow, beyond the edge of the meadow where the trees with their delicate spring buds stood silent guard, beyond the unseen hillside, beyond someone else's farm or the Count's forest and deer and squirrels, beyond the unseen roads and farms and other hills and towns that led to Paris and the King, all places and people and wondrous things she couldn't see now and had never seen before. All alongside a river that she knew eventually led to the sea, because she'd been told truly that all rivers lead to the sea. Livie turned once more and frowned deeply. This was just her mind playing tricks with her. There was nothing down there except people and shopkeepers and a market for farmers to sell their wares, a place that she might never visit.

Livie sat on the cold ground, gathering her skirt around her knees. She didn't feel much like going back down the hill to finish her chores. If this was how things were going to turn out, well, she had a right to just sit down and think. *So what?* the Voice said. *So you never travel to the sea, or the forest of the Count, or see the King in Paris, or float down the Rhone. This is what it is, you know? Your destiny.* What is destiny? Livie asked. *The way things were meant to be,* said The Voice. Livie sat there, wondering at that. And what if I don't want this to be my destiny? What if I think that it is rubbish? Livie asked herself. *Ah, well, that's a good question. But maybe you're stuck with it.*

She stubbornly pushed The Voice out from her mind. Standing up, she brushed her patched dress down as neatly as it would allow.

"No," she said aloud to the sun and the sky and the meadow. "No. I am not stuck with this."

Jumping up, she ran home at full tilt.

****

"I will take the vegetables to Market," she told Maman in the kitchen. "In my wagon, pulled by my oxen." She put her hands on her hips and then dropped them to her side. Hands on hips was just asking for trouble. Livie was nearly out of breath from having run down the hill, losing and stopping for a moment to fetch one *sabot* as it kicked off her foot into the weeds. She sniffed determinedly and waited for Maman's wrath.

Maman stared at Livie, her own hands on hips. She blinked.

"Is this so? I don't think so. This is not market day," Maman replied evenly. Livie bit her tongue so that she wouldn't smile. If that was Maman's only objection, then...

"Well now, when you do go, your brother must come with you. You cannot go to town alone. Never can you go alone to town, do you understand?" Maman continued. Livie nodded. Then Maman turned and absent-mindedly picked up her wooden spoon out of the cooking pot where it was floating after her daughter's interruption. Livie braced to be swatted, perhaps for her mouthiness, or for being wishful,

136

or for nothing at all at this point, but instead Maman spoke softly to herself and used the spoon to help her emphasize her thoughts.

"We haven't much to take to market. It's very early. Of course..." she waved the soup-wet spoon which spattered against the kitchen table and the stone floor. "...we have some good root vegetables. Rutabagas do well after a cold winter and we have plenty. There are also turnips. And parsnips and the small potatoes. And you are how old? Old enough. Hmm. Yes. We could go to Market. That is, you could go. If you go with your brother." Maman nodded.

Livie's eyebrows went up in wonder. Perhaps Maman had the same kind of conversations in her head that she did. And she did remember her birthday! Were there any more discoveries she was going to make about her own mother? She wanted to hug Maman from behind, but didn't for fear of upsetting something or other. Being under foot. She bit her tongue again to keep from smiling or cheering or both. But she left her look of surprise on her face a little too long. Maman turned.

"Did you think that you would be alone? Are you out of your mind?" Maman waved the spoon at her as if she was about to spank her with it. Livie flinched and shrugged at the same time, hoping that one or the other was enough for Maman.

"Which brother," she asked Maman.

"I don't care which. One of them. One will go with you. Pick. I don't care," replied Maman with clipped words.

"Yes, Maman. Alright," Livie said. "Now?"

"Not now, silly child. When they come in. Now, no more about it. Go wash your hands and face for supper." Livie fairly flew from the kitchen. Always go while the going is good. *No more about it.* These were always Maman's final words.

****

Papa, on the other hand, was not so inclined to talk about it. He and Maman and the brothers were at the kitchen table. Livie sat in her seat, silently listening to Papa shout.

"You want to go to Market?" he growled, then grunted, eyes down on his bowl, chewing each word as much as the turnips in his soup. "Hmmph. You want to go to Market?" Papa shook his head, then nothing. Another head shake. Livie kept her own head down, steadily spooning soup into her mouth, eyes peeking out of loose hair over her face. *Keep your mouth shut, Olivia*, reminded The Voice. *Maman has already said yes. Papa has to come around to her way of thinking in his own way.* I know, she thought. There's no good reason for him not to.

"It is a waste...," he mumbled through his soup.

"Someone has to go," Maman said quickly. "Picoult..." She stopped. Papa looked at her. Picoult isn't going to Market for us anymore, Livie thought.

"You're not old enough," he growled. Livie's eyes clenched shut. Oh, no.

"It's her birthday today, foolish man. She is old enough. And she won't be going alone," Maman said.

"Well I'm not going with her," Papa said with a dismissive wave of his hand. "I hate going to Market."

"I know that you do," Maman said. Livie hadn't known that. She always thought that it was just too difficult to walk all the way to town and Monsieur Picoult was going to town anyway and that was why Papa didn't go. Hmmm. He didn't like going. She wondered why. Then, as if he heard her unspoken question, Papa shook his head at Maman.

"It's talking to those people. They think that they're so much finer than me. As if they don't eat turnips. As if they don't care to know who grows the turnips they pretend they don't eat. As if they're all Calvinists and don't get their fingers dirty under the nails. I don't want to talk about it anymore. I'm not going. You're not going." He wiped at his nose with his shirtsleeve.

"But that's not fair!" Livie squawked, then clamped her mouth shut. She flinched under the heat of Papa's gaze. *Don't stop now*, The Voice coaxed. *How much more trouble can you be in? I'm sure there's* plenty more trouble, she thought, but pressed on.

"Papa, just because you don't like going to town? Just because you don't like Calvinists? I don't care what a person is. I'm just glad they'll eat turnips." Livie clamped her mouth shut before more words spilled out without thought behind them. She held her breath.

But instead of exploding like a thunderbolt over her, Papa huffed and puffed without speaking. Like a storm passing without rain, he controlled himself, looked down and took another bite of his soup. Livie shivered, although it wasn't at all cold in the kitchen. It was a strange silence. She glanced at her brothers, but they were looking at Papa, silently waiting for whatever happened next.

"Suddenly you think you know everything." Papa's voice was eerily soft. "But you don't, you know." He set his spoon down in his bowl and, closing his eyes, pressed his lips together as if he'd tasted something bitter and impossible to swallow, but had swallowed it anyway.

"You could have asked Monsieur Picoult if this is true, and he would have said yes, indeed." Livie grit her teeth at Papa speaking about her friend. But she said nothing.

"No one in town loves us, up here on this hill," Papa continued; softly, this time. "Old Purgatoire went to Market because somebody had to. I can tell you that there are no farmers in Ardeche that own their own farms. Almost none, anyhow. Once there were so many. My father, your grandfather, had his, and there were others. Oh, there was always *crown* land. Land owned by The King. Men worked those farms and were paid some and lived in a crown hut that they paid rent for the use of. And there were the notables, like our own Count with his fine *chateau*, who had their own good land and their own peasants to tend their fields and gardens. But Ardeche also had a good share of men who owned tiny plots down on the flat land alongside the river, or rotten stony hillside fields like ours. They were men who'd come back from their time in the army and settled here to farm, because the weather here doesn't get too hot nor too cold. 'There are worse places than Ardeche, and some better,' your grandfather would often say.

But not many."

Livie hadn't known her grandfather. He died, her brothers had told her, before she was even born. And she had never once heard her Papa refer to their farm as *rotten*. She'd always thought it was a fine farm, a wonderful place for growing. Why had Papa not liked it? He seemed to read her mind, and heaped his scorn on their farm.

"You couldn't grow good sweet grain on such slopes, and it was the wrong side of the hill for grapes. And it drained rain poorly, so it was only good for planting rye, and some small quantity of oats. Your grandfather hated this farm as much as he loved it. There were no fields here when he as a young man – it was just a hillside then. He'd been a soldier and they gave him land for his pension when he left the army. Did you know that?"

Livie shook her head slowly.

"Well, then. Your grandfather married a nice girl from Annonay, because he owned property. They had two sons, and he planned for them to share the land. All of his life your grandfather pulled rocks from the ground, to make fields so that he could grow crops. Sometimes it seemed as if he'd planted pebbles, because the fields grew stones every winter after harvest. His sons helped him as soon as they were old enough to carry a rake or lift a stone out of the dirt. They grew up broad-backed and hard working. He and his boys pried the rocks up out of the frost and barrowed them to the edges of the field to make walls, or back to the farmyard. He built the cattle-byre, and the stone walls of the farmhouse with those rocks. It was difficult to make things grow on the hillsides, but they did. Things never went too well, but everyone ate and everyone had something to do.

"He had cows, your grandfather. They pastured on the hilltop and made sweet milk for market. There was a bull, on Picoult's farm. He made good calves. Picoult was luck..." Papa's voice fell away to nothing before he could finish the word. Livie knew why. There was no luck. Nothing was lucky. Nobody had better luck than another. It was always a matter of hard work and good timing because of making good

140

decisions. Those were the words that Papa said at the supper table to Jean-Charles and Guillaume, while they nodded with mouths full. There was no such thing as luck.

Papa raised his hands and shook his head to wave away of that line of thinking. He grumbled under his breath and started again, quieter, less angry.

"All of his life, your grandfather knew that when he grew old he couldn't give the farm to both of his sons, but would have to divide the land between them. He wanted to buy more land, even more of the lousy hillside, but there was no money. There was never money for that. Divided, each farm would have not provided enough for a family. Your grandfather kept this thought to himself his entire life - as he grew older, as his sons grew up - that he would never be able to give them both land for their own.

"But the sons were also brothers. They worked their father's land with backs that grew strong, and they brought in crops on that stony hill. They worked together, and sometimes they disagreed with each other, but they were always brothers. And as they grew up, the sons also wanted to marry and get on with their own lives. The sons - the brothers - knew that the farm was too small to support two families. So your grandfather had to pick. He had to make a decision that he didn't want to make. He gave the farm to his elder son. No one was surprised by the decision, but the younger son was frustrated. As it often does, that frustration turned over into anger and then resentment. Perhaps it was impossible to prevent it from doing so. The younger son left; left the girl he wanted to marry, left his father and brother and walked away into the west, to find some other way to spend his life, away from his family and what might have been his family. And he never looked back."

Papa took a deep breath to continue, but let it all back out in a whoosh, as if he'd picked up something too heavy to carry anymore. He sat in his chair, head down, staring into his empty bowl.

Livie watched Maman's face, looking at Papa darkly.

"Go on. Tell her," Maman said. "It is time that you told her."
What was she talking about?

"No. It is not time for that," said Papa. He raised an empty hand, roughly waving the family away, but not before making his decision. "But it is time for market and Livie will go."

Chapter Fifteen

Livie found that she had to speak sternly to herself just to keep from galloping around the farmyard like Apollo the horse. It was all she could do to keep from shouting aloud. Market! I'm going to Market! Who could ever believe such good fortune? Papa wasn't really happy about it, not happy at all, actually, but he still said that she could go. That was good enough. That was fine! *Now, let's not get in trouble before market day. No running. No silly questions to Papa. Do all of your chores,* scolded The Voice. *Don't argue with your brothers.* Yes, yes, of course, she thought. But it was difficult, that was for sure.

Now, suddenly, those days that had seemed to be fairly skipping by dragged like boots slogging through deep mud. Oh, Livie was busy, alright. Feed the chickens. Weed the gardens. Help with lunch. Fetch the water to wash. And still each day took too long. Time takes...too much time!

And spring teased with warm sunshine then slapped with cold rain as punishment for reasons unknown. The rain beat the new plants down onto the muddy soil. At least no frost, Papa grunted at the sky after each rainstorm, his head nodding affirmation, but he frowned each time he said it. A frost now would be terrible, Livie knew, killing the new shoots of rye and the tender potato plants and the young tomato vines. Maman always held seeds aside for replanting against such an awful possibility, but she worried about the idea of having to do such a thing. A frost now would cause such a late start that the dry summer months would take their own toll on the fruit and grain. Well, Livie thought, with a little luck. Like Papa, Livie didn't really believe in luck either, but still she was careful not to do anything that might just cause something. So she did all of her work without complaint. And it was extra...lucky that Papa and Maman could see how grown-up she was, doing things without first being asked. And the first Market crept closer, like a snail, like a caterpillar.

She wondered who else would go to Market with her? Surely Maman also wanted to go. And would Papa pick Jean-Charles or Guillaume? Her brothers had to be pulling out their scraggly beards wondering which of them would be so fortunate. They were probably just like her, staying busy just trying to keep her mind off when, when, *when!*

Livie leaned against the stone wall of the cattle-byre. The breeze played in her hair, and she looked through it as if gazing through the gauze of a *tulle* window curtain. What if, right at that very moment, Joseph-Michel was going up in the new hundred dress balloon? Right now! What if he had tried to let her know, but couldn't? It could be that there wasn't enough time, or the weather had gotten in the way for him, too. Or what about the possibility that his mean brother wouldn't let him out of his sight to send her a message? There had to be a way for her to find out. But there had been no opportunity to run up the hill to see, or, rather, smell, the paper-making, not if she wanted to stick to her chores. Then Livie smiled to herself. She would have to try and look from here, somewhere.

Like from high atop the cattle-byre roof.

Kings George and Louis lowed softly when she came into the byre. She patted each of them on the rump and slowly lifted Papa's ladder from the wall. It was very heavy and she did her best to balance it on her shoulder. The rungs were scarred and splintery from use. Carefully she sneaked outside.

The slate roof of the cattle-byre joined flush with its stone walls. With a grunt, Livie set the ladder down on the ground and lifting one end up, dropped it against the roofline with a dull thump. This will work perfectly, she thought. Stepping up onto the first rung, she felt her *sabot* slip a little bit. She thought a moment about kicking them off, but didn't want to go barefooted on these ladder rungs. It's alright, just don't slip, she told herself, and climbed up.

On the tilted roof, however, Livie no longer trusted her *sabots*, so she crawled off of the ladder instead, holding her palms flat against the sun-warmed slates. Her breath came fast. It was thrilling to be so high. Skittering on hands and knees, she worked her way to the roof peak. She perched there, sitting uncomfortably and holding on each side of the peak with her fingers.

Pretty. But not a balloon to be seen, said The Voice. *Time to get yourself down from here.* I know, Livie thought. But she looked out over the farmyard instead, past the fields, and down the slope of the hill, beginning to turn the full bright green of spring. Beautiful! She felt like she was special; to be seeing this, to be up here where she could see so much. Although it was not the same as the view from the hilltop, it was still pretty nice. Then another thought settled over her; that it was also very nice to know this was her family's farm and that she was part of her family - although she had to admit that she was but a small part. All of this, the byre, the house, the yard and fields and garden, each was a bit of her life. And part of what she now knew was a very large world. And that was quite something. *You are a strange child*, said The Voice In Her Head. I suppose so, she thought. She wished very much that there was someone to share these ideas with. Maman and Papa wouldn't do, nor would her brothers, who were more likely to laugh and say the very thing as The Voice. What she needed was a friend like Picoult; but this time, if possible, someone her age. That would be good, wouldn't it?

A breeze wafted over her and she closed her eyes to enjoy it. It was time to climb down before she was caught. Another idea had come to her, she should check the baskets for the vegetables to go to Market, make sure they were soundly mended. It wouldn't do to be caught up here, daudling. Livie opened her eyes, squinting at the sharpness of the blue sky. She let one hand go to shade her eyes. And she slipped.

One moment she was balanced, the next she was falling. Livie felt herself sliding on her backside, down the slate roof. Oh! she thought. No! Her stomach lurched up into her throat in dread. Don't fall! Don't! Livie's feet splayed out in front of her to try and stop her slide, but the wooden *sabots* skidded against the slates. Her fingertips scraped at the roof-peak and she held on with all of her might. And somehow she stopped sliding.

Now what? Livie asked herself, panting with fright. She kicked off her *sabots* and they tumbled over the edge of the roof. Her bare feet held in place on the warm slates. Carefully, Livie turned over onto her stomach. On her hands and toes now, she shimmied down to the ladder and climbed on. She didn't stop until she was down on the ground. She sat at the foot of the ladder, her heart thudding in her chest. Then she felt tears burning down her cheeks. She wiped them away with the sleeve of her apron.

Once again, where were her *sabots*? She found them and put them back on. Pulling the ladder down, she carried it back into the cattle-byre, setting it beneath the rafters. Climbing into the cattle-byre loft, Livie tugged some hay loose and tossed it down in front of George and Louis. George shook his head in surprise and backed up.

"It's just hay," she giggled. "Eat." George stepped forward and sniffed, irritated.

"Silly old ox," Livie said.

The produce baskets for Market were carefully stored in the rafters of the cattle-byre. What if the mice had gotten into them and nibbled them? If they needed repairs, Livie didn't want to wait until just before market day to find out. Climbing halfway down, she could see them, leaning in a stack, one inside the other. She fetched them down one-handed, slowly, carefully. Setting them in the straw on the stable floor, she un-stacked them, running her fingers over them, checking each basket. The thin wood staves were gray with age but sound, as was the split-vine which wound the staves together. Livie was reassured. Next!

She checked the rutabagas in their cold-storage, the fat round roots covered with crackly-dry oak leaves she and Maman had gathered to protect them from winter frost. She pulled one from the bin, turned it over in her hands. It was good and hard, dry on the outside with no earthy-smell, no soft places that peeled under her fingertips. Gently she placed it back in the bin. Lifted a potato. Not so hard as when it was first harvested, but still good. She rubbed the eyes from it as she had seen Maman do before. It keeps them from rotting from the inside out, she said to herself. Parsnips and turnips, also good and firm in their nests of oak leaves. Carrots, limp but still bright orange. Not brown, not wet with rot. They would do.

Crunch. What was that noise? Crunch again. Livie turned. One of the boys moo'd gruffly, annoyed.

"Oh, no," Livie groaned, dropping the vegetables in their bin.

She'd left the baskets on the stable floor. Scurrying over, she yelped at what she saw. George had stepped forward and put his hoof through a basket-bottom, then backed up to get it off, punching his foot through another.

"Stop!" she shouted at George. The ox moaned, troubled by the things attached to his feet. He kicked, but the ornery basket wouldn't let go, so he stepped down hard through a third and fourth. Livie pushed at him, but George was frightened now. He bumped back against the little girl, knocking her hard against the wooden wall of the stable. She slid to the straw-strewn floor. Still George couldn't free himself from the baskets. He backed up again. Livie scuttled back against the stable wall. Crawling past the unhappy animal, she stood where he could see her.

"George, George! It's alright," she whispered. The creature swung his head to see what was grabbing his feet, his horns grazing against the stall pillars. In the other stall, Louis moaned in sympathy. Livie grabbed the last two baskets and pulled them out of the way of the frightened animal's hooves. Then as carefully as she was able she reached down, still whispering to him - hush, hush - and the ox was quiet while she drew the broken basket from his front hoof. Just as carefully, she got the others away from his back feet.

Nesting one broken basket inside another, and those in the last, good, baskets, Livie cautiously placed them back in the rafters. She tried to calm herself. This wasn't a real worry, was it?. Just some baskets. *Just most of the baskets.* She leaned against the stone byre wall and wiped sweat from her face with her sleeve. From a bucket hanging on a nail, she took a double-handful of oats and placed it in George's feed-bin. On a moment's further thought, she did the same for Louis. There was no point being angry with the oxen, none of this had been their fault.

Then she waited, listening to the steady breathing and constant chewing. She looked at the byre doorway. Surely everyone in the family must have heard the commotion in the cattle-byre. But no one came. Not her brothers, not Papa. Well, then. Livie started for the doorway and slowed to a stop. At the very least, the right thing to do was let Maman know. That was the *responsible* thing to do. It would be alright. Maman could mend them, couldn't she? But how did this happen? Maman would ask. Yes, I understand that you were checking on them, and you left them on the floor. Well that's what oxen do. They step on things. That is why you must pick up after yourself, Livie. Let's tell Papa, and see what he thinks. Livie groaned aloud.

Papa mustn't find out about this mishap, she thought, or he would change his mind. Pushing her hair out of her eyes, she decided. For now there would be no telling. She could do the mending herself. *Not without help*, said The Voice accusingly. *What do you know about mending baskets?* Alright then, Livie thought, her mind spinning in circles. Not one thing. So, when it was time to load the baskets to take to Market, she would do the loading. No one needed to know that there were broken ones. They would be left up in the rafters until she could explain to Maman and then learn how to mend them. *After going to Market.* And anyway, they probably didn't need them before then. Oh, but what if they did? For now, though, never mind. It was time to go wash up for supper. She pulled the cattle-byre door around and closed the latch.

See how the days are longer, she tried to sing to herself, looking up the hill at the pink sunset. Spring was back, everything moved along at its own pace, one bit after another, large or small. Even if the remaining lilies didn't sprout, didn't bloom, it would be...alright. See, Monsieur Picoult. I am not disappointed about it. They would have been lovely, but I'm going into town, taking the boys and baskets of goods to sell.

But now everything weighed on her shoulders. She stared at the strips of clouds that colored the darkening sky. Did these mean rain, or fair weather? What if it rained tomorrow? If the weather was bad would there still be a market-day in Annonay? She suddenly couldn't recall if Picoult came with his wagon when the weather turned. *Olivia! Of course he did*, said The Voice. *People still need potatoes on a rainy day as much as a sunny one. And parsnips. Not turnips so much, though.* Livie made herself smile and watched the clouds change color again, to a deeper pink.

She tried to remember the sounds that he had made with the box, the *virginal* he'd given her. How lovely to be able to create music.

"So, little sister. Up bright and early in the morning, right?" Jean-Charles said, passing Livie after washing his face and hands at the well. "Papa says that I'm going with you tomorrow." She tried to hide her surprise, at how he spoke to her and that he already knew he was going with her. Still she stopped and stared.

"You. With me?"

"Of course. You can't go alone, can you?"

"Maman?"

"No. Just me." Her brother didn't seem to notice her shock, but kept on going, kicking his dirty boots off at the kitchen door and clomping inside in his stocking'd feet.

Market day tomorrow! Not tomorrow, she thought. That was too soon. She splashed her face with cold water from the well-bucket, which set her to shivering. And going with Jean-Charles – he'd just said so, so he must be sure of it. So they'd been talking about it, then. To Market. To Market. To *town!*

****

Livie couldn't sleep, could barely keep herself lying in bed with her covers clenched to her chin. Every shadow on the wall was something to stare at and try to figure out. Every sound in the night was someone coming to tell her that it was time to get up and prepare for going to Market. Get up before everyone else, she told herself. I can go outside and put the broken baskets on the wagon, fetch the vegetables in the good baskets and carefully place them in the broken ones. No one had to know that they were broken until they got to town. She smiled in the dark. Everything could be moved gently. It would be just Jean-Charles and her.

What was it going to be like? That was the one question she couldn't answer.

"Can we help?" squeaked Beatrice, startling her from her thoughts. "I'd really like to go to market. After all, you promised." The girl-mouse had climbed up onto the foot of her bed. In the dark she was just a small, deep shadow. Something else skittered across the floor. The boy-mouse, Pierot.

"Oh, I think I'm in trouble," Livie said. "I've broken the baskets. Well, George broke them, but it was my fault."

"Why did you take the baskets out?"

"I thought that mice might have eaten them."

150

"Really now? Mice don't eat baskets, you know," said Beatrice. "Not even if we are very hungry. And by the way, George is sorry."

"What? I didn't know that," Livie said.

Livie stared at the little girl-mouse, but couldn't see her face. How did she know what George was thinking? She shook her head.

"I need to be asleep. I have to get up early to load the wagon. How else can I hide the broken baskets?"

"I don't think you can," said Beatrice. "You know, a lie is always worse than the truth, even when the truth is bad."

"I didn't lie," Livie whispered keenly. "I didn't tell anyone about it at all. I didn't know that we were going to go to market tomorrow. I thought I had time and was going to mend them."

"Ah, so you didn't tell anyone that they were broken," the little girl-mouse squeaked, her paws on her waist.

"No."

"Well don't just sit here. Get up and do it now," scolded Beatrice. "You can fix the problem."

Livie sat up. Yes. She could go downstairs and load the baskets into the wagon. Get all of the vegetables out and ready.

But she couldn't sneak outside past her parents, past her brothers. The house was just too noisy.

"No, no. It's not a problem," squeaked, Pierot, climbing up into view and leaning against the footpost of Livie's bed. "I can show you the creaky spots. It's easy."

Livie pushed back the covers. As she turned to slip her feet into her *sabots*, Pierot scampered over to her.

"No, no. Carry them," he hissed. "Follow me."

Pierot led her on the safe path down the stairs. It was still creaky beneath her, but not nearly as noisy as it would have been had Livie clomped down on her own. Beatrice ran alongside.

"You know," the girl-mouse said softly, as if she was talking to herself. "This isn't at all what I meant. I thought that you should tell your parents about the baskets, not try and hide them."

151

"Oh, we can't hide the baskets," Livie said. "It's all we have to carry the goods to market."

"Right," said the little boy-mouse. "We're just going to put them in the wagon. Get everything loaded. We're helping."

"Tsk-tsk," said Beatrice so softly that Livie could barely hear. "A lie is a lie. You know that."

They rounded the corner at the bottom of the stairs and stopped. Livie listened, but could hear nothing but her own breathing. A bed upstairs creaked, its frame stretching under the weight of a sleeping body. But with the help of the mice, she had been so quiet that no one had awakened. In the kitchen, she could see the banked coals in the fireplace, and the door out to the farmyard.

"The kitchen door creaks badly," she whispered to Pierot.

"Grip the handle firmly with both hands and lift the door up as you pull it open," was his advice. "Go as slowly as you can."

"How do you know this?" Livie asked.

"Your brothers do it that way when they sneak out, of course," replied Pierot. Livie froze. "No, truly. I've seen them."

She started to ask what her brothers snuck outside to do, but there was a noise upstairs. A cough. Papa mumbling something. Was he awake, listening for the strange noise downstairs?

"Let's go," said the little boy-mouse.

"Shh," Livie put a finger to her lips. To be caught right here would be the worst end.

"Oh! Your Papa is coming," Beatrice squeaked from the doorway to the living-room. She scampered across the kitchen floor. "We must go right now!"

No time to think on it. Livie took the door handle and lifted, pulling with all her strength. The door opened silently. Would Papa feel the night's breeze? Yes or no, she would soon find out. Beatrice shot between her feet, out into the dark night. Pierot went the other way, into the living room.

"Close the door, Livie," squeaked Beatrice. "Pierot never gets caught." Livie pulled behind her, turning the handle again and making the door snugly shut. Yes! she thought. The little boy-mouse would get Papa's attention away from them. He would be *the noise downstairs.*

The sky was not black, not filled with the twinkle of stars as she thought it might be. Instead it was lit by the moon through a thin blanket of clouds, the faint glow permitting her to see even her bare feet and where her feet were walking and the little girl-mouse looking up at her.

"Don't stop here," Beatrice said. "We still have to get past the black wolf." Livie smiled to imagine Nick the mean dog as a wolf. *Do you suppose that if you were as small as a little mouse,* asked The Voice, *you just might think the same thing?*

They padded across the farmyard.

"He's a good dog now," she said to the mouse, who hopped over the hummocks of new spring grass. "He listens to me."

"Well then, we will probably be alright," Beatrice replied. "But if he starts barking, it's over. If he decides to gallop about and wake the chickens roosting in the low bushes, that'll be enough to bring your Papa out." Livie nodded at this, even though no one was looking.

"I know what to do," she said.

"Good," Beatrice said. "Because the dog's not asleep." Then, to Livie's surprise, the little girl-mouse ran away.

Suddenly, as if blown by a silent breeze, the black dog was there, standing between her and the cattle-byre. She flinched at the musty sourness of his breath. Talk to him, she thought. Sweetly.

"Hello, Nick," she said as tenderly as she could. "That's a good dog."

The big black dog's snarl was full of menace.

Chapter Sixteen

Three things can happen here, said The Voice. *He can bark, and Papa comes outside and you're in trouble. He could bite you and you're in trouble. Or he could bite you, and bark.*

Livie rolled her eyes. Thank you, she thought. You're not very helpful.

As if to bring her back to the here-and-now, Nick growled again, threateningly. Livie heard a hen rustle nervously in her sleep-roost.

What was his problem? Didn't he know it was her? He was growling as if she'd never been outside before. Wait, she thought. I've never been outside at this time of day. Maybe he doesn't know it's me.

Livie growled, rumbling in the back of her throat like thunder in the distance, trying to sound just like the dog. Don't make me bite you again. At that thought she leaned forward and bared her teeth, snapping them together with a sharp click.

With a soft whine, the black dog tucked his tail under his rump and crouched on the ground.

Livie reached out and patted Nick on the back, and the big dog rolled over for her to rub his belly. Well, now, she thought. How do you like that? She obliged him for a minute, thinking that she didn't need Nick happily barking, either. Then she took the frayed rope and led him back to the cattle-byre. At the doorway, Nick turned around and settled on the dusty ground. Fine, Livie thought. Now she had to get to work.

Inside the byre it was as dark as if Livie had closed her eyes. She tried to remember where everything was. There was the sound of the boys breathing, steady and slow as if they were asleep on their feet. The wagon was to her right, in front of the doorway. Sliding her hand against the wall, she found Papa's ladder.

"Everything is alright," she said to the oxen to reassure them. "I'm just climbing up to get the baskets."

Livie leaned the ladder against the rafters and took her first step. Everything was more...well, wiggly than before. Not as much fun as in the daylight, she decided. Well, should she keep going or try to sneak back inside and explain everything in the morning? She climbed. Gripping the ladder with one hand, she felt around in the rafters for the nested baskets. There they were. They seemed heavier than they'd been just that afternoon.

Climbing down one-handed she felt the nervous sweat beading on her forehead. Her eyes had adjusted to the dark as much as they were going to, and still she was surprised when her foot touched the ground.

She stood the baskets up in the bed of the wagon, humming to herself and the boys the music that Picoult had made on the *virginal*. What she could remember of it and could make her voice produce, anyway. Eight baskets. Three with gaping hoof-holes. Three had no bottoms at all, they'd been kicked out completely. Only two were left undamaged.

"Well, then," she whispered aloud. "We'll use those to carry things from the bins. Let's get to work."

Going by touch alone, Livie opened the potato storage and began lifting potatoes out one at a time, feeling each for eyes and soft spots, sniffing them to see that they still smelled like clean farm dirt and vegetable with no hint of rot. Each one was carefully laid in the bottom of the basket. She didn't take any chances. When the basket was about half-full, about the length of her forearm, she stopped and carried it to the wagon, grunting to heft it up onto the bed.

Climbing up herself, she began gently transferring the potatoes one by one to the first of the broken baskets. They would make the trip safely, she guessed, and when they got to town she would tell Jean-Charles what had happened. He could help her with the broken baskets. It would be alright. Finished, she climbed down and crept back to the potato bin. Half-filled the basket again, and hefted it to the wagon. It was slow hard work, and she kept at it. When two of the broken baskets were full of potatoes, Livie started on the parsnips, checking each root for sweet smell and un-bruised flesh. Three more broken baskets were filled with these. She turned again. Now to the turnips.

"A shame that you work so much harder in the dark than during the day," said Papa. Livie felt her legs wobble beneath her, as if she was still standing on the ladder.

"Oh, Papa," she croaked. He was a shadow looming in the doorway, the faint glow of moonlight behind him.

"Be quiet. No words," Papa said. His voice was soft, but she could sense the anger in it. If she could just explain...ah, but there was no chance for that now.

"Why would you think it correct to be out here in the middle of the night? Safe for you to work by yourself in the dark? Why?" Livie couldn't see her Papa's face, and he couldn't see her in the blackness. She could hear him sigh, though. She also knew that the questions weren't for her to give an answer.

"Olivia. There are so many things that can happen in the middle of the night. And you don't have to be a little girl for them to happen to you. To hurt you. Do you think that your Maman could survive if something bad happened to you? No. Her heart would break into pieces." Papa stepped back into the moonlight. He waved to her to come out of the cattle-byre.

Livie stepped out into the night-time. There was Nick, contentedly sleeping on his paws in the dust. That was why she hadn't heard him, she thought. Papa was wiping his face with his big dirty handkerchief, as if he had also been working hard. He turned and started to walk across the farmyard. After a few steps he looked back and waved her forward to join him. But instead of going back to the house, he headed for the lane.

"Let's take a walk," he said.

Papa was silent as they made their way up the lane towards the top of the hill. Livie walked beside Papa trying to match his steps. She listened to the scuff of their feet in the road dust, and the late night creatures: the tentative chirping of the first crickets of spring, hidden frogs singing together softly, the cooing of an owl in a tall tree somewhere. She had the sudden odd realization that she wasn't afraid at all - to be out here in the night, to be off of the farm - because Papa was here, too. She felt like reaching over and taking his hand. She didn't, though. He was still angry, of that she was sure.

At the top of the hill, Papa slowed. He scuffed the toe of his boot in the dirt, making it crunch. The sky was still glowing with the light of the moon. To Livie it was strange, as if she was in the middle of a storm that had no wind or rain or thunder.

"You come up here sometimes? Even when there is no need to feed the chickens?"

"Yes, Papa," she answered softly.

"It's beautiful. Do you like it up here?"

"Yes, Papa."

"I do, too. Anyway, I used to. When I was a little boy, I would come up the lane and help your grandfather. This was the place where he hoped he would make his success. A field where he could plant his vines and grow grapes. You know, it's always cool in the morning here. Then the sun finds its way up and over. Warm and sunny by midday. Cold again at night. Perfect." Papa looked out over the meadow.

Livie looked at him, at the deep shadows of Papa's eyes. How could Grandfather have grown grapes up here? What did Papa mean? There was no field here, just a meadow full of weeds.

"We plowed this field very deep. Not with that *araire* your brothers must use. Your grandfather had an iron plow and a dray to pull it. You could dig as deep as you wished but he said it wasn't safe. The stones, Livie, the stones. Every turn of a row brought them up like dragon's teeth. 'Slowly, lads, slowly,' your grandfather would remind us. 'We don't want to pay the blacksmith for a new blade, now do we?' So we went as slowly as old men hobbling. We turned the top, and turned it again. And again a third time. If you would have seen it you might have thought us mad. But grape vines like to send their roots deep to escape the frost, so we broke the ground deeply. And we had a wagon, like the one Picoult gave to you, to carry the stones we dug up down the hill. There was soon a pile in the yard as tall as a man and as big around as..." His voice as soft as the breeze, Papa stretched his arms wide, then as if they were too heavy, dropped them. He turned and looked at Livie. She couldn't see his face.

"This meadow would have been part of my farm, when your grandfather was old. He and I would have worked it together. Then my younger brother would have had the lower fields, and I the vineyard. There was plenty of stone to build another farmhouse for his family, whenever he was ready to settle down and have one. When we went into town, the girls looked at my brother because he was handsome and he was going to own his own farm. He had a white linen shirt your grandmother made for him. As bright as a sunny day. All the girls came to buy potatoes from him, if you can believe it."

Standing next to Papa in the dark, alone on the hill, Livie found that she had stopped worrying about being in trouble, about what would happen when Papa asked her about why she'd been in the cattle-byre. She wanted to ask him what happened next, about how things had ended up so different. Why had she never met Papa's brother? Why did he leave? Why Papa never called him 'your Uncle'?

"I don't understand, Papa?" she whispered. "What happened to Grandfather's farm?"

But Papa didn't speak. He wiped his face with his sleeve the way he did when he was tired and sweaty from toiling in the field. Papa seemed to be pressing the memory down deep inside, to rid himself of it forever. Livie had a sudden sense that this was the last chance she would ever have to find out about her family.

"Papa, I broke the baskets. Most of them, anyway," she said.

"Oh, is that so?" he said softly. "Well then, you'll have to mend them when we come home from Market."

"Yes, Papa." Her heart suddenly raced. If she was going to have to mend them when she came home, then she was still going to town. She was still going to town!

"Family is a fragile thing," Papa said. "Something as regular and simple as winter can break it. A winter a tad colder, a bit deeper with snow and ice. There was one like that. It was cold like you've never seen. Then your grandmother fell sick. Oh, we were just able to make ends meet, it had been a good harvest. But we dipped into the storage bins more than in a usual winter. By the time March came we had no parsnips or potatoes left. Do you think that you ever are tired of turnip soup? I went every day with that bitter taste on my tongue, so that a sip of water wouldn't wash it out. I almost couldn't wait for spring, just so that I could nibble the new green shoots of grass. But then came the first Market day, and there was nothing to bring. Your grandfather was not terribly worried about this, and even less so because your grandmother had recovered from her sickness. We plowed our first furrows, and piled more stones. Everything was going to be alright."

"Then it was alright?" Livie didn't see what Papa's point was. What had happened to the farm, and her grandparents and...her uncle?

"But it had also been a bad winter for everyone else as well. Your grandfather hadn't thought of that, either. Even the Count's farms had been hit hard. But then the King's spring taxes didn't change. Because they never do."

Staring out into the darkness, Papa explained how each spring the tax collector came to Annonay. He had soldiers and assistants and Livie's grandfather listened to the tax collector as he put the new number in front of him. Some number of francs for each farm, due before June. There would be no chance to plant more potatoes, to sell beans and parsnips and make the money. No opportunity to plant grape vines, let them grow and mature. Her grandfather had stalked about the farm, frustrated and angry. If he didn't pay his taxes, the farm would be lost. To pay the taxes, part of the farm had to be sold. They had labored so on it, but there was no other way.

Suddenly Livie understood. Her grandfather had sold the new vineyard, or what would have been the new vineyard. The top of the hill, which had been part of her grandfather's farm, was sold to pay taxes. But to whom?

"My brother was quiet about it," Papa said. "When we'd been growing up, he'd helped carry the stones, helped plow the furrows. He'd been working so hard. He'd been dreaming about us having a vineyard. But now he saw that everything was changing. He realized that none of this work was going to be for him, none of the farm would end up his. Your grandmother tried to explain to him that if we all kept working hard and were patient that we could buy the vineyard back again, or maybe even different land somewhere close to our farm. But he couldn't make himself listen to what we said. He thought he knew better than that. We had to sell part of our farm. Maybe it was even the best part. He and I both thought that it was. And it would never be there again. My brother decided that our *chance*, our luck, had gone."

Livie looked up at Papa's face. There was a sheen of tears on his cheeks.

"Oh, Papa. I'm sorry," she said.

"Picoult made us a good offer for this field. As a favor to your grandfather. And we were able to pay the taxes. After my brother left, your grandfather didn't let himself become angry about it any longer. Maybe he loved my brother differently than he did me, I don't know. Possibly it was me who should have left. I would have liked to talk with him about it more."

"Why didn't Monsieur Picoult grow grapes here?"

"I don't know, *cherie*," Papa said. Livie gulped. Papa never called her *cherie*, his 'dear'. "I think that he was always waiting for us to buy the field back from him. I think that he was a good neighbor."

Livie turned and looked out over the darkness that was the town. Her eyes were heavy and her shoulders slumped under their own weight. *No wonder*, nagged The Voice. *You've been awake all night.* Her nose tickled, too, as if she might sneeze. She rubbed it with the back of her hand. Strange smell, she thought. Sour, like Maman's soup.

"Is Maman already awake?" she asked.

"No. That's coming from town. Something burning." Papa sniffed and wrinkled his nose.

I can see his nose, Livie thought. It's lighter than before. The sun must be coming up. But what is that smell? Not something burning, though. Rather like a stinky old dog. Her eyes opened wide. A *stinky old dog*. 'When we start again in the spring, you will know that I am back at work,' was what Joseph had said. 'You will be able to smell the paper, right? It will smell as sour as a wet dog.'

Montgolfier was working on his balloon!

161

Chapter Seventeen

"Well, then. Let's see this *petit belle jardin* of yours," Papa said. Livie startled. She'd never told Papa about it, and assumed that Maman hadn't either. Well, you couldn't put much past Papa, she thought. She took his hand - it was warmer than her own and felt strong and hard, but surprisingly smooth - and led him toward the plot that she and Maman had scraped in the meadow last fall.

"Oh, Papa. It's not doing well," Livie said. "Nothing had sprouted when I last looked. I think the bulbs were poor. And the deer got into it."

"Ah," said Papa softly. "Did you manure it?" No, she thought. I didn't think that I should. It was a new garden and nothing had been planted there before. *Except the weeds, of course,* said The Voice.

"No, Papa." Of course, that might have helped, she thought. Why hadn't she?

"Good," Papa said. "Maybe this fall we will give it some manure. But too soon will make the bulbs weak; they'll sprout but send no blooms. Lilies are sulky but proud. When they work hard, they like to show off. Up here on this hill, I would think they have to work hard, right?"

Livie smiled. Yes, Papa, she thought.

The little patch of garden was just ahead. She could see her feet now, and Papa's, in his big worn boots. So Papa's brother - her *uncle* had left so that Papa could have the farm without dividing it further. Dividing the family.

"Look here," Papa said. "Nicely done, *cherie*."

She stared at the dark place on the ground that was the garden. Spread sparsely across it were shoots, poking up through the bare dirt. Some had even spread their first leaves. Were these her lilies? *Of course*, said The Voice. *Who else would have planted flowers at the top of a lonely hill?* Somehow, in the few days since she had last been here fetching chicken food, the bulbs had sensed that it was time to come up, to come out into the sunshine. Not that it was shining right now.

"Papa, I promise - they weren't here before."

"I believe that they hadn't sprouted yet. But they were here. Perhaps these lilies are shy ones. They only felt safe coming out in the night." He knelt down and reached for one of the shoots, gently touching it with his fingers. "They get the morning breeze, which makes them sturdy. But in order to be strong against the wind, they won't be so tall. This one should have a good bloom."

"When, Papa?" Livie crouched beside him, reaching out and touching one of the new plants herself. So many bulbs had sprouted, she couldn't even count them all. Oh, if each one would bloom, what a garden this would be.

"I couldn't say for sure. It depends on the weather, the sunshine and rain. Very soon, I think."

She'd never felt so close to Papa before. He was always there, always hard working and strong. It felt safe having him as her Papa, but never like this. Like she was hugging him, even while she wasn't. It was quite something.

"Papa, what happened to my uncle?"

Papa nudged the dirt with his fingers, poking at it, and then rubbed it between his palms. Maybe he didn't want to go on with the story.

"For a while he lived down in Annonay. I suppose he was a hired-hand on someone else's farm. Then there was the fighting. I heard he was caught in that."

"Fighting?"

"There were fights between the Calvinists and men of the Church. Catholics, like us. Wandering groups of men, armed with knives and rakes and clubs. In the fields they fought. At the river bridges, trying to keep each other from crossing. Even fighting at Market."

"Why did they fight?"

"Who can guess such a thing. A wrong word, maybe. A look someone didn't like, or a misunderstanding. Men fight for foolish-nesses of all kinds."

"Is that when Monsieur Picoult began taking our goods to town?" Livie asked. Papa looked over at her and smiled.

"No. That came after. But now my brother had a cause to fight for. Something he could point his anger and frustration at," Papa explained quietly. "And when the Count sent soldiers, well..." Papa shrugged.

"It was your grandfather and I that brought him home in the bed of a wagon. He'd been knocked hard in the head and was...asleep. He didn't wake up from it. Your grandmother took it badly. And my brother...your uncle...had been correct. But it was the end of our *bon chance*, our good fate. For a while, anyway."

Papa stood up and took Livie's hand, helping her stand. It was time to go home.

"So," he said as they walked down the hill. "What happened to those baskets?"

****

"I know that you can do it, but what do you say I hold the traces

164

for now, eh?" Jean-Charles gave them a shake, and the boys leaned against the yoke. With a jolt and a shake, the wagon rolled forward. Livie couldn't keep from grinning, looking over her shoulder at Maman and Papa, waving at her. She threw her hand up and waved back.

"Be good, Livie. Listen to your brother," Maman shouted. "And don't wander off! Don't drop anything! Be more careful with the baskets!" Maman might have gone on all morning if she was allowed to, but while Livie watched Papa took her arm and turned her around. Maman may have been crying, too - she was holding a handkerchief - but Livie couldn't tell because the wagon was rumbling onto the lane now, and so she turned around to see where they were going. Pretty soon they would be somewhere she had never been before, the downward slope of the lane towards town. The boys were pulling happily, their hooves clomp-clomping along on the dirt road. Livie imagined that they knew they were headed for Market - they'd done this many times before. Were there any special little things that Monsieur Picoult used to do for them after their day's work pulling the wagon? She decided she would find some sweet oats for them when they got home.

The sun was climbing steadily into the blue sky. Livie sniffed. She could still smell the stinky dog odor. She'd said nothing to Papa of Joseph's promise to her to send up another balloon. *Don't you think he wants to know?* asked The Voice In Her Head. *What do you think that keeping it a secret from him is called?* Nothing, she thought. Not a lie. *Ah,* The Voice said. *Just because you say so does not make it right.* Never mind, she thought. I don't even have a plan to go see Montgolfier. She didn't, of course. But she didn't want to think about this right now. It was just too beautiful a morning.
****

In that way that nature has of making some days more special than others with more everything - the sky a surprising variation of blue that draws your eye, the breeze lifting a teasing perfume of fresh spring grass and the new spread of leaves in beech trees, the sun just a bit brighter somehow and its light flickering playfully down – this day was almost too much for her, and made her heart skip a beat. Livie was tired, she hadn't slept a wink all night, but didn't mind. She was also hungry. Maman had made mush for breakfast, but it wasn't oats or anything tasty, just the boiled sourness of cracked rye, and she'd only eaten a couple of spoonfuls. But then Guillaume had surprised her, slipping a two-penny piece into her hand as she climbed onto the wagon. She'd looked at it, then at her brother, and he'd winked.

"Get yourself a bit of barley-sugar, eh?" Guillaume whispered. "And save a tiny taste for me."

"What's barley-sugar?" Livie'd asked.

"My goodness. I'm not telling. You'll find out when you get there. Ask someone." And even Jean-Charles had nodded at this.

So she wondered what barley-sugar was, and watched as the lane widened as they came down the hill, and saw the first farm. It was not too different from theirs, she decided, except that it felt more compact. The fields were neater, the straw-thatch on the roof of the farmhouse newer.

"They're raising wheat. Not so many stones in those fields, I'll guess," Jean-Charles said with a touch of envy. Her brother held the traces lightly in his hands. The hill was behind them – the road to town was level now.

Fence lined one side of the lane. Beyond it, out in the field, Livie could see a man on a horse. Was that Joseph? No, of course not. Montgolfier was not a farmer. It was probably another rich man, for she was certain that only rich men owned horses for riding.

"If it were not Market, there would be many people out working in those fields, Livie," Jean-Charles said. "Those are good fields for sweet grains like wheat, but you have to keep the weeds down. Otherwise they will take over the field." She nodded at this. Weeds were trouble everywhere.

Next they passed something odd - a fenced-in meadow. To Livie's amazement, there were cows grazing on the new grass. Cows! Brown and white, with short-curved horns. Like small oxen, they lowered their heads to bite off the greens, then raised up to chew and watch the Bien wagon go by. Livie couldn't help but giggle at them.

At the following farm, they saw a wagon like theirs beside a small barn. Two boys – much younger than her brothers – were carrying a basket filled with something bound for Market. These farmhands hefted the basket onto the wagon bed and waved at Livie and Jean-Charles. Livie lifted her hand tentatively.

"Do you know them?" she asked as they continued down the lane.

"No. They are just farmers, like us. We may see them at Market. You never know. Perhaps you might go and introduce yourself, young farmhand." Her brother grinned and nudged her with his elbow.

The morning breeze turned, brushing her hair from her face, and Livie again could smell the sour pong that she was certain was the paper of Montgolfier's factory.

"Do you see?" Jean-Charles asked. "Up there, through those trees?" He pointed with one hand.

What? She glanced up, couldn't see anything yet.

"The church steeple," Jean-Charles said. "We're almost there."

Then everything seemed a whirlwind. They were in Town!

****

There were, Livie saw, stone houses built next to each other. Pretty, funny houses, leaning on one another as if there was suddenly not enough room in the world to place houses. And also there were buildings bigger than houses, bigger than barns or cattle-byres. Some made of stone, others of wood, stacked and fastened together and painted shades of white, with windows placed into them like deep-set eyes.

Her nose tickled. Yes, she could smell the paper, but there was also something else. Something new and wonderful. She asked Jean-Charles what it was. He gave a sniff.

"Ha! Someone's grilling meat. Beef, probably. At market, they put it on a skewer and sell it." Livie could understand why. If she had the money she would buy it for sure. And bread. Somewhere, someone had a pan of bread baking. Maybe two. But not like home. Maman sometimes made bread, putting the dough in a small iron pot and covering it with a lid. She would set it in the kitchen fireplace after everything had burned down to a crackling warmth, and use the scuttle shovel to cover the top of the pot with the dark red coals. Maman's bread was always awfully chewy, and sour, the flour being typically rye. But this bread smelled sweet. Her mouth watered.

But Town also stank a little.

"Don't they muck out the manure?" she whispered to her brother. He shrugged and smiled.

"Not as well as we do, I suppose."

Livie could hear the growing noise. Wagon wheels turning in the grit. People talking. Men shouting to other men. *Bonjour!* What? I said *Bonjour!* Oh, of course! Did you bring your wife? Of course! I always bring my wife! Oh, of course you do! Otherwise she would make you sleep outside!

She wanted to cover her ears, and laugh at the same time. Now they were among townspeople. Louis and George seemed to know how to push forward into the crowd without stepping on anyone. And the crowds seemed to part for wagons, patiently and without even noticing that they were being nudged out of the way. Amazed, Livie felt her head turning left and right, back and forth, and over her shoulders at things she missed. She stared as a girl that looked her own age leaned out of a doorway, with yellow hair and blue eyes, boldly staring back at her. The girl smiled, and Livie smiled at her. Then the girl stuck out her tongue at her and slammed the door. Livie blinked at such a thing. Well then, she didn't expect everyone to be friendly, anyway, did she?

"Where do we go?" she asked Jean-Charles. He nodded his chin forward.

"Up here. We'll find a place. It's different every time, I suspect."

He looked at her with a slight smile. "It's been a long time since I've been here, too, you know."

Livie thought a moment.

"Do you ever sneak out to come to town?"

"Who said such a thing? Guillaume? Do you think that maybe he was lying?"

"No. It wasn't he. The mice told me," Livie said, and then bit her tongue because it sounded so silly.

"Oh, the mice told you," said Jean-Charles. "Well, I suspect that they ought to know, then." Then he shrugged at her.

Yes, Livie thought. It was a different kind of day. A wondrous strange kind of day.

The boys truly knew where to go. They joined other wagons rolling full of goods and then they were rolling into a field full of carts and crowds and small buildings that had a temporary look to them and brilliantly colored banners and flags, where more men were shouting and Livie could even see children running around playing, and Louis and George still kept going, slowly and carefully weaving their way through things.

"See, here's a good place for us," Jean-Charles said, and he pulled between two wagons and tugged on the traces. The oxen stopped immediately and lowered their heads together to pick at the grass beneath them.

"Let's take off their yoke," her brother said, and Livie helped remove it and set it in the wagon. They used the traces to fasten the boys to the wagon the way the other farmers had tied up their animals.

"I will set up our baskets, and we will sell some turnips, eh?"

"Don't forget that the baskets are broken," Livie said softly.

"I will be careful with them, don't you worry," her brother replied, rubbing his chin-whiskers. Then he picked up a wooden bucket.

"Do you see the tall flag there?" he asked Livie, pointing. A tall banner wiggled in the slight morning breeze. "That's where the well is. Take this bucket and you can get wateryou're your oxen. Quickly!

169

Tout de suite!" She was excited to have something important to do, and set off immediately.

Livie passed other wagons with their own baskets of potatoes and parsnips and other root-vegetables. There were wagons with hay in them, tied in small bales. Piglets squealed from wooden coops, and the black noses of brand new white-woolen spring lambs stuck between bars of taller cages. Then she saw the carts of peddlers that weren't farmers, shouting about cloth and wooden dowels and nails and smithied tools and all sorts of things that Livie had never seen before. Here! Door hinges, guaranteed not to rust or seize! I have for you a special iron wire that will bend but never break! Come, come! Beautiful thread all of the colors of a rainbow, by the spool or by the inch! Just look! Rabbit-felt hats softer than the bare skin of your youngest child, but even more water-repellant than the roof of your house, if you can imagine such a thing! Livie couldn't help but smile so widely that her face hurt from it. One farmer, set a little away from the others for obvious reasons, had a wagon filled with manure, which he was selling by the bucket. Livie shook her head at that one. People will even buy manure? *Well, why not?* said The Voice. *But not us!* The farmers looked so much like Papa, she thought, very stern and hard-working, their hats clamped down on their heads and occasionally pulling their dirty handkerchiefs to wipe the sweat from their faces. The other men, peddlers and merchants had a more sophisticated look to them. They kept their hats on their heads, but tilted jauntily. They looked like they didn't work quite as hard. Lazy, Livie decided, but then changed her mind. They were different from farmers, she concluded. They work hard at those things that they do. We all have different work.

She reached the flagpole that marked the well. There was a line of people already waiting before her, with buckets like hers and iron pots and even cups and mugs to be filled. The well was manned by a troupe of boys. Their faces were dirty, and their trousers and shirts had splotches of mud on them, but they worked the handle that wound a rope-bucket up from the depths and splashily poured the water into the containers that people brought with them to be filled. The boys took turns at the heavy handle, gritting their teeth with the effort to wind the rope as swiftly as possible. One rough looking, pinch-faced boy a bit older than the others was obviously in charge and supervising the pouring. The line moved.

"Does it cost money for water?" Livie accidentally asked aloud, then blushed because the woman in front of her in line turned to look at her. She was holding a small cooking pot.

"No, dear, or I'd have brought my own for soup." the woman said in a friendly way, waving her pot. "Those lads are paid at the end of the day. Everyone selling today chips in for the market rent and the clean up."

Livie nodded. The woman took her container up to the well where the pinch-faced boy tipped the new rope-bucket over, pouring fresh water into her pot. The woman toddled off to make her soup, carrying her full pot with both hands.

"Keep 'er movin'," the pinch-faced boy said. "That's the way." He knuckled his hair out of his eyes and waved Livie up to the cobble-stone-well while a little boy wound the handle so hard that he was jumping up and down with the extra effort.

"Who're you?" the pinch-faced boy asked. "Aint seen ya here never before, have I?" He seemed to snarl at her, then spat on the ground.

Livie blushed even harder than before. She didn't want to answer the boy. He was scruffy and bold. Something about him was special. He wasn't pleasant to look at, but she couldn't take her eyes off of him.

"Oh, she's new she is," puffed the little boy on the well-handle. "Never seen her before, so mus' be she's new."

"Keep it quiet, Rat," the scruffy supervisor said, slapping the little boy gently on the top of his head with the flat of his hand. "You need your every breath to pull that water." The little worker doubled his efforts, puffing all the way. The pinch-faced boy turned back to Livie.

171

"What izzit? Cat gotcher tongue?" He grinned at her, showing a couple of front teeth missing. His brown hair stuck up in front and in the back, like feathers that wouldn't sit smooth. He had an old black tri-corn hat that hung on his back from a line around his neck. He pulled the hat onto his head; it didn't fit, but he tipped it forward so that suddenly he had an air of dashing about him. Apparently it was a feature of his authority over the other boys at the well, because they all stopped working and looked to him. He lifted the bucket full of water onto the well's stone-edge. The little boy working the handle puffed a sigh to have a break from his efforts. In spite of herself, Livie shyly smiled back at the rough boy.

"We're here selling winter roots," she said.

"Ah. You're farmers? Good people, then. Close to the earth I expect? Well, folks gots to have yer parsnips, s'pose. Make a franc or two this day, then," said the rough boy. "Maybe you get you a new apron."

Livie knew that her apron was old and stained, but stood defiant-ly.

"Are you always rude?"

The boy put his fists on his hips.

"Sure, I suppose so. But don't trust my say-so. Ask around. Everybody at Market knows that I am. Why don't you?"

"I've never been to Market before," Livie said.

"First time? Well, then, farm girl. Take yer bucket back'n water yer animals," he said with a wink, holding out his hand for Livie's bucket, into which he poured the water. "Do some sellin', so's you don't waste all yer time here at the well on this fine day. Then, you know what to do? You sneak off to the band stand. That's where we'll be gatherin' to do some mischief."

It all came at Livie like a storm. Who was this bold fellow? How did he know that she was watering the boys? Where was the band stand, and what was a band stand? What kind of mischief?

"Back to work, you slovenly scamps," the rough boy commanded

172

his cohorts. The little boy at the pump jumped to begin cranking the handle and pull up another bucketful of water.

"Go on then, girl. Then back at the band stand, later." The pinch-faced boy waved a hand at another part of the field of flags and carts and crowds of people. "Can't miss it. Promise." He motioned forward the next person in the line and Livie hefted her bucket and began making her way back to the boys. Then she stopped, turning.

"They call me the Prince," the pinch-faced boy said, looking at her as if he had known that she would ask. "Prince Bullyboy."

Chapter Eighteen

Her brother had moved the baskets to the edge of the wagon bed, and stacked turnips, parsnips and potatoes on the bed itself in small pyramids for the customers to see.

"Papa showed me how to do this," he said. "I was probably your age back then. I liked Market day, that's for sure."

"It's wonderful," Livie said.

"Guillaume and I alternated coming with Papa. I always thought that Guillaume got the better of it. Somehow, you know, he always got the sunnier days. Or when we had the best produce to sell. It wasn't really that way, but at ten or eleven it's hard to convince you otherwise."

Livie climbed up on the wagon so that she could watch everything. Customers strolling past talked with the farmers, picking through the wares, asking questions, making decisions. Some farmers chose to shout out what they had to sell, and others had little flags with shapes drawn on them, of carrots and beans and other things, although how they had such fragile wares to offer so early in the season, she couldn't imagine. She asked Jean-Charles.

"They put them up in pots," he told her. "Pickled or brined. They're as dear as they can be. But some will buy, just to have them."

"Ooh, I love pickled beans," said a little voice beside her. It was Beatrice. She must have hidden beneath the baskets.

"I wasn't sure you were here," Livie whispered.

"Couldn't miss a ride to Market," said the little girl-mouse. "I thank you kindly for letting me come along."

"Not at all," Livie replied.

Then there were two women talking to her brother about potatoes. They carried baskets on their arms and each of them bought a handful, and paid him their coppers. Livie clapped quietly for the sale, and Jean-Charles turned and gave her a grin.

"Good potatoes," Beatrice said. "You've done well. Not everyone knows how to winter them, keep them from getting frost. Ah, well. I've got to run. See you later then?" Livie nodded, and the little girl-mouse skittered down from the bench and away. More women were talking with Jean-Charles, as he picked out parsnips for them. More coppers changed hands.

Jean-Charles flipped one to Livie. She caught it in her apron.

"Remember I told you about the grilled meat? Can you find it on your own, bring it back for us? Beef on a skewer. You should be able to sniff your way to it." Livie jumped down from the wagon.

It was just as easy as he'd said. She ran through the crowds towards the smell of cooking. There were a number of vendors making all sorts of wondrous treats, sweet smoke rising from kettles and pots and wire-mesh grills set over small cooking fires. An enormously fat man wrapped in a long leather apron and with a tiny leather cap perched on his head turned a huge leg of meat on a spit over coals. She stood stock-still, entranced. The meat dripped juices sizzling onto the coals, the perfume of this almost making her dizzy. He looked at her with eyes crinkling at the corners.

"Are you hungry, my darling?" His voice was high and squeaky, not at all what she expected.

"Oh, yes," she said, almost choking on her words. "I have a penny to pay."

The fat man chuckled.

"Well then, let's get you fed." He pulled a skewer from his apron, a sharpened sliver of wood. In his other hand a sharpened knife materialized as if by magic. With the knife, he sliced daintily at the meat over the fire, and stabbed it with the skewer at the same time. In this way, the meat threaded onto the skewer as he sliced, so that when he was done slicing, it was on the stick.

"That'll do you?" he asked in his high voice.

"One more for my brother, please," she told him.

"Ah, then. Very kind of you to fetch for him, then," said the fat man as he prepared another skewer. "Make sure you tell him to be polite to you, or you won't give him his lunch, right?" He chuckled again at his own joke. Livie gave him the copper and made her way more carefully back to the wagon. She almost couldn't stand it, the food smelled so fine.

"Try it," Jean-Charles said when she handed him his. She nibbled at an edge and then took a big bite. Salty, sweet, tender and chewy all at the same time. Her eyes closed. Oh, my, why had she never had such a thing before? It made her mouth hurt it tasted so good.

"I expect you'll be sneaking out yourself now," said Jean-Charles, smiling at her. "We'll have to lock your door and window." Livie gaped at him. So that was what he and Guillaume did. They snuck out to go to Market. Did these crowds go on into the night?

Another customer, and Jean-Charles handed his skewer to Livie to hold for him. We will probably sell all of our potatoes, she thought. Wonderful. They finished their lunch, and went back to work. Soon they had to move up another basket. Livie helped, so that nothing spilled onto the ground. They made another pyramid of potatoes, sold more, repaired the stack. Jean-Charles' pocket jingled when he patted it.

"You didn't get your barley-sugar yet, did you?" Jean-Charles said, squinting up at the early afternoon sun. "You'd better go find it before it's all sold away."

"Where?" she asked.

With a smile, he waved his hand at the whole crowded, crazy Market field. Out there, somewhere, he seemed to say. You go find it.

The day was full of surprises. Yes, Jean-Charles would let her go to the band stand. He knew exactly what she was talking about when she asked. *But you didn't tell him about the boy*, said The Voice. No, she thought. *Or the mischief.* No, nor that.

Livie knew she was near the band stand before she saw it. Her heart jumped in her chest. There was music: she could hear it although it was nothing at all like the sounds that had come from the *virginal* when Monsieur Picoult had played. Noises as varied as differ-ent birds waking up in the summer at first light, but somehow meant to be together. Whistling, controlled and mournful and beautiful. Humming sounds, reliable and sure. When Livie could see past the crowds of people gathered to listen, she saw men standing on a wood-en platform. In their hands they held things, stick-like things which they put in their mouths. Boxes with handles over which they waved their hands. She made her way closer; none of the grown-ups there seemed to mind that a child pushed past them to hear. The boxes had strings stretching from one end to the other. Ah-hah, she thought. That was what made the humming. Like the strings inside the *virginal.* The sounds they made together were more beautiful than anything she'd ever heard. It teased her, made her want to move around, or tap her foot on the ground, or wave her hands about her head, or cry tears she couldn't explain. It called her closer, nudging in to see the move-ments of fingers on the strings or over the sticks. Livie could hear one thing's sound in her left ear and another's in her right. Like...food for my ears, she thought. Tastes I've never sampled before. Sounds I've never heard before. She closed her eyes again, so she could listen only to the music, pushing away the other noise of the Market crowd.

"It's no time or place to go to sleep," said a voice next to her. Livie startled. Turning, there was a girl standing next to her, as young as she, maybe a little younger. Pretty, she thought. Familiar, but why? The girl stuck out her tongue. Oh! Livie thought.

"You're the girl in the doorway," Livie said.

"You really are a *bumpkin*," the girl replied. Her eyes were a fierce blue, and her yellow hair framed her face under her white cap, which she had tied beneath her chin. She wore a pretty dress of light gray that made Livie wish that she had more than one dress and that she was wearing the other one.

"What is a bumpkin," Livie asked, although she already had a pretty good idea.

"A bumpkin is you. A person like you. Someone like you," the blue-eyed girl turned it into a sing-song, punctuating each phrase by sticking out her tongue. She danced out of Livie's reach, as if she expected to be hit by her.

"Well, I am not a bumpkin," Livie said, almost to herself. She just decided that she wasn't. She'd never even heard of one before, but suspected that it had to be more than just how you looked. It had to be how you behaved as well. So how could this girl know she was a bumpkin if Livie had never been to town before?

"You are a country girl," the blue-eyed girl said. "You have no style." *She's rude*, The Voice said. I know, Livie thought. But she's also right. I have no style. *And so what?* said The Voice. *It's still rude to say so.*

"Well," Livie replied. "I know mice with better manners than you."

"No you don't," the blue-eyed girl said softly, coming back over near Livie. "Take it back."

"Oh, but I do," Livie said. "They live in the cattle-byre, and they're very polite and helpful."

"What're their names, then?" asked the blue-eyed girl.

"Beatrice and Pietro," Livie replied.

"Pietro? He must be Italian," the blue-eyed girl said. "Is he?"

"I don't know. I've never asked him. He's funny and very smart, though. He can drive a team of oxen." That wasn't entirely true, because she knew that she'd been asleep in Monsieur Picoult's kitchen when the mouse had driven the wagon, and so that part was probably all a dream. But still, Pietro was very smart. "And Beatrice is friendly."

"I don't know any mice," the blue-eyed girl said, suddenly wistful. "I would like to have one as a friend."

"You'd have to be nicer than you are right now," Livie said in a low voice. She's a lot like Nick the dog, Livie thought. Mean at first, then abruptly nice. Defensive. I guess people can be like that, too. So you have to be careful with them, treat them differently than you might have thought you should. "You can't be so mean to people."

"What's your name?" the blue-eyed girl asked, as if ignoring what Livie said.

"Olivia - but people call me Livie."

"I'm Jeanine," said the blue-eyed girl. She stood next to Livie, watching at the men playing music, and said nothing. She must have decided that I'm not so...bumpkinish, Livie thought. *Strange little girl*, said The Voice. Yes, Livie agreed. But I think I like her.

"I see you found the band stand. Well, come on, then," said a voice, also familiar. "Things to do, things to do." Livie and Jeanine turned around together. It was the pinch-faced boy - Prince Bullyboy.

"Who's this, then," he growled. His shock of brown hair stuck out in all directions.

"This is Jeanine," Livie said.

"*I know* who she is," Prince Bullyboy said. "I wanted to know how she knew who you were, if you've never come to Market before." He frowned at the little blue-eyed girl and she looked at the ground, speechless.

"Her name is Livie. I just met her," Jeanine said.

"Well, so you say," said Prince Bullyboy, frowning in a way that said that he didn't quite believe her. Then he looked up in the air, sniffing like a dog. "Time to get things done, my ladies. We need your 'sistance. This way, if you please." He waved his arm like he might bow, and Livie stifled a giggle.

The afternoon Market crowd was standing around talking more than shopping. Livie was pleased that there was such a place for people to meet to talk, laugh, just say hello to people you hadn't seen in a while. She couldn't imagine Maman and Papa standing around during the day. Papa always had to be back at work in the field, or fixing a tool with a frown carved in his face, straining to pull out a rock, muscularly swinging a scythe. How grand it would be to be able to meet people and talk with them, share a cup of cider or even some fresh sweet milk.

"Faster, now. No daudling. Opportunity doesn't come along every moment," the boy hissed. "so's you must be ready." They were passing behind a wagon stacked with wooden poultry cages. There were still some chickens in the cages, and they were tired, aggravated birds, squawking at everything they saw. Livie watched as Prince Bullyboy reached up onto the wagon. He's going to steal a chicken, she thought. For what? To sell to someone? *Is that what all this is about?* asked The Voice. *You're following a thief around. And stealing is wrong.* I know, she thought, but she was also fascinated by this person who so confidently wandered through the Market it was as if everything was here solely for his entertainment. As quick as a rat sneaking an egg, he pulled his hand back. But it didn't contain a chicken at all. Instead, he had grabbed a bottle of something. Without running, he slipped the bottle behind him, tucking it in the back of his trousers and dropping his shirt over it. He waved the girls forward. Livie looked at Jeanine, who was goggle-eyed at the theft, but who waved her forward silently with a shooing motion. Don't stop here! Livie scampered after the pinch-faced boy, expecting a shout or a heavy hand on her shoulder, but no one had noticed a thing.

Prince Bullyboy stopped next to a vast stack of firewood that some-one had cut and split. It had the sour-wet smell of oak. He turned and looked at the girls.

"What is it?" she asked. "What did you take?"

"Wine. The man's own bottle," the boy replied without removing it from the small of his back. "Can't take wine from the wine-mer-chant, because he keeps it in barrels. Well, I supposed you could, but we'd need help of a few more fellas to lift it." He laughed.

"It was stealing," she said. She had to say it, just to see what he was thinking.

"Why, sure it is, and I'm well on my way to Hell, along with me own father and the Count and the King's tax man," Prince Bullyboy said. "And I'll give you odds on who's the worst of them all."

Livie didn't reply. The tax man, again. He had to be the most evil man in the world, if everyone thought so poorly of him. She thought of what Papa had said about taking the vineyard away from Grandfather. Prince Bullyboy looked hard at her, as if trying to hear her thoughts. Then he turned to Jeanine.

"Now you," he said to the little blue-eyed girl. "It sure would be nice to have a sweet-loaf. Everyone's hungry, right?"

"I've never taken a loaf before," said Jeanine. Livie looked at the little girl. Had she stolen before?

Prince Bullyboy shrugged.

"No different than nicking anything else. Be quiet. Keep calm, don't run. Oh, and cry real tears if'n ya gets nabbed." He ticked off these rules on his dirty fingers.

"What's nabbed?" Livie asked. Prince Bullyboy gave her a look of exasperation.

"Someone collars you, puts the finger on you. Grabs you. Get it?"

Livie nodded. It didn't surprise her that nearby there was a cart with baked goods on it. A fat man stood in front of the cart, talking, chewing a bit of bread. The baker, yes? The pinch-faced boy certainly had looked over this part of the Market. Loaves of wheat and rye bread. Roasted oats piled loose in a clay pot. Other enticing treats, the likes of which she had never before tasted. Small sweet loaves shaped like ears of corn, resting in a basket lined with a cloth. Long breads of some sort that smelled so fine Livie couldn't help but smile, until she looked at the pinch-faced boy staring at her.

"Think you can fork out coppers for such gifties? They're not meant for us, that's for sure. Let the gentlemen buy them. Now pay attention, girl. How will you know what to do when it's your turn?"

Her turn? Oh! No, no. She wasn't going to steal. Not on her first trip ever to Market. Not ever. But there was Jeanine, quietly walking past the wagon. So small that almost no one noticed her, except that she was a pretty little girl, with a neat bonnet over her clean yellow hair. Why didn't anyone see her? Livie could still hear the soft and beautiful sounds of music on the other side of the Market field and wished that she was still standing by the band stand. The baker was patting the short man on the shoulder. They were both laughing at something one of them had said.

"Watch this..." the pinch-faced boy hissed.

Jeanine looked back behind her, back at them, as if she had forgotten something. Her eyes were wide, not frightened but aware. Then she did it. Livie almost didn't see her do it, but the moment the little blue-eyed girl was glancing over her shoulder she reached out and without looking picked up one of the loaves of sweet-bread and in one motion tucked it under her arm. She kept on walking at the same pace. The baker and the other man were still laughing. They hadn't noticed.

"See?" whispered Prince Bullyboy. "So easy it can be done by a child."

He beckoned her and set off. Livie followed. They didn't walk by the baker's cart themselves; that would have been asking for trouble. Instead they went the other direction and out into the Market crowd. *He knows exactly where he's going*, she thought.

"But what about Jeanine?" asked Livie, not even sure that the

182

pinch-faced boy could hear her.

"If she forgets where we're going next, well, then she forgets," he answered without looking back at her.

At a part of the field furthest from the town road were some small buildings. They were just shacks, really, but except for the band stand they were the only permanent dwellings she had seen in the Market. Prince Bullyboy stopped near one of them. Livie sniffed, having so far found this to be a reliable way of knowing what was being sold.

"Your turn," the pinch-faced boy said in a soft, friendly way. "Like I said, easy does it."

"I don't think so," Livie replied, looking down.

"Should be no problem," he said, without changing the tone of his voice. "Really. Even for a first time."

"I don't want to have a first time," she said, keeping her eyes down.

"It's just a game, you know. S'not like stealing. Not really. The merchants sort of expect it to happen, from time to time." Livie looked at him; he was smiling down at his hands, and using one fingernail to thoughtfully clean the dirt from beneath the others. She wished Jeanine were here, because the boy had a way about him. Like he could make you do something without using force. *Perhaps that's why he's called Prince Bullyboy,* said The Voice. I think so, she thought.

"Flowers?" she wondered aloud. The pinch-faced boy grinned.

"Truly? Flowers?" She was skeptical. He shook his head. "Hardly. Smells nice and all, but it's candy. The boys'll want something sugary, right? That's the sweet shop."

Prince Bullyboy explained to Livie how to go into the sweet shop and not bring attention to herself.

"You're a girl," he told her, "so that's in your favor, but you're poor and your dress is shabby, so the shopkeep will wonder how you can afford anything he has to sell. Not like he doesn't have penny-candy, but he imagines that he makes all of his sweets for the Count himself. The man's mean as a snake and doesn't like children much, so don't mess around in there. Just grab and go, eh?"

Almost like a dream, Livie thought when she found herself walking through the sweet-shop door. It was propped open, so that made it easier, but now she was inside and all around her were wonders she'd only imagined before. Wooden trays of sugar-cakes. Clear glass bowls of hard candy that looked like red and yellow jewels. Crystals hanging from strings, reflecting the lamplight. On a table, mysterious brown clay jars of different sizes. She peered into one, smelled something spicy, but couldn't see what the mystery was. A couple of other people were in the shop, a man and a woman. She was so nervous and excited she couldn't look at them.

"You like honey?" asked a man's voice. Livie spun. A man in a cloth cap, with a big belly that his waistcoat couldn't cover completely, and a shiny round face.

"Me?" She was startled, and felt her face flushing warm.

"Cinnamon honey. In the jars there," he pointed at the mystery containers.

"I've never had any before," Livie said, her voice the croak of a frog. "Do you make it?"

"God makes the honey ," said the man with a slight smile. "Not me. He taught the bees how to find it in the blossoms, and they give it to us. I grate the cinnamon and add it, of course." He came over beside her.

"What is cinnamon?" Livie was nervous and confused. The man's eyes went wide.

"You've never had cinnamon? Oh my! I think you should taste it. No one should go through their childhood without knowing honey or cinnamon." He pulled a small flat stick from his waistcoat pocket and dipped it in one of the clay jars.

"No, you shouldn't do that," Livie said, clapping her hands to her cheeks. "You'll get in trouble."

He smiled wider, his cheeks causing his eyes to nearly shut.

"I don't think I will, *cherie*. Here, try this." He'd pulled the stick

184

from the jar and spun it so that the thick and gooey stuff wrapped around it and slowly dripped towards his fingers. "Hurry."

"Oh, sir, but the shopkeep is mean as a snake."

"Is he really now?" said the man in the cloth cap. One eyebrow arched upwards. "Who told you that? Well, we'll have words with him when he comes, then. Now taste the honey before it slides off."

Livie took the little stick and licked at the honey sliding down. Sweet! Her mouth hurt it was so rich and sweet and wonderful. She gave a little groan.

"Bees?" she mumbled through the stickiness. "Make this?" The man in the cloth cap nodded, smiling at her.

"Every ounce of it. And whikle they're at it they make every single flower bloom. Quite a deal for us, isn't it?"

"Oh, my," was all she could think of to say. She licked the little stick clean, while the smiling man in the white hat wandered around the little shop.

"Most people don't, but I like it even better than barley sugar," he said. Livie turned. Barley sugar! That was what Guillaume had said for her to get. He'd even given her the coin for it. Barley sugar must be wonderful! But the cinnamon-honey, still tingling in her memory. Incredible!

"My brother told me that I should get barley sugar," she murmured.

"He's wise. It's very fine stuff, no doubt about that," said the smiling man.

"I've never even seen it," Livie said. The smiling man walked over to one of the tables where sweets dangled from strings, flickering in the lamplight.

He pulled down one of the strings of crystallized sugar.

"So. Do you still want to steal something?" he asked, his smile perfectly in place.

Livie froze.

Chapter Nineteen

Scream! shouted The Voice In Her Head. *Hurry! Burst into tears! Or run!* But Livie couldn't move, or look away from the smiling man. She felt a terrible embarrassment pouring hotly across her face. The man shook his head slowly.

"It's alright, *cherie*. I would guess that every child that comes into the shop thinks about it. And those that don't come in, well, sometimes they think about it, too."

"It wasn't my idea," Livie said, but then shook her own head. "But that doesn't matter. I still let him talk me into it."

"The boy outside?" asked the smiling man. "The one who says that I'm mean as a snake?"

"Yes, Monsieur. He calls himself the Prince," she replied, still feeling the burning flush in her cheeks. The smiling man closed his eyes slowly, knowingly. Livie suddenly realized that she was speaking with the shopkeep himself. She groaned inwardly. *Am I more of a fool because I was caught or because I was going to try and not be caught?* Livie

186

asked herself.

"So what were you going to take?" asked the round-faced man. "What looked so good that you couldn't resist?" His smile was tighter, grimmer, but still there. Did she detect his head shaking at her?

"I don't' know," she said. "I've never seen so many wonderful things before. I don't know most of them."

"Really?" The shopkeep stopped smiling now, but leaned forward with interest.

"We don't have sweets. Maman doesn't make them."

"No? Not even a little bit? Something for holiday?" The shopkeep apparently didn't believe her. Everyone had some sugar, something sweet from time to time. What was the point, then? Terrible. He frowned deeply. Livie felt badly for him, that her news had affected him so. Then she perked up, remembering.

"But we've sold some potatoes and turnips today. My brother gave me a coin to buy barley-sugar," Livie said. She pulled it out of her apron pocket and held it out.

"My, my. Five whole centimes. That's a lot of barley-sugar, my dear," said the shopkeep. "What do you want to do?"

"I don't actually want to steal anything," Livie said. "But I don't want Prince Bullyboy to..."

"To what?" asked the shopkeep. "Laugh at you? Is that what you're afraid of?"

She shrugged. "Maybe. I don't know." What she really wanted to do was scurry back to her brother, to the wagon and the boys, and just sell parsnips and potatoes. This felt like she'd fallen into a strange dream.

"I've always thought that if you spend all of your life worrying about people laughing at you, you'll spend all of your life worrying," the shopkeep said.

Livie smiled. She didn't know enough people to worry about being laughed at. The man nodded at her.

"Well we'd best hurry, because that boy out there will wonder what you've been doing so long," said the shopkeep.

"Maybe I could buy the barley-sugar?" She handed him her brother's coin.

The shopkeep pulled down a four strings of the crystalline candy

"A centime's worth?"

"Yes, please."

"And a bit more for your honesty," the shopkeep pulled a fifth string down. He handed them to Livie who tucked them in her apron pocket. Then he gave Livie four new coins, one centime each, which she also dropped into the pocket.

"You're a good girl. Stay away from that boy," said the smiling man.

"I know," Livie nodded.

"Perhaps I'll see you again, then," the shopkeep said. "You still have some sweets-money left. Some other time?"

Yes, thanks," Livie replied.

"Out of here. Go sneak some cider to go along with that," he said with a wink. "Now, get!"

****

Prince Bullyboy tilted his head to look hard at Livie, like he might learn something more about her from this askew angle. He and Jeanine were out in front, behind an empty cart. Livie hadn't been able to see them, but the boy's shrill whistle had turned her in the right direction to see his hand waving beneath the cart's wheels. She'd handed over the candy as soon as she'd crouched beside them, keeping her coins secreted in the apron pocket.

"Hey, you did pretty good," he said, holding them up and counting, before tucking them into his pocket. "Not too bad, New Girl To Market. Five strings of rock-candy? On your first try?"

"The shopkeep wasn't watching. I took three, but wasn't sure it was enough," she fibbed, staring boldly at the rough boy. "How many are we, anyway?"

"Oh, well, that's none of your business. We're not a *we*, not just

188

yet," Prince Bullyboy grumbled at her. "And your friend here needs to go back for another loaf. That little tid-bit she grabbed before won't feed a family of mice."

Jeanine frowned. "I don't think I can do it again," she whispered. Livie felt relief that Prince Bullyboy's attention turned from her amazing "theft" to the little blue-eyed girl. She could see clearly, though, that Jeanine didn't want to do this anymore, either.

But Prince Bullyboy was having none of it. "Oh, come on. Sure you can. Aren't you hungry?" he joshed her.

"I don't want to," she continued. "They beat you if you're caught, you know. With a cart switch for horses." Jeanine sniffled.

"No, no," he argued. "That's just a tale. No one would beat a child, 'specially a well dressed girl-child like you." He stood carefully and taking her by the arm began leading back through the crowds to the baker's cart. Livie hesitated and then followed, The Voice In Her Head scolding her with every step.
****

Jeanine stood motionless in front of the baker's cart. Livie could guess how she felt: heart thumping loudly in your ears, legs feeling too heavy to lift. Feeling like everyone's eyes are on you, burning into you, wondering what it is you are thinking about doing.

"Never stop! Not right out there in the middle of everything," whispered Prince Bullyboy. He held up a grimy finger as if counting off another rule. They were standing near another empty wagon, where they could clearly see the baked goods on display, and Jeanine as she casually walked past. The baker was still eating, his chubby cheeks waggling as he chewed a tasty bit of one of his loaves. "Ya see? If you stop and stand still then everyone wants to know why you did. They think something's wrong. Or they wonder if you're going to buy something. Or maybe that you aint. And if you aint going to buy something, then why'd you stop? So, how is she going to make the grab now and not be seen?"

Jeanine glanced over her shoulder, like she'd done before.

"S'too late now to try and be casual like that," Prince Bullyboy said. "Just making it more obvious that she's on the sly."

"Go stop her, then," Livie hissed in spite of her fear. What in the world was she even doing here? She knew that she should have said something to Jeanine, tell her not to try it. "This is a stupid game. If she's going to get caught, then stop her."

"Can't," he replied. "Me going out makes it worse for all of us. 'Specially me." He snickered, and Livie frowned at him.

"Girl, don't give me the stink-eye, neither," the rough boy growled. "I didn't make her go out and do anything. She likes to."
Don't do it, Livie thought. But then Jeanine reached out for the loaf anyway.
****

They ran! Behind them, the shouting grew.

When the baker turned and roughly snatched Jeanine by the hair hanging out of her bonnet, shouting 'Thief!' Livie scampered forward and kicked him in the shin with her *sabot* as hard as she was able. It was a surprising, terrible thing to do, yes, but she couldn't let Jeanine get in trouble. She was just a little girl, after all. The baker yelped at being kicked, and let go of Jeanine, turning instead towards Livie. 'Holy smokes!' Livie heard behind her, as Prince Bullyboy ran up and pelted the baker with what looked like a clump of dry mud, but on bursting open on the man's chest turned out to be a clump of manure. Probably horse, Livie thought fleetingly. The baker yelped once again, and Livie took Jeanine's empty hand, her other still grasping a loaf of sweet bread. Prince Bullyboy grabbed Livie's empty hand with his filthy one and pulled her behind him, into the Market crowd. The rough boy squeezed her hand harder as he led her past the ropes that tied up tents and the backs of carts and wagons. Don't stop, the squeezing said. And don't let go. She did the same with her other hand, passing on the message as she tugged the little girl behind her. And whatever else you do, don't fall, she tried to make her squeeze say.

"Hang on to that loaf," Prince Bullyboy shouted over his shoulder.

"No point throwing it away now."

Their escape took them over to the band stand again, and Livie once again felt the music washing over her, but this was no place or time to stop and listen. The rough boy apparently knew where he was going, so although she wanted to let go and make her way back to her brother and the boys and the wagon, she hung on to Jeanine and let Prince Bullboy lead the way.

Behind them, another shout went up. *Thief!*

"It's just sport, I promise you," the rough boy said as they ducked behind a wagon. Two horses nibbling on a small mound of hay gave the children a look, then ignored them. "They want to catch me, but just as many want me to get away again. It's the same every Market. There's a wager or two going on, if I know what's what."

They remained crouching by the wagon while Prince Bullyboy peeked around. Jeanine stayed tucked right next to her. The little girl smelled warm and sweaty, her hair was disheveled, and her bonnet hung down on her back, but she held Livie's hand faithfully. This is an odd way to make a friend, Livie thought. Not at all what I thought going to Market would bring.

The commotion on the other side of the field grew, and it was probably not a good idea for them to venture back out yet. But that wasn't Prince Bullyboy's thinking at all.

"Come on."

"I need to go back to my wagon," Livie said, when he crouched back beside them.

"You'd be nabbed as quick as a rabbit," the pinch-faced boy replied. "And we sure don't need that kind of trouble."

"What then?" asked Livie, surprised at her own boldness.

"Let's go," he said.

"Where? We can't go out there now, you just said that they're trying to nab us."

"Yeah, but if you stay with me, we'll scoot right past them before they know we've been," He had that tilted grin on his face again.

"Where?" Livie repeated.

"Into the woods. I have a castle there." What woods? Livie wondered. She hadn't seen them coming to town with Jean-Charles.

"I don't like it in the woods," whined Jeanine softly. Livie could tell that she was still frightened by the baker having caught her. The rough boy rolled his eyes.

"Never mind. Let's go. Everyone else's already there." Prince Bullyboy set off, pushing through the crowd of grown-ups as if they were in his way. Livie ducked her head, expecting at any moment to feel someone snatching her by the hair. But amazingly no one seemed to notice them, so Livie stayed right behind the boy, with Jeanine right behind her. Not quite sure why, she pulled the little girl closer, tucking her hand under her arm, so that she wouldn't lose Jeanine. She'd never done anything like this before. It was like...sneaking out at night, but a different kind of scary. Even worse. Or better, she couldn't decide. Everyone was waiting, trying to catch them. Everyone who? Her heart was in her throat, beating madly. They wove through the people, past the wagons and carts and stands of other goods to be sold, the empty baskets and boxes. Prince Bullyboy moved as if he didn't really care that they kept up with him. Maybe he really didn't, Livie thought.

On this side of the Market field were low leafy bushes, and beyond them a wood of tall trees just spreading their bright green spring leaves. Here at the edge Prince Bullyboy stopped and turned.

"Come on, then. Waiting on you like one pig waits on another." He pulled his tri-corn up on his head and cinched up the cord at his throat. Hands in front to protect his face, he dove into the bushes. Livie looked back at Jeanine, letting her hand go. What a strange turn this day had taken. Was this little girl going in with them?

"How do you know Prince Bullyboy?" she asked. But the little girl said nothing, just motioned with her chin towards the place in the bushes where Prince Bullyboy had gone. She shrugged. Livie put up her hand and pushed her way in.

192

The thorny branches pulled at her clothes with misplaced vengeance. They tugged angrily at her hair. Better to keep eyes closed, she thought. Was Jeanine still behind her? A squeal of pain told her yes.

"Quit snapping them at me," the little girl accused after a springy branch hit her in the chest.

"I'm not doing it on purpose," Livie replied just as one slapped her in the neck. "There must be a better way to go." But then they were through.

"No better way," said Prince Bullyboy, who was standing in the shadow of the woods' edge, leaning with one hand on a gnarled trunk. In the other he held a bottle, from which he tipped and took a drink. He puffed out his cheeks and exhaled loudly when finished. He held out the bottle to Livie.

"Thirsty?"

She was. She took a careful gulp. And gagged. Coughed. Oh, it was sour and bitter. Awful stuff. Closing her eyes, Livie spit out what she still could.

"What is this?" she coughed. He snatched the bottle back from her.

"For crying out loud! Don't waste it on the shrubs. It's good Rhone wine," Prince Bullyboy laughed. "What's wrong with you? Never tasted Rhone wine?"

"No." She could imagine, though. A drink made from a river? "It tastes nasty. Even nastier than my mother's turnip soup." Livie's eyes were watering. She swiped at them with the sleeve of her dress.

"I told her she was a bumpkin," said Jeanine. Livie turned, but the little girl was smiling at her, a warmer kind of smile. The kind of smile that good friends might give each other. Her voice had changed, too. The teasing about being a bumpkin was different, somehow.

"Well, at least I don't let the baker pull my hair," she said, and Jeanine giggled. Livie giggled back and knew right then that she had her first real friend, ever.

The rough boy hushed them. He tucked the bottle back in his pocket.

"This way. Let's go," he said. He turned and led them. Livie could see that he was on something like a path; leaves kicked out of the way, old footprints in the dirt. Jeanine took her hand again, and held it tightly.

It was darker within the woods, and quieter. Even though she wasn't chilly, Livie felt a shiver roll down her back. The noise of the crowd was muffled behind them, as if it didn't want to follow them into this gloomy, shadowed place. The level Market field turned into a downhill slope. Livie felt her sabots slip on bared roots. She didn't want to fall down.

"You never been anywhere like this before, I think," Prince Bullyboy said. "Scared?" Yes, Livie thought. Her mind kept returning to wishing she was back in the wagon, throwing hay to the boys. Tasting a piece of her barley sugar she'd watched him put in his pocket, instead of running away from shopkeeps. She didn't want to tell him that, though.

"No," she said. "I was once in a thunderstorm. Lightning all around. Rain falling as hard as stones from the sky."

"Well, we'll see," he said, as if he wasn't listening to her at all.

"Are they following us?" Livie asked.

"Are who following us?"

"Shopkeeps. Merchants."

"Maybe the Count's soldiers, even. I don't know. Who cares? They'll never find us, I know that," Prince Bullyboy said. Livie was skeptical, but there was no noise behind them anymore.

The rough boy followed the path around some large rocks. The slope grew steeper. It was difficult for Livie to balance herself and hold Jeanine steady as well. She noticed that the little girl's shoes were nicer than hers. Leather, with a pretty metal buckle over the top. Fancy, but no more practical out here than her *sabots*.

"Here we go," Prince Bullyboy hissed as he rounded a large tree trunk and stepped down onto a slippery, moss-covered stone.

"Where are we going?" Livie asked. Her *sabots* were unsure on the many autumn's worth of slippery old leaves.

"This way," the rough boy replied without looking back. "It leads down to the river. Eventually, I mean."

They skirted around another large tree, and Prince Bullyboy stopped. In front of him was a monstrous fallen log; an ancient tree that had come crashing down to lay across the slope, blocking the view of what lay beyond. The trunk was thick with old moss and vines still attached, as thick as a man's arm and running the length of the fallen log, splitting and winding around many times in as many directions. In falling, the once-mighty tree's torn up roots had made a deep, raw hole in the earth on one end, and in the other direction Livie could see its high branches now made a wall of green across the slope of the woods floor. Maybe it was the same terrific rainstorm last summer that had done it, she thought, or some other great wind, but in any case the fallen giant hadn't been on the ground for very long. Its branches were newly green with Spring leaves, struggling to find nourishment from the bent roots remaining in the ground, and from whatever sunlight could reach it on the floor of the forest. Livie looked upwards, squinting. There was an opening the fallen tree had once filled, through the forest canopy on up to the sky. The sunlight poured in as if darkness was a barrel and the day was trying to fill it. Prince Bullyboy raised his hand triumphantly.

"Welcome," he said. "...to my castle." Livie looked around, but there was nothing here but the tall trees and the fallen log. What castle?

Heads popped up on the other side of the fallen log. Little boys' heads.

"Girls?" asked one head in a half-groan. Among them, Livie recognized the stalwart lad from the well, the one who had tirelessly turned the crank to lift the bucket. Rat – that was his name.

"Aw, what'd ya bring girls for?" asked Rat. The others nodded without speaking.

"They aint girls. They're thieves. And how about you shut up?" said Prince Bullyboy. "You don't know someone isn't still following us." The heads vanished one by one. He turned to Livie and Jeanine. "Let's get inside."

The rough boy scrabbled up over the log and one at a time pulled Livie and Jeanine over as well. On the other side the boys were gone, as if they had indeed just been heads and somehow had mysteriously rolled away.

"Where did they go?" Livie asked matter-of-factly. She looked at Jeanine, but the little blue-eyed girl shrugged. On the forest floor there was sign that people had been walking around, but where had the boys disappeared to?

Prince Bullyboy watched them exchange looks. With his hands on his hips, he smiled at Livie. He pointed at Jeanine.

"She aint never been here before, neither. So, I show you this secret and then you belong," Prince Bullyboy whispered. "But, you tell this secret and we all come after you. No more Market for you. No more coming into Annonay. Maybe we even chase you home up your own hill. Right?"

Livie looked at the rough boy. Suddenly he looked different. Darker. *And how does he know that you live up the hill,* asked The Voice. *Olivia, it's time to get out of here. Don't you think that you should be going back to help your brother?* Yes, she thought.

But her feet didn't move. Instead, Prince Bullyboy showed where the boys had gone. Bending over, he reached down where the roots of the great tree still entered the ground, where they hadn't been torn apart by the storm that had topped the giant. He stood, lifting something that Livie hadn't seen. A plank, covered with moss and dirt and old leaves. Beneath the plank was a hole in the ground, wide enough for boys to be hidden within.

"Well?" Prince Bullyboy said mock-gallantly. "After you."

Chapter Twenty

The outside of the hole was mud stirred up by many boy-feet. At first, the two girls stood hesitantly above the entrance. Prince Bullyboy had squatted down on his haunches and disappeared into it. As he'd said, quick like a rabbit.

"You've never been here before?" Livie whispered to Jeanine, who stood in front of her.

"Oh, no," said the little girl, who crouched on the ground by the hole, holding her skirts close and trying to peer inside.

"I thought you were friends with them," Livie said.

"Oh, no," Jeanine repeated, sniffing at the very idea of being friends with the boys. "Why would you think that?"

"Well," Livie started. She wanted to remind Jeanine that the little girl had made fun of her being from a farm, being a bumpkin, in front of the boys at the well. But then she held her tongue. It was nice having a friend and she didn't want to spoil that. She decided to compliment her instead.

"When you took the bread, it was like you'd taken things before. I mean, you were very skilled."

Jeanine backed away from Livie and patted her hair with her hand, as if she hadn't actually done the deed. It was that same unpleasant look of superiority that Jeanine had worn when they met at the band stand. A smear of dirt across her face contradicted her attitude, however.

"This is the first time that I've ever seen those boys," she said. "We don't go to Market much."

"Really? How could you live in town and never before go to Market?" Livie asked.

"Because we just don't, that's all. My father and..." she started, but bit off the words. She looked down where The Prince had disappeared. "It's not what I expected. This is very strange."

"I think so, too." Livie said, wondering what Jeanine had not wanted to say. "It's a hole in the ground, like a gopher's."

"I don't know what a gopher is," Jeanine replied. "Like a puppy?"

"No. Like a big rat with no tail," Livie said. Jeanine scrunched up her face in disgust and shuddered.

"Maybe we shouldn't go, then."

"Maybe not."

But it was too late for that. Prince Bullyboy poked his head out again and hissed, "How long you gonna wait before you get on in here? 'Til the constable comes and you get us all caught? They'll give you beatings as well as us, you know. That won't do, will it?" Livie didn't know what a constable was, and the crashing about in the woods behind them had stopped, but maybe the rough boy was right. She didn't want to be caught and punished, didn't want a beating. Prince Bullyboy shimmied out of the hole again and helped Jeanine climb down and in by holding the hand that Livie wasn't holding. Livie didn't take his hand, but squatted down herself and crawled in, wishing all the while that she wasn't there, hadn't run into the woods or gone over to the band stand. *Do you regret going to Market?* the Voice asked.

No! Never, she thought, making all of her other regrets of the day weaken considerably.

Inside the hole it was shadowy and smoky, because the boys had somehow lit some very poor candles, and when Prince Bullyboy dropped the plank back down over the entrance the last bit of daylight disappeared. There was nowhere else at all for the smoke to go. The wall was packed dirt, but they crumbled whenever one of the Livie bumped against it. Like cold storage for potatoes, she thought, and she shuddered although she wasn't at all chilled. But it also stank unpleasantly, like dirty little boys and their sweat and sour breath, and something else as well; some sort of animal had been using the hole as a place to sleep, perhaps back during the deep of winter. It was hardly a place to be at all, and Livie wanted to say this, except that the boys were all grinning at the marvelous *hiddenness* of it, the great secret they'd kept from all of the grown-ups. She looked behind her at Prince Bullyboy, on his shadow-dark face and wide, gap-toothed smile. He looked absolutely proud of himself.

The roof of this gopher-hole was the fallen log, but the floor sloped downward and soon Livie could stand up. It was drier inside, although it was still packed dirt beneath their feet. Livie couldn't tell how big the place was; it seemed full of boys and the odd things that they had gathered to bring inside, as if they were squirrels saving nuts. Prince Bullyboy stood close behind her - too close really - but she couldn't move away. In truth she didn't want to; Livie felt the awful pressing weight of the monstrous log above her and didn't want to be deeper down in the hole.

"Come on," the Prince said, standing with his back bent so that he wouldn't bang his head. "No one can find us here. Nobody knows about it. We can feast in peace." He took out the first loaf that Jeanine had taken and tossed it to Rat, who pulled off a hunk before it was snatched from his fingers by the other boys. He stuffed his hunk into his mouth so no one would take that, although Livie wouldn't have been surprised if one of the other boys, nearly invisible in the smoke and gloom, had gone after it with their prying fingers. How many grimy boys were there down in this hole?

Next, Prince Bullyboy pulled out the bottle of wine, yanked out the cork and took a gulp before passing this around as well. Jeanine didn't take a sip, but the bottle came to Livie and it still had some in it. She thought about how nasty the sour and bitter liquid was and felt her gorge rise in her throat. Still she tilted the bottle and let it pour onto her tongue. Her eyes watered from the wine and from the smoky air.

"We needed a good place. Rat found it, and we all burrowed it out. I found the door." He pointed at the plank covering the entrance. "And we all made it nice. It's mostly dry 'cept when it rains hard, and a sight better than getting caught for taking a sausage from the fat man with the grilled meat."

"This is terrible," Jeanine squeaked. "What do you find 'nice' about it?"

"Ah, you're a girl, what do you know, anyway?" squeaked Rat and snatched at the bottle, which Prince Bullyboy pulled away, out of the little boy's reach.

"Rat, where are your manners, boy?" he growled and took another sip of wine. "Don't you know nothing about *hospitality?*"

The little boy shook his head, his cheeks bulging with bread. The others were a grubby mass of fidgeting noise in the smoky gloom, barely recognizable as boys. Livie noticed that Prince Bullyboy didn't pass around the strings of barley-sugar crystals. Perhaps those he kept for himself. But I paid for those, she thought.

She looked at the rough boy, who was suddenly sitting. He'd pulled a plank like the one that covered the entrance from a cubbyhole which had been dug into the dirt wall of the place and slid it across until the end was resting in a cubby-hole on the other side, like a bench. Clever, she thought. He leaned against the dirt with his feet up on the bench and crossed. The candles flickered shadows over his face.

"Hey, it's not very comfortable, but it'll do in a pinch," he grinned. In the ill-lit space, his teeth seemed to be stained dark by the wine.

Jeanine snorted. Prince Bullyboy coughed back at her.

"If you don't like it," he said menacingly. "...you'n her can leave. Go home to your pretty house. Tie your bonnet on straight before you go, though. Spit on a cloth and wipe the dust from your face. Pull up your stockings, ladies."

Livie didn't know what was making him so angry. Maybe he was sort of the way Nick, the mean black dog used to be. You could never tell what he was thinking and what would make him bark.

"But when the baker grabs you by your ear and takes you to the constable, what you gonna say?" Prince Bullyboy growled. "Oh, I'm so sorry, Monsieur. I didn't mean to steal your bread. I'm sorry candy-maker! Pfah!" He shook his head, while the other boys giggled and poked each other.

"No! That isn't right. It was your idea," Jeanine squeaked.

"But I'm not the one climbing out of the castle. They won't catch me," he scoffed. "Just you."

"Tell 'em, Prince!" shouted Rat in a ragged squeak. Everyone looked at him. "Tell 'em the story about that time when you was caught! Go on! The time when you was caught!"

"Alright, I'll tell it. Stop shoutin', ya fool, before we're all caught," Prince Bullyboy growled. But he leaned back again on the dirt wall and seemed to relax.

The other boys settled down where they were, Livie knelt and found that the air wasn't as smoky down here. The ground was cool and only a little damp and so she gathered her dress beneath her and sat on it. She tugged Jeanine's hand and the little girl crouched beside her. Livie could feel Jeanine's heart racing, like a frightened animal's.

"OK, then. Once was a time my Ma stitched for fine folks. She's a good seamstress, with strong fingers and clear eyes. So she stitched for them as would pay for it, you see," Prince Bullyboy's voice was low

201

now, calmed. Livie could tell that he'd told this story before, maybe to the boys or others like them.

"And what about your dad? Tell 'em about your dad," Rat interrupted, excitedly.

"Shut up, Rat," the older boy barked, swinging the flat of his hand at the little boy, who ducked. Rat shut his mouth with a squawk and the click of teeth. Prince Bullyboy settled back down again.

"We lived near the gorge. You know, the stone shacks by the river bridge? The walls leaned on each other, and the damp seeped in, but Ma kept it clean. It was a lot of work, but she always worked hard. She took on washing, too, on account of we was near the river and all. When folks mucked up their duds dragging hems in the street, or sluiced some mud on their dresses, Ma washed them out. I even helped some when I was a short-pants tot, as much as I could. I fetched and carried the clothes, you know? Heavy bundles of fine folk's clothes. I didn't have no cart, but a even tot can fetch and carry. Not too much to ask, I told myself. Ma 'preciated the effort, anyways. *You're the good boy*, she said. *Always there for me*, she said. And don't you expect the fine folks would toss an extra coin your way now and again? Annonay aint no big city, aint Paris, but now and again is pretty good, right lads?"

The other boys murmured their agreement, and Livie even found herself nodding, although she knew nothing at all of what it felt like being paid to work.

"But then one day things changed. The fine folks started not wanting Ma to wash their clothes. *Thanks, anyway*, they told her. Not all together, not all at once. One by one, like. Like they'd been talking to each other, or someone. Someone who said something about Ma that they didn't like. Like suddenly her work weren't good enough anymore. Well now, she didn't understand it at all. Talked about it with me in the dark after she blow'd out the candle. She knew I was awake, knew I didn't settle down to sleep until she did. *I does it right, don't I?* she said. Yeah, Ma, I told her. *I use good lye soap, clean as a bird's whistle.* Yeah, Ma. So Ma had to work harder with her stitching to make up the difference. *We gotta eat,* she said, when she was stitching by candlelight, mending torn out hems or making more room in the waistcoats of fat gents. She didn't know why they didn't need their clothes washed by her anymore, but so she worked even harder with her sewing. After a while, when we couldn't afford candles for burning at night, she took to stitching by the light of the moon. *Look for the stars,* she told me. Sure, Ma. *Clear nights with a moon is best,* she said. She was sewing by touch more than anything else. Sure, she got pains in her head, from working in the dark, trying to see what she could. Can you 'magine what its like doing stitching by moonlight, trying to get it to reflect off of a broke bit of windowpane I found? Fingers as cold as death, as stiff as twigs on a tree? Naw, I don't think you can."

Now all of the boys were crying "No! No!" Their shouting sounding like the quiet hungry lowing of the oxen in the morning. Someone bumped one of the candles and it tipped over and went out, throwing different gloomy shadows around the strange space.

"But then little by little, nobody brought their torn bits around anymore. Me and Ma was getting by, but just barely. She went to one of the tailors in town, to ask him for his piece-work. You know how that goes, eh? Tailor got the work, gave it to Ma to do. Ma did all the work. I ran it back to the tailor, who got paid, of course. Then he'd toss a coin or two to Ma for all her effort. *Not very much,* she said, next time she seen the tailor. *Well,* says he, looking all serious in his eyes. *You're right. But it's a small job,* he hissed at Ma. *I suppose I coulda done it myself. There's plenty who will do the work for this, you know. But I thought you needed help.* And so Ma hadda bow and scrape so as not to offend the tailor. But that weren't enough for that tailor. He was like a snake, like something from off of the ground. He started telling me to bring things back to Ma. *Her sewing is crooked* he would say, or *see here; them stitches too large.* I looked at him, to see if he was playing me for a fool, but there wasn't a smile on his face. Maybe they were or maybe they weren't, but Ma was working in the dark of night. I was running back and forth carrying clothes. Ma was worn to the quick, and the tailor was just as smug as one of the fine folks themselves.

Livie could feel the anger roiling in her stomach. He should have just hit the tailor with a rock, she thought. Right in his head, with a big old rock. What if Maman had to do that, because there was no farm on the hill? What if there was no sour rye growing out in the fields; that sour rye that you hate to eat in mush? And no Papa? She wondered where Prince Bullyboy's father was. She couldn't imagine not having Papa.

"One fine day Mr. Needle 'n Thread told me I gotta take something back to Ma. *Tell her to wash this*, says he with a sneer on his mug. *You've dashed street-mud on it from your running too fast. Right*, I says, *But Ma don't wash clothes anymore.* I let it slip outa my mouth by accident. I didn't mean to, because Ma always said that our own stuff and non-sense was private, but I didn't like this fella any more than I could throw him. And this skinny twig, this tailor, he tells me, *I don't believe you!* Hissing it at me, like a street-tomcat. No, it's true, say I. The folks don't bring their wash around no more. Tailor smiles e'en wider. *That's because you Prods aint fit to do the work.* Well I didn't know what he meant. So I ask him what's he mean by that? What? *You're a Calvinist*, he snarls. Howling at me like some kind of dog. Then he sets to mumbling. *Leastwise, your father is. Not fit to live here. Not fit to do work of good people. Ought to be run out of town, every last one of you.* Then he picks up a stick from his table and takes to swinging it at me. Well I lit out from the place, still holding the bundle of clothes he wants Ma to clean. I got down the street and I flings the bundle in front of a carriage and the horses reared up and squealed like something bit 'em, and they trampled those fine folks' clothes. The tailor was chasing and shouting at me all the way, at least up until he saw his money-work go under those carriage wheels.

"I went home and told Ma most of what happened. She shook her head. Said as she mostly expected it. Then she switched me anyhow, for being rude about it. He was rude with me, says I. Said we was Calvinist. *Words don't hurt nobody*, she said, and went to sit by the fireplace which was cold as river-stone because we got no coal nor wood. Ma was mad, but not so much mad as sad, you know what I mean? So that's when I knew I hadda help out with things. Best I could come up with was doing a little sneaking."

The older boy leaned back against the dirt wall again, but Livie couldn't see all of his face in the dark. Only his pinch-faced smile with a couple of teeth missing. It wasn't funny. What was he smiling about? Apparently Calvinists felt the same way as her Papa did? Maybe everybody felt like someone else hated them for something, at least sometimes. And what was the point of it all? She had no idea. When Prince Bullyboy spoke again, however, it was barely a whisper.

"*Words don't hurt nobody.* That's what she said. I said yeah, Ma, I know. You're right. Words can't really hurt you. Thy don't put scars on your back or your face, like when your Pa has too much wine in his belly and wants to thrash someone, because he let the hate build up inside him. Words don't hurt like when he leaves and tells your Ma how worthless she is, and how much you remind him of her. And words don't hurt a bit when folks on the street tell you to step out of the way because you're Calvinist, and you don't hardly know what they're talking about until they hit you with the end of a walking stick, and it raises a lump about the size of a spring potato on the side of your head. Ma said words don't hurt."

"But she was wrong!" blurted Rat, whose nose was running and mixing with the dirt on his hands and giving him the look of a little man with lip-whiskers. This time Prince Bullyboy said nothing to scold him. He sat still for a moment in the smoky gloom.

"But she was wrong. Words hurt plenty. They keep things the way they are, every time. A man of means don't want nothing to change. He'll beat you down if he can. Them's in charge of things don't like anyone nipping at their heels. Right? So you know what I did first? Went back and nicked that old tailor's hat, right out of his shop when he wasn't paying enough attention. This very hat."

The little boys all gave a cheer and quieted right back down, as if they were controlled by reins like horses. Livie again felt Jeanine startle next to her at the noise.

Now Prince Bullyboy stood up, looming over everyone because they were all still sitting. He humph'd to himself, as if thinking deeply.

"I'm sorry," Jeanine said softly. "About your Ma and all."

"What's that?" he said.

"I'm sorry about your mother," she repeated. "It can't be nice being hungry."

"No it aint. And Ma worries 'bout me all the time, so she says. She don't want no thief in the house. But I'm not a thief, not really. I never take what don't do Ma no good. Nothing that can't be turned right into a couple coins, so's she can eat and pay the rent. We don't take purses, because there's them that do that, an' they're fierce. Bet you didn't know that, farm girl." He looked right at Livie and she shook her head, not sure if he could even see her in the darkness.

"But so here we are, the terrors of the market stalls," the older boy hissed. He punched a fist into the air, then slapped it on his other hand. "Stinking bread-men, wine merchants and sweet-makers look for us, but cannot see us. The man grilling spiced meat, the fat sausage stuffers, cake-makers. They all know we're here, but only after, when we've come and lifted away their goods. You're right, town girl. Man's gotta eat."

Jeanine startled again, clutching her hand painfully. "She said she was sorry," Livie yelped. "I'm sorry, too."

"Who cares what you say," the older boy growled. "You don't know anything. You don't even know what you're doing here. Do you think that just because you talked the candy-man into a couple strings of barley sugar, we'd leave you alone? Let you go? Nobody ever stole from the candy-man before. He never takes his eyes off his goods. How'd you do it? You had a couple pennies with you, didn't you? Paid him? We was watching everything you did. Nobody fools Prince

Bullyboy."

"And you!" He pointed at Jeanine, who shuddered now, eyes clenched shut. She tucked in close to Livie. "You can't take a loaf of bread without mucking it up, can ya?" Livie felt her heart racing. She stared at the older boy. His face was changed, not friendly at all, not a hint that it had ever worn a smile. "You'll get us all in trouble. Bring the constable down on us."

Jeanine croaked out again that she was sorry. She whimpered, on the edge of crying.

"What's a constable?" Livie asked, surprising herself.

"My God, you're the dullest one yet, aren't you?" groaned Prince Bullyboy. There was nothing at all nice about him anymore, Livie decided. He was just mean. The other boys in the gopher-hole giggled and snorted. "Constable upholds the law. He'll tell you that himself, when he catches you. That is, when we put you outside to be caught. Someone has to be caught, or they just keep looking. Keep on looking until they find us. Got no intention of them finding us, of course." He sneered and his missing teeth made his face look even more fierce. Livie winced. The hole smelled worse to her now than before, because she sensed that the animal odor was just these boys. These weren't just bad boys taking cakes from the market. They were evil.

Chapter Twenty-one

Now it was Livie who suddenly shivered, so hard she was sure that Jeanine could feel it. She wanted to abruptly stand up and shove past Prince Bullyboy, but he blocked the entrance to the gopher-hole so that even if he fell down - if she could push him down - he would still block her way. She looked over at the little girl with her. She couldn't leave Jeanine here, just let her go and make her own escape.

"So," Prince Bullyboy put his hands on his hips. "What do we do with these two, then?" He was looking back at the gaggle of boys in the hole. They all started to answer him at once, and the sound was like the barking of a pack of dogs.

Rat was jumping up and down, and one of the other boys was trying to hold up the remaining candle to see everything and it caused the murky light in the gopher hole to flicker.

"Let's thump them," the little boy shouted. "Let's thump them."

Livie's eyes widened. What in the world was thumping? Did they want to beat her? Hit her with a stick?

208

"Or do we take them outside and strap them to the tree?" snarled another boy, back in the gloom. "Throw stones at 'em for a while? Yes, we could do that." The candlelight jostled again as the boys hooted and bumped against each other. Throw stones! To the tree!

Livie glanced down at her skirts, and at the top of Jeanine's head, tucked under her arm. At the dirt floor of the cave. Almost invisible, she saw it. The tiniest of movements. A mouse, scrambling in the dirt. The creature stopped and looked up at her. Beatrice? she mouthed the name. The mouse shook its head. Do you know Beatrice? The mouse seemed to nod with a toothy smile, then disappeared in the dark.

"I want to go," Livie said. The boys were all talking too loudly to hear. She took a deep breath.

"Let us go!" she shouted, jumping to her feet and spilling Jeanine on the ground. At that moment, the mouse scrambled up the leg of the little boy, Rat. He screamed, jumping up and down. Livie shoved him in the chest with all of his might. Rat toppled into the boy holding the lit candle and it snuffed out as they both fell. All of the boys began tussling and shouting. The gopher-hole was pitch black and dusty, and Livie struggled to not cough.

Someone grabbed her arm and she reached out and scratched their hand to a satisfying yelp of pain. She ducked down on the floor again, felt around until she touched Jeanine's skirts. She grasped the little girl's hand and yanked her close. Jeanine squealed.

"Stop! It's me," Livie hissed in the little girl's ear. "Stay down. Let's get out of here." She didn't wait for an answer but began crawling up the incline towards the covered entrance to the cave. Something skittered over her hand.

"This way, girl," Livie thought she heard the mouse squeak loud enough to be heard over the tussling of the boys behind them.

"Oh! Rats!" another boy shrieked, perhaps also hearing the mouse.

"I'm right here!" shouted Rat. "Get off my leg!"

Livie saw the tiny bit of light coming through the plank cover. She crawled quickly, keeping one hand behind her clenching Jeanine. It wasn't easy this way, but she was afraid that the little girl might not follow her. At the muddy top she pushed the cover out of the way.

"Now! Quickly!" she said, letting Jeanine go and climbing quickly out. The mouse that knew Beatrice scampered out, too, slipping under the leaves and away. In that shortest bit of a moment, Livie had the sudden realization that it was only a mouse, and just a voice in her head, but Jeanine was her real friend, and she was right behind her and they were both in real trouble. On her knees, Livie turned and reached back to grab Jeanine's outstretched hands. How heavy she was! With a grunt, Livie tugged and the little girl slipped most of the way through the cave's entrance, squealing. Livie's hands were muddy and she felt them slipping.

"I don't think so," shouted Prince Bullyboy with a snarl. His body blocked the entrance. He was holding on to Jeanine's ankle, his hands and face even dirtier than before.

Well, alright then, Livie thought. She grabbed a handful of mud and leaves and shoved them in the older boy's face. He sputtered and cursed, but didn't let go of Jeanine. So Livie sat back and kicked at him with her wooden *sabots*. Prince Bullyboy grabbed at her, now, but one shoe hit him on the nose and he howled. Blood spurted onto the muddy ground. Livie jumped to her feet and tugged Jeanine away. The little girl was filthy now, and crying.

"Come!" Livie said and, holding Jeanine's hand, they ran.
****

"Please-ease stop," Jeanine panted, pushing her bonnet back and wiping her face with the back of her hand. Unfortunately, she was putting more dirt on than removing it. The grime had mixed with tears and she looked as if she were wearing a mask. She couldn't breathe without hiccupping. "Livie. Stop."

They were galloping down a path, Livie pulling the little girl as much as was necessary to keep her going.

"Not yet," Livie said over her shoulder. "Can't stop. They're after us now. They can probably run faster than we can. Come on!"

Accidentally, Livie had run the wrong direction, not back out of the woods the way they had come. She had no way of knowing if they were heading into a deeper forest. This slope leads down towards the river, Prince Bullyboy had said. *What if it does?* asked The Voice. *What are you going to do then? Cross it?* Yes, she thought. If we have to, that's precisely what we'll do.

But instead of continuing down the hill, Livie stopped. She turned left, off the path. It was slower going, because many years of fallen, rotting leaves had made the ground soft and slippery underfoot. Well, she thought, at least there was no brush and thorns grabbing at them. But the boys can still see you. We have to keep going!

They ran.

Suddenly, Livie felt the little girl's hand pull taught as her feet slipped out from under her. Livie was pulled from her own feet, and the two of them tumbled into the damp leaves, sliding to a stop. Had it been any other occasion, Livie would have laughed at such a thing. She wasn't hurt, but could feel the leaves in her hair and in her dress. She stood and shook herself off. Jeanine, however, didn't move.

"It's alright. We're fine. You didn't hurt yourself, did you?" She checked the little girl's legs and arms, but there were no new scrapes or cuts. She was just frightened.

Livie helped her up and they continued, walking now. Jeanine was moaning. Livie stopped, turned and put a finger to her lips. Every breath the little girl took was an exhausted gasp.

"We must be quieter, right?" She smiled, hoping that her own dirty face didn't look make her look scary. "We don't want them to catch us again." Jeanine nodded. Then, off in the woods, a bark, like a dog but not quite a real dog. Another bark, less real than the first one. The boys! They were coming.

The ground sloped downward again.
****

Livie could hear it now. The rush of water splashing over stones.

211

She hadn't meant to do it, but somehow she'd led them down to the river anyway. And even though Livie had tried to keep Jeanine quiet, the little girl was weeping, and talking.

"It wasn't my fault-ault, you know," she gasped. "I don't like them at all-all. He was going to hurt us, wasn't he-ee?"

Livie stopped and crouched next to the great rough trunk of a tall tree. She pulled Jeanine's hand and the little girl tumbled down onto the ground next to her. Her eyes were nearly swollen shut from crying. If she didn't calm her down, Jeanine was going to get them both chased right into the river.

"Do you know where we are?" Livie asked, but the little girl didn't even look around to see.

"We're in the woo-oods," Jeanine sobbed softly. "The forest."

Livie thought, maybe I could hide her here. Hide her safely and then go get Jean-Charles. Her head suddenly spun. Her brother had to be wondering where in the world she was by now. Perhaps he was imagining her lost in the market, crying, dirty. Just like Jeanine here. And where was the little girl's family? she wondered.

She shook her head. No. We stay together.
She heard more barking up the hill, now. So we won't go that way, Livie thought. Down the slope then. *No, not to the river*, said The Voice. *You don't want to be at the river*. Well, we can't stay here.

"I'm afraid of dogs," Jeanine said, so softly that Livie could barely hear.

"It's just those boys, that's all," Livie said, squeezing the little girl's hand in what she hoped was a reassuring way. "They're trying to frighten us. Not really dogs."

"I'm afraid-aid of dogs," Jeanine repeated with a hiccup. She isn't listening, Livie decided.

"I was afraid of them, too," she replied. "We have a big mean dog on our farm, all greasy black fur and yellow fangs. I named him Nick. He barks a lot, and I think he would bite, if he could. But the one time when I had to choose between being bitten by him and..." Livie felt her face grow hot as she remembered about Beatrice. The little mouse had saved them, hadn't she? Was she alright?

"What hap-happened?" Jeanine whispered. Livie looked at her. Tears had cleared two paths down through the dirt on her face.

"I bit him," Livie said. Jeanine nodded. "He was being mean so I grabbed him and I bit him right on the ear until he whimpered. When I let him go, he took off. It felt good, just like before when I kicked that prince of bullies. Did you see his nose crack? He squealed like a newborn piglet." She hoped that Jeanine might smile at that, but the little girl kept sniffling. Livie helped her pull her bonnet back on, tucking her away inside the stiff, dirty cloth.

"He took off, that dog did, when I bit him. Stopped barking at me, too." Livie fixed a loose bit of Jeanine's blonde hair. "I don't know why he was the way he was, but he's never barked at me again. I expect that he would bite me good if he could get away with it, though. That's just a mean dog's way."

"You bit the dog?" Jeanine mumbled.

"That's right," Livie smiled. "Although I'm not happy about it." She brushed off the loose leaves and dirt from Jeanine's skirts.

"There now," she said with as much of a smile as she could muster. "Not clean, mind. But it's an improvement." She felt like she was Maman, making the little girl try to feel better and safer. *Growing up*, whispered The Voice. *That's what's happening to you.*

"So, is this the way?" Livie tried again, pointing towards the sound of splashing water. "If we go down to the river, will we be able to make it out of the woods?"

"The Deume," said Jeanine in a dazed way. At least she'd stopped crying.

"Yes?" Livie said. She remembered Joseph talking about the river in Annonay, and squeezed the little girl's hand again.

"It's not very wide in town," Jeanine said. "But it's deep and fast. Deep."

"Do we need to go across it?"

213

"To go where?" The little girl's eyes scrunched in a frown of thinking.

"To get to town. Where there are people," Livie said.

"I don't know. Why can't we go to Market?"

"We can't go back that way, towards Market. That's where the boys are, and probably the constable." Livie brushed her own hands off on her apron. "So we'll go to town, and find some help."

"Stay here, then," Jeanine mumbled. She was starting to close her eyes. Livie stood and put her hands under the little girl's arms, lifting her up.

"No. We can rest when we're out of these woods. Let's keep going." Carefully, they descended the slope.
****

The splashing noise in front drew closer, louder, and the barking was still behind them. But that, too, was growing louder and Livie's heart skipped as she could hear the distinctive voice of Prince Bullyboy, howling in frustrated anger as much as trying to disguise himself as a dog.

The air smelled damp and cool. Her sabots threatened to slip on the leaves, and Livie stepped as quickly as she could without pulling down Jeanine with her in another fall. Sunlight on the ground between the tree-trunks told Livie that they were making their way out. She slowed.

The trees ended abruptly, and they were standing at the top of a stone cliff. Below them was the river, tumbling past huge stones as it made its noisy way. The water was black where it wasn't falling, and kicking up foam and foggy mist where it crashed over itself and around the mighty boulders, which looked like they had been placed there to try and slow the river down. Well, Livie thought, at least the boulders are out of the water. We can cross from one rock to another. Livie watched the mist rising, and knew that this was where the dankness in the woods came from.

"Is this the Deume?" she asked.

214

"Yes," Jeanine said, squeezing her hand as she looked into the gorge.

"I thought you said that the river was deep and fast."

"It is. Very fast. And see how deep?" Jeanine pointed down, at the boiling rapids. "It's much worse after it rains."

Livie nodded. "Which way do we go?"

"Downstream." Jeanine pointed a dirty finger.

"Towards town?"

"Yes. There are bridges in town that go over the river. Not here, though."

Livie wanted to sit and think, but there was no time for it. Like a pack of dogs hunting for them, the barking boys were coming. *Can't go back*, said The Voice. *Can't stay here.* What then? she asked herself. She stared at the water, at the cliff wall. Like stones laid one on another, mortared together. Like the wall of the cattle-byre. She could climb it. Down as well as up. *That's silly thinking*, said The Voice. No, it's not, she thought.

Livie leaned close to Jeanine.

"We'll climb down, then go over the boulders," she said, as firmly as she could. It was as if she was somebody else, someone braver than she was, more sure of herself.

"I don't think I can," Jeanine said, but she wasn't whining or whimpering anymore. She looked up, and Livie looked right in the little girl's eyes.

"It's an adventure. We can climb down. Just do what I do, right?"

"I can't swim," Jeanine said.

"Well, me, either," said Livie. "So let's not fall in."

The rocks looked as slippery as morning dew on a slate roof so Livie took off her *sabots* and her stockings and tucked them in her apron pockets. She tapped Jeanine's foot with her hand and the little girl took off her own boots. Livie tied the laces together and slung the boots around her own neck.

"Don't lose them," Jeanine said. "My Papa will get mad."

"I won't," Livie replied with a forced grin. "I promise. Follow me."

She sat down and reached her foot out for the first rock. It was cold with the mist from below, and she gripped with her toes as well as she could. It was terribly steep and looking down made her flinch.

"My stomach feels bad." Jeanine, above her, crouching to climb down to the ledge she was on.

"Mine, too. Don't watch the river. It makes you feel dizzy. Watch the rock you're on instead."

The river crashing over the huge rocks was everything. They couldn't hear each other without shouting, so neither girl spoke. Jeanine was a good climber after all, and slowly and carefully they descended into the gorge.

Livie's fingers were sore from gripping the canyon wall, and cold. Her feet were also chilled from the wet stone, and she was afraid that they would slip. Her arms felt tired. But with one more sliding step, she was at the bottom. She wiped her face with the sleeve of her dress, which came away brown with mud. I must be a frightful thing to see, Livie thought. She held up her hands to help Jeanine, who also slid to the ground. It was so loud here that the little girl covered her ears with her hands.

She leaned next to Jeanine's face in her bonnet.

"We must keep going."

"Can't we rest?" shouted Jeanine.

Livie waved her arm across the splashing, foaming river.

"We can cross on the rocks, but then we still have to climb back out again!"

"I'm cold!"

"Me, too. And I could use a bath. Come on!" Livie smiled and took Jeanine's hand once again, and they stepped out onto a big boulder perched in the water. It was even more slippery than the side of the gorge, and Livie crouched down, pulling Jeanine with her, to cling to the rock with both hands and feet. *Too slippery*, said The Voice. *It was difficult enough to climb down. How are you going to climb back up?* I'll figure that out when we reach the other side, she said aloud.

Like being in the middle of a thunderstorm, the cold, wet breeze swirled around them. Livie licked her lips, tasting mud, spitting it out. Between each boulder, the river was a brown torrent of foaming water. Livie looked at Jeanine, and she too was dripping wet, with lines of clean cutting through the dirt on her cheeks. Her bonnet was soggy now and drooped over her face, but that didn't matter. She didn't need to see around it.

"Just step where I step and hang on to my hand with all you've got!" she shouted. Jeanine nodded as she had before. Livie couldn't feel her feet anymore. She needed to sit down and warm them, rub them, but they'd reached the middle of the river, and water was splashing up and soaking them, trying to pull them in. Get to the other side, she thought. Slowly and carefully.

"Oh!" Jeanine squealed. Livie looked at the little girl. "You've cut yourself!"

Livie looked at her free hand. It was seeping blood onto the boulder they perched on. It didn't hurt and she shrugged at Jeanine, and tried to smile. Probably looked more like a grimace, but she squeezed the little girl's hand and got a return squeeze.

"Almost there!" she shouted. Suddenly she felt a sharp, terrible pain in her shoulder. What was that? She groaned.

Jeanine screamed.

A stone clacked the boulder they stood on and bounced up, just missing Livie's face.

Livie looked up.

Prince Bullyboy stood at the top of the gorge, staring down at her, showing his teeth in a snarl just like a dog. He hefted another stone in his hand.

Turning his head, he barked.

Chapter Twenty-two

Clutching Jeanine's hand firmly with one and clinging to the boulder with the other, Livie found she had no free hand to rub her aching shoulder. Instead, she rolled it around, up to her neck and back again. It was hot with pain. She hoped it wasn't bleeding, because that would scare Jeanine. We must keep moving, she told herself. We're right out in the open. She watched as the older boy barked again. He's calling his gang, she thought. Yes, we must keep going.

"Come on!" she told Jeanine and reached her foot out for the next boulder.

The mean boy's aim was good. The next throw glanced off the boulder in front of them and thudded off of Livie's shin. She stifled a yelp and grimaced. No. Don't scream and don't let go. We're almost there, she thought. Over the thunder of the river she heard the older boy laughing or barking, or perhaps even both.

Then her foot slipped and she skidded on her backside. She kicked to get her feet under her, but slid even further. Please, no! The river washed over her feet, pulling at her. She was drenched. But Jeanine held her hand firmly and yanked hard. That wasn't enough, and Livie went into the river.

She couldn't breathe. That is, she wanted to breathe, was even willing to take a breath under the water, where she surely was. But her muscles were frozen into uselessness from the river's icy-cold. It was as if she had mistakenly fallen into a drift of snow and it wouldn't let her move. Her feet couldn't kick, and her head couldn't turn. She didn't actually remember a snowfall like that, one with a really deep blanket of snow, covering the winter-bare fields and the cattle-byre and all of the tree-branches with white so startling that it made your eyes hurt. Wind picking up the snow in sheets and pushing it around, into your face, your eyes so that you can't breathe and can't see a thing. So that you can't see a thing. Can't see a thing. *Why not?* shouted The Voice over the river's thundering noise. *Why, why why?* Don't know. My good...it was too cold even to think. And still she was thinking; thinking how one by one the cattle-byre's roof slates were skidding out from under her feet. Oh! Watch out, Louis! Watch out, George! I don't want to fall. I should keep my hold on the peak of the roof, even though my hand hurts and my shoulder hurts. Take a deep breath and pull, she thought. But she couldn't take a deep breath. Why why why? *Because you're in the river, not on the roof,* said The Voice, more quietly now, closer to her. Oh, of course. So cold. One arm above her and one dragged by the force of the river. No help at all.

But then, somehow, there was help. Her head came up and out of the water. Livie opened her eyes. There, on the boulder, Jeanine still held her hand and had grabbed her wrist with the other. The little girl was pulling as hard as she could, teeth gritting, eyes closed. Livie's shoulder sang with pain as she rolled onto her belly against the rock. Still she couldn't get her feet under her. With a howl, Jeanine gave another huge pull and now Livie's shoulders were out of the water and on the boulder. With her other hand Livie clawed at the rock and pulled herself back onto the boulder. Water streamed from her hair, as she gasped for air. She looked at the little girl who had pulled her out of the river. Jeanine sat there silently, still tightly holding her hand. Another stone clacked nearby, bouncing harmlessly into the river. There was no time even to thank Jeanine for fetching her out of danger.

"Don't fall-all in," Livie said, her own voice hiccupping from the cold. Jeanine nodded.

Livie climbed down from the last boulder to the stone embankment. Prince Bullyboy's friends hadn't arrived yet, she thought, and it was hard to throw this far. She reached up for Jeanine and helped her down. They crouched behind this boulder, out of sight from the top of the cliff.

"Climbing up won't be as steep as coming down," Livie said, leaning close to Jeanine's bonnet. She shivered. She was colder from the river than she was sore from the stones.

"But I'm so tired," Jeanine said.

"Me, too. My leg really hurts now. But we can't stay here, though." She looked up where Prince Bullyboy had been. At the moment he wasn't there. Jeanine followed her gaze.

"No. I suppose not," she replied. For some reason the little girl seemed suddenly calm.

"He must be getting the others. Or maybe he's hiding from someone." Livie wrapped her arms around her knees. "The constable?"

"Yes. Perhaps he is hiding," said Jeanine.

"You don't think so?"

"I don't know. What if he's gone 'round?" asked the little girl.

Livie shook her head. She didn't understand. Gone 'round? Around what? She looked at Jeanine, her eyebrows raised.

"What if he crosses over the bridge to town and is waiting for us to climb out of here?" Jeanine asked.

"N-n-no. He's still getting the other boys to come out of the woods." Livie hugged her knees even harder. "Or if he has, then we'll go back across the river and climb back into the woods. That would fool him." But neither of them wanted to try and cross the river again.

Livie shrugged. "In any case, I'm freezing. Let's get out of this place." Again, Jeanine nodded.

Livie's shoulder ached terribly, but there was nothing she could do about it. Each time she gripped the rock, she hissed with the pain.

"Hold on where I hold and step where I step," she called back to Jeanine. The little girl yelped something, but Livie couldn't hear.

It turned out that it was easier going up than down, although Livie couldn't have explained why. Every place she needed something to grab onto, there it was. Each time she thought that it was far too steep or that she might slip and fall, there was a spot a little easier to climb, somewhere to stand still for just a moment. As if she'd been lifted up by a magic bird, or even a strange balloon, Livie was suddenly out of the gorge. She sat on the top of the cliff, panting and shivering with cold and exhaustion. She hauled Jeanine up beside her and looked around. There were no boys across the river, not as far back as she could see into the trees. There were trees on this side of the river, too, but the woods were not deep. Livie could see right through the trees to the other side, where it looked like a farmer's field, still bright in the afternoon sunlight.

And she was soaking wet, but at least her *sabots* and stockings were still in her apron pocket. "Put your boots on," she said. Jeanine sat on the edge of the cliff without thinking, and Livie stifled a gasp, but said nothing. Instead she helped the little girl on with her wet boots and they set out together, walking slowly along the edge of the river gorge, downstream, towards town.

Not surprisingly, the first thing Jeanine did was complain.

"My feet hurt." They had to step carefully. The grass path was slippery with mist from the river.

"It's because your shoes are wet. You don't want to stop, do you?"

"Yes, please," Jeanine replied. Livie shook her head.

"Oh, Jeanine, *cherie*. We have to get out of here, make our way to town. I don't know how far it is," said Livie. "We'll rest when we're certain that we're away from Prince Bullyboy. Alright?"

"But I'm cold," Jeanine whined softly.

"I'm sorry. I'm cold, too," Livie said, squeezing the little girl's hand. Cold, but not scared. That was good.

"It's because my dress is wet, too."

"I know," Livie said, pushing lank hair out of her eyes. "Mine is soaked right through. I'm the one that fell into the river, after all."

"Well I pulled you out," Jeanine pouted. "Mostly."

"Yes, you did." Livie smiled. She found that she couldn't be mad at Jeanine, no matter how foolish the things were the little girl said. Perhaps this is what having a friend is, she told herself. A real friend. *You mean not a mouse or an ox or an old man who misses his family or a fellow that chases balloons? And why can't those be your friends?* asked The Voice. Because a real friend is someone you can talk to, and learn from and who helps you through difficulties. *Exactly,* said The Voice. Livie had to conclude that she couldn't think of a good reason at all. Apparently she had to find a new friend to discover that she'd had other friends all along.

And so, although it had been a very strange day, a strange and somewhat uncomfortable, exhausting and scary and painful day, it had also been amazing and wonderful and funny. A very good day. Livie's smile widened to the point where she found she wanted to laugh.

"You know what?" she said to Jeanine. "My garden won't bloom."

"You have a garden?" said the little girl tiredly.

"Yes, but it won't bloom."

"Why not?" asked Jeanine, as if the subject of flowers had been something they'd been thinking about together the whole time.

"I don't actually know. My mother and I planted them on top of the hill," Livie said softly. "They're lilies." She told Jeanine about the little plot of bare earth and how her friend Monsieur Picoult had given her the lilies. Jeanine wanted to know more about Monsieur Picoult, so while they rested Livie told her about the terrible thunderstorm, and making soup, and listening to the *virginal* and planting lily bulbs and the deer eating the bulbs and how now they didn't seem to want to bloom.

"That's too bad," Jeanine said. "About the flowers, I mean. And for Monsieur Picoult."

"Yes," said Livie, and Jeanine leaned against her shoulder and the two of them sat silently for a moment. Then Livie leaned forward and peered around the brim of the little girl's bonnet. Jeanine sat up. With her damp and grubby apron, Livie wiped at the dirt on Jeanine's face. It helped a little, because the little girl's face had become crusted with dust and river-mist into a muddy mask. She knew she was accomplishing something when Jeanine said *ouch* and pushed at her hands, the same way she herself might have done with Maman.

"Thank you for that," Livie said, looking into her friend's face, into the tired eyes and dirt and tears.

"For what?"

"For saving me from the river," Livie said.

"Oh. You're welcome." Jeanine shrugged. "That was scary."

"Yes, it was," Livie smiled.

Now she knew it wasn't over yet. They had to get off of this path. If Prince Bullyboy was actually going around to cross a bridge and come back and get them, then he would come this way and they would be blocked again. She pulled Jeanine towards the woods, and this time the little girl came without complaint.

"Promise this way will still lead us to town?" Livie asked. Jeanine's bonnet waggled a nod. "Let's get out of sight, then."

The ground was clear of brush and fallen branches and as much as they could they galloped past the tall trunks. Livie hoped that Jeanine was correct, that this was at least a roundabout way towards town. She ached in so many places that she felt like lying down among the roots and napping for a while. But Livie could also tell that they were getting there, somewhere, getting closer to town. She could smell a faint breath of smoke. They stopped next to a large gnarled trunk and caught their breath.

"Someone's starting dinner," Livie said. "Smell?"

Jeanine sniffed.

"I don't...no, I do!" She gave Livie a weak smile. "Oh! It smells fine. Better than my Maman's." At that she looked down shyly.

"My Maman's food doesn't taste so good either," Livie said. "We always eat a lot of turnips. I get so tired of turnips." I do get very tired of them, she thought. She thought about how supper seemed like the same thing, day after day. How her life, before...what? Not just today, surely. But before, it was so much of the same, one day after another. Now she could say that it wasn't. She knew. Not really. Each day was distinct and strange and interesting. Still, even turnip soup, she decided, would be fine right now. Her stomach felt as empty as a dry wind.

"I'm hungry," Jeanine said, as if she was reading her mind. She sounded much younger now, just a little girl. Livie couldn't keep talking to her. Each breath was a weary, panting gasp. Could she truly be even more exhausted than Jeanine? The little girl was depending on her to get them out of this mess. If Livie could just get back to her brother, it would all be better, wouldn't it? She looked at her little friend, hair hanging out of her bonnet, dress smeared with mud, arms dangling at her sides. Then she thought about how she herself looked. *You're filthy, that's for sure*, said The Voice. *Maybe Jean-Charles won't understand that you've had been chased by bullies.* Livie hadn't considered that. "How did you come to be with bullies in the first place?' he would ask her, eyebrows furrowed and frowning, pointing his finger at her soaking, muddy dress. Then, looking at Jeanine. "And who is this little girl? What did you do to her?" Wait a moment, she would say. What had she done to Jeanine? Nothing, except that she'd helped rescue her from Prince Bullyboy. "Well, then, I guess you've had quite the adventure," Jean-Charles would say next. Still frowning, as if he didn't quite believe her. Oh, and if he had been searching for her instead of selling potatoes? That couldn't go well. But there was also a chance that he'd be smiling at her. Maybe he'd had a good afternoon of selling and remembered that he, too, might have run around getting into messes like this very one if he was still her age. He would have relished a great adventure, wouldn't he? He wouldn't have traded it for anything. Well, then...me, too, she told herself. At least, so far. Because they weren't *away* yet, and not rescued at all.

The yapping of a dog. Behind them, somewhere. Whether a real dog, or a bully-boy dog Livie couldn't have said. And she couldn't tell if it came from the nearby farm, or the woods. A sharp crack. Someone stepping on a dry stick? Was it closer? She stretched her neck to see, but the forest revealed nothing. A movement caught her eye, but whatever it was didn't move again, gave her no more clues. So had that been a distant bark, or just her own heart's own odd thump in her chest, the wheezing of Jeanine next to her, beyond tired? Then something else.

"Liiiiiivieeeeeee!" Someone was shouting her name, stretching it out so it sounded like the howl of a dog.

You must run! said The Voice. *Don't wait until it's too late.* But it was already too late. She was too tired and cold and wet to run. *Run anyway,* said The Voice. No, she told The Voice. Better to stay here and hide. Rest a little longer, think on it a bit more. *Livie!* said The Voice, calling to her like Prince Bullyboy out in the woods. *Livie!* Only this time The Voice was different than before. Scratchier, more quiet. *You can't hide anymore,* it said. Whose voice was it? Livie wondered for a moment. Then she knew. Monsieur Picoult. I miss you, she thought. *It's not really me, you know,* said Monsieur Picoult's voice. *It's your own smart little self, thinking things through, taking what you've learned and using it.* Really? thought Livie. I don't know anything. *Every day you know more,* said Monsieur Picoult's voice. *And now it's time to get up and out of the storm.* In the distance, behind them, Livie could still hear the crashing water of the River Deume. She shivered again. No I can't, she thought. I'm so tired...and Jeanine is so tired. The little girl was nearly asleep, her shoulders twitching as if she was weeping in her exhaustion. I can't do this, Livie thought. I can't carry her. I can barely carry myself. She's in the way, but I can't leave her here. What do

I do? Just like being in the storm, said Monsieur Picoult's voice. I was so afraid, then, Livie thought. So scared and tired that I couldn't move. *But right now you can get up,* said Monsieur Picoult's voice. *Don't you remember how you ran through the wind and rain and thunder? You didn't really need me to come for you at all. You could have made your way home all by yourself. You're a big girl, now, and smart.* But I'd have to carry Jeanine, Livie thought. She's too heavy. *You won't have to carry her. Not really. Just wake her up, Livie.*

Livie sat still for a moment longer. In the distance, among all of the tree trunks and shadows she saw a patch of dark green, looking oddly like a hedge growing in the forest. *Laurel,* said The Voice, returned to its old place in her head. *Bushes as thick as a rock wall. You can get beyond that and keep going.*

Livie squeezed Jeanine's hand, hard and strong.

"Come on. You can do it. We'll go into the brush over there. See it? No one will be able to see us over there. One more run, alright?" With a groan, she pulled the little girl to her feet.

Once on the other side of the hedge of laurel bushes the girls walked slowly, holding hands. They tried to step as carefully and quietly as they were able. Livie wanted to ask Jeanine if they were still heading in the right direction, but didn't. She wasn't sure that the little girl even knew anymore. It felt to her like eyes were watching them from behind every tree, ready to jump out at them. Well, what were they waiting for? She felt like snarling out into the shadows. Come on, you boys! Just try something! She squeezed Jeanine's hand again and kept half-walking, half-running. Hopefully, they were heading towards town, following the way of the river. They had to get somewhere soon.

Again, there was barking. It was far off, but Livie could clearly hear it. Jeanine could hear it also, because she was running faster, some hidden strength coming to her. They clung to each other's hands tightly, painfully.

"Next time, I don't want to go in the woods," Jeanine said softly.

Next time! Livie thought. Next time I will stay with my friend in the Market with my brothers. And we'll eat barley-sugar.

"Alright then," she said. "I promise. No running through the woods."

"What do we do? They're almost here," the little girl panted.

"No, we're going to be all right," Livie said, knowing that it was a lie. She saw something ahead. Another thicket of laurel bushes. Oh, no. After all this, had they been going in circles? But no, this was different. They had been going down hill the whole time. She was sure of it.

The laurel branches were woven together in their search for daylight, and with one arm Livie scrambled into the bushes, hoping to find a place to hide, somewhere for the two of them to stay out of sight. The twigs yanked her dress and tore at her hair, but she didn't let go of Jeanine's hand. With eyes clenched tightly shut, she leaned forward and pushed.

Livie fell. Her eyes stayed shut, but there was sudden, surprising flash, as if she'd bumped her head and was seeing stars. But if she had indeed bumped her head, oddly there was no pain. No, it wasn't stars.

It was sunlight.

Chapter Twenty-Three

Livie blinked. The glare of the afternoon sun was so bright it stung her eyes. She smiled anyway, a tired, crooked kind of smile that no one else saw. Jeanine leaned against her like a sack of potatoes. Well now, at least they were out of the woods. Well, sort of. The road – it was really just a wide dirt path – was deeply rutted from cart wheels and hoof-prints. Apparently it was well traveled, and the thickly twined laurel bushes had hidden it from them. There were even little flowers growing beside it, tiny yellow blooms.

"Can you tell where we are?" she asked the little girl. But Jeanine shook her head without even looking. Alright, then, Livie thought with a shrug and a frown. They would keep going down stream. That was supposed to lead them to town, right? So which way was down stream? Livie wasn't sure.

But she certainly wasn't going to wait for the mean boys to tell her, either. She made a decision.

"We must keep moving," she said, putting her hands under

Jeanine's arms and lifting the little girl to her feet. "Let's go this way." And they set off on the dirt path with the sun at their back.

As they trudged down the lane, Livie counted all of the things that were wrong and right. She wasn't sure she was headed in the right direction. Well, sort-of sure. But she was still soaking wet, from her dunk in the river, although at least most of the mud had washed off of her. Her feet hurt tremendously, but she hadn't lost her *sabots*. Jeanine was tired and Livie was partly carrying her, but she hadn't left her behind. And she was suddenly terribly hungry.

Wait! There *was* something cooking. Grilled meat. It smelled wonderful! Maybe they'd found their way back to Market. *No,* said The Voice. *You crossed the river. Market is back on the other side.* Alright then, Livie thought. But that's food, and we're going to go towards it.

The first buildings of town were rickety-looking wooden affairs, looking for all the world like hen-houses. Do people live in these? Livie asked herself. *Everyone needs to be somewhere,* said The Voice. I suppose then I'd rather be in my own home, with its stone walls and thick warm thatch, and even Maman's turnip soup cooking. Or maybe potatoes. And Maman herself, holding her still and roughly combing the dirt out of her hair while grumbling about how much trouble Livie could get into if left on her own. Clucking at her like a mother hen. Yes, right now all of that would be nice.

The fragrant smells of cooking were everywhere now. Supper. Had Market already closed for the day? Livie had no idea. Here were more houses, side by side, almost leaning on each other, with the wooden walls brushed white with lime-wash.

"That's pretty," she pointed for Jeanine to look. The little girl nodded, hidden inside her bonnet.

"Mine's prettier," Jeanine mumbled.

"You're probably right," Livie said, her arm around her friend. "I'd have to see it again to be certain, though. But that's not a bad little house, is it?"

"I'm so hungry," said Jeanine, ignoring her.

"Me too."

Livie looked around at all of the houses, at the closed doors, and at the windows and chimneys. There's no smoke coming from the chimneys, she thought. Where is everyone? Or was this the time of day for Market's great meal? Did Market have a great meal? Something she'd imagined but never before tasted - roast chicken, perhaps, and fresh loaves of bread and soup and little sweet cakes and candies and all of the goodnesses of spring brought together, wafting on the wind, calling everyone in town out of their homes into the center of town.

There would be no one to call to for help if Prince Bullyboy and his mob suddenly appeared in front of them. She didn't say what she was thinking to Jeanine. Instead she decided that the best place to be right now was Jeanine's own house.

"Which way would take us to your home?" she asked.

"I don't know," the little girl replied, but whether this was whining from exhaustion or really not knowing, Livie couldn't tell.

"If we could just get *you* home, everything would be alright," she said, trying to nudge her friend into looking around and helping find their way.

"Not really," said Jeanine.

"What do you mean?" asked Livie.

"It won't be alright. I know it," the little girl said.

Livie frowned.

"What won't be alright?" she asked, confused.

"It won't be alright at home. It will still be wrong." Jeanine pushed back her bonnet so that it hung limply on her back. Her eyes flickered back and forth. Livie could see the little girl's tears again. What was this about? Didn't Jeanine want to go home?

"Well then. We can find my brother, Jean-Charles," she reassured the little girl. Jeanine nodded. "That's what we'll do."

The smell of smoke was stronger, now, but it didn't smell as much like food as something burning, like brush or logs in a fireplace. Well, if there was a fire, people would be gathered around it, anyhow. Livie tugged on Jeanine's arm playfully as they walked down the lane. Hurry! she thought.

Livie's *sabots* rang out with a clip-clop. Now how do you like that? The road was suddenly cobbled beneath their feet. The stones were worn smooth from years of people and wagons and animals walking over them. The girls rounded a corner where the first stone house stood. This was more like it, Livie thought. They were actually in town. The road ahead was a curving rise, with sturdy stone walls on either side. Once again, she could still hear the distant-thunder sound of the Deume tumbling and crashing over rocks. Eyebrows raised, Livie looked at Jeanine and the little girl nodded. This was the bridge they'd been were looking for. The little hand in hers squeezed fiercely. Because - and Livie wasn't even a little bit surprised - the bridge was not empty. Leaning on one of those sturdy stone walls was a sweaty, frowning Prince Bullyboy.

His nose was still rimmed with red from where she had hit him with the *sabot*. In his hand was an egg. He tossed it gently in front of him and caught it again. No, not an egg but an egg-shaped stone, like a cobble picked from the road. Did he plan to throw it? Throw it at her? Here, in town? Her thoughts raced from one place to another, as if in a storm. Surely someone would see him and stop him. Or at least be there to punish him after he did it. But as soon as she thought this, she knew somehow that there was no one around. Everyone was whereever the great roast was. They were wherever the wonderful smoke was coming from. And that was where she and Jeanine had to go to get away from this boy. But that place was over the bridge.

Still afraid of the storm, said The Voice; now partly the old voice, but also some of Monsieur Picoult. She couldn't decide where one bit ended and the other began. *That's the problem,* it went on. *This boy is just thunder and wind.* Yes, but he hit me with a stone before, Livie thought. *He did indeed do that,* said The Voice. *Did it hurt?* Yes. *Enough to keep you from crossing that river before?* No, she admitted to herself. *You're going to have to get by him, anyway.*

She looked down at her *sabots*. The dust and gravel between the cobbles on the lane was loose, if she knelt down she could grab a handful to throw in his face, but she didn't think she could get away with that trick again. Just run, she thought. Run right at him. Let him try and throw his rock. No, *make* him throw it.

"Where are the others?" she asked the big ugly boy.

"They're coming. Not as fast as me, I'm guessing." Prince Bullyboy puffed out his chest.

"Maybe they're coming slowly because they're not interested in being around you very much," Livie said.

"Yeah? Maybe you should shut your mouth," the boy smiled, showing his yellow, doglike teeth. He clenched the rock in his fist, as if readying himself to throw it. If he hit her from that close, it was going to hurt badly.

"I'm scared," moaned Jeanine, too loudly.

"You should be," said Prince Bullyboy threateningly, tossing his rock and catching it again. "Nobody's going to hear you, you know." He was right. The river's noise over the rocks was like thunder again. But Livie wouldn't give him the satisfaction of seeing her fear. She glared at the big ugly boy.

"No," Livie spat. "She shouldn't be afraid at all. She's just a little girl. She should be home, or with her family, eating a piece of barley-sugar at Market. She should have a big brother who protects her from mean, stinking things like you." For a fleeting moment, Livie wondered again what was wrong at Jeanine's home. But there was no time for that right now.

"You..." Livie pointed a dirty finger at Prince Bullyboy. "You want to spoil that. You want to ruin this day. This day that was very good before I saw you. This is the day when I made a friend." She took Jeanine's hand and held it firmly.

"And what's wrong with you?" she continued, leaning towards the boy. "Do you think that it's fun to make little girls cry? That's your joy in life? Then it's no wonder that nobody likes you. Right now, this very moment, your own gang of rascals doesn't want to hang around with you if they don't have to. You're no prince. Just a bully." Livie knew that she sounded silly even as she said it, but it had the right result. The agitated boy was tossing his rock higher in the air, catching it, tossing it again, and higher still. He was puffing with frustration.

"You girls are so stupid that you don't know nothing at all." Prince Bullyboy was still smiling, but he was red in the face. "Don't you think that they're coming? Some of them had to cross over the river and keep following you. The others were behind me, but I was running fast just so I'd beat you here."

"Well now. Is that so?" Livie fumed. "Do you know what? I don't believe you,"

She stalked forward, squeezing Jeanine's hand.

"I don't *believe* you!" With that, Prince Bullyboy's jaw dropped. The egg-shaped rock went up into the air in one final toss. Livie sprang at the big ugly boy, yanking Jeanine along. She screamed like a wild animal.

Prince Bullyboy's eyes went wide. The rock came down towards his hand, but instead of catching it, the stone dinged painfully off of the tips of his fingers. He yelped, and fully expecting Livie to try and knock him over, he flinched. Somehow, all by himself, he fell on his backside with a thump. A fleeting thought went through Livie's mind. There, wasn't that easy? There's the prince of bullies for you. But Prince Bullyboy wasn't done yet. He reached out with his hurt hand and grabbed at Livie as she passed. She swatted at his face. The boy snatched at Jeanine, who squealed and hopped to the side away from him.

"Faster. *Faster!*" Livie hissed at Jeanine. She heard the big ugly boy growl like a dog. Her ankles turned painfully on the cobbles, but she kept going, holding on to Jeanine.

Prince Bullyboy shouted at them, so angry that he made no sense. Livie and Jeanine skittered across the bridge. All they needed was one person, to see them, to shout to for help. How could everyone be gone from an entire town?

All of the houses on this side of the bridge stood next to each other, their gray stone walls touching or shared one by another. It was quite something. Livie would like to stop and look at them – never having seen so many different buildings at the same time in the same place – but this was certainly not the time. Isn't that odd, she thought. All I've done is run around since coming to town. I haven't really seen a thing. I still know it better from the top of the hill at home than I do from down here. If Papa asks, I will have to make something up.

"He's coming closer," panted Jeanine. Livie was pulling her now, and the little girl's other arm was flapping like a bird's wing. *That's it, then,* said The Voice. *Good try.* No, she thought. *Let her go, and the bully will stop chasing you.* No! *But he's going to throw that rock of his. Turn here!*

Livie dared not look back. At the corner of the next house, she jumped and pulled Jeanine behind her.
****

The horse reared up and kicked out at the two girls who had frightened him. Clutching desperately to Jeanine, Livie squeezed her eyes shut and waited for something terrible to happen. But nothing did.

"Now, now! That's enough of that!" The voice was gentle and soothing, and Livie thought she recognized it. She opened her eyes. Above her was a big black horse, iron-shod feet clattering on the cobbles. The man on the horse was leaning over the front of his saddle and was patting the creature's neck. He was very well dressed and his wig was neat and powdered. His black boots gleamed and his hat had silver braid. Livie had never seen anyone so fancy before. Perhaps he is a Count, she thought, and suddenly spun and looked down the street. At the corner, Prince Bullyboy stood, hands on hips. The man on the horse waved his hand at the big ugly boy as if he were an annoying insect, shooing him away. Prince Bullyboy shook his head in disgust and frustration and ducked out of sight back the way he had come. The man on the horse then turned back to Livie and Jeanine, who huddled together below him.

"*Mademoiselles?* Are you alright?" asked the man on the horse. Livie looked up, dazed. Then she smiled.

"I know you, don't I?" She stared at the man. The big horse nickered softly at her words. The man on the horse chuckled.

"I'm afraid that you have me mistaken with someone." The man pushed his tri-corn back and frowned. His eyes searched the two girls.

"But this is Apollo. I recognize him," Livie insisted. The big horse heard his name and gently nuzzled Livie's hair.

The man's eyes widened quizzically.

"But how do you know my steed, miss?"

"Oh, monsieur. We've met before. He let me ride him. He is a fine horse and was very careful when I was on his back." Now the man laughed outright, but it was not a happy laugh.

"Ah-ha! And there you are, right to the heart of the matter. Once again, my scalawag of a brother has taken my horse without my permission. Why am I even surprised?" He slapped his satiny breeches with his gloved hand.

Livie blushed. "Oh, no, Monsieur. This was a long time ago. Last summer it was. You must be Jacques-Etienne, the brother of the great inventor Joseph-Michel Montgolfier." Livie had the presence of mind to curtsey, although she realized that she must look a fright. The man on the horse frowned again, eyebrows knitting. But standing in the saddle, he lifted his tri-corn and swept it down, bowing from the neck and closing his eyes. Then he sat back on Apollo, slumping his shoulders, gazing down the empty street where Prince Bullyboy had just been, talking to himself as if the girls weren't there. Livie and Jeanine stood silently, watching.

"Oh, well, of course that's who I am. Etienne, the brother. The brother who makes paper bags. Not the smart brother, or the clever brother, or the hard-working brother. Everyone always says that it is

Joseph who is the great inventor. Why? Because he spends all of his time telling everyone so. And where would he be without me? Who makes the paper for his balloons? Who lets him buy all of the taffeta that he needs for his project? And where did that money come from? From my paper bags. That's where." He plopped his hat back on his powdered wig and looked to the two girls for agreement.

Livie and Jeanine nodded, as if they knew all the time that Etienne did all the very hard work.

"Exactly. Thank you," said Etienne, furrowing his brow. "He's like that foul-tempered little tax-collector, the Great Lavoisier! The man doesn't pay attention to his real job, so everyone around is as corrupt as the breath of an old dog. But he's a genius, of course. Inventor extraordinaire. Do you know what I mean?"

Livie shook her head, and Jeanine, looking at her for guidance, copied. The man on the horse rolled his eyes in frustration.

"It doesn't matter. I've explained it over and over to Joseph, and he doesn't understand either. What else can I do?"

"I don't know," said Livie. This Montgolfier brother was a funny one. She decided that she liked him. He'd chased away the bully with a wave of his hand. And she'd never met someone so comfortable holding a conversation with himself. Then she giggled. He was just like her, wasn't he? He must have his own Voice.

"What is so funny?" Etienne sat up straight, trying to seem serious and severe. Jeanine flinched, but Livie just shrugged.

"I was thinking that I know just what you mean. I have two brothers and sometimes it is hard to get along with them." She curtseyed again, just in case.

But Etienne pointed at her with a smile and looked around as if there were others in the empty street who could hear her.

"Yes, precisely! I'm the one that has to keep the blessed paper-bag business going. I'm the blessed clerk, for God's sake! Nobody ever wants to be the clerk, but someone has to be."

"I'm the chicken-feeder and garden-weeder," Livie said. Etienne stared at her. "At home, on Papa's farm," she clarified.

"Right! And who wants to be that?"

Livie shrugged again. Nobody *wanted* to be the chicken feeder. It was like the young man said. Someone must be.

Etienne nodded with a purse-lipped smile, as if concluding that this was a smart, if quite dirty, little girl.

"And she knows Apollo, and Joseph-Michel. It's quite the mystery," he said aloud. Livie gave him a crooked smile. So he *does* have a Voice In His Head.

"Alright then. Well, we'd better get back to the launch, and you two can tell me how you got so filthy."

The launch? Livie thought. What launch?

Oh, my! The balloon!

Chapter Twenty-four

Livie walked beside Etienne Montgolfier who walked beside Apollo and held his reins. She glanced up at her friend, Jeanine, who rode on Apollo because Livie and Etienne had explained to her when she shook her head about doing that very thing that all princesses and warrior queens rode mighty steeds. Despite the mud in her hair and on her face and dress, he had lifted her onto the horse. The little girl had a tired smile on her face and clutched Apollo's mane with knuckles whitened beneath the grime.

"So then what happened?" Etienne asked again. He'd asked Livie that a lot, as they plodded casually along through the empty town. He'd wanted to know everything: from what she liked to be called – Olivia or Livie – to how she had met Joseph, how she had saved the balloon, and ridden Apollo and she naturally had to tell him about her Papa's farm and her family and the storm and Monsieur Picoult and the gift of George and Louis the oxen and the *virginal* and almost tumbling off the cattle-byre roof and coming to Market and being chased by Prince Bullyboy and nearly falling into the river Deume and finally getting Jeanine and herself safely here into town. It was a long and convoluted story, and Livie had to admit to herself that even she was confused by how and why events had happened. She started by telling this young man, this stranger she had only just met, that she was anxious about revealing to him all of her story.

"Why?" he asked, eyebrows raised.

"Because there have been some strange bits to my life," she shrugged. She wasn't sure why she had called them *strange*, after all she had nothing to compare. But the Montgolfier brother nodded knowingly.

"I see," Etienne said. "Well, if you are uncomfortable then perhaps you shouldn't tell those parts, Olivia Bien."

"No, it's not that," Livie dismissed the thought with a wave of her grubby hand and a shy smile at hearing her full name, and explained that she felt like she knew him, probably because he was Joseph-Michel's brother and, in her opinion, not so very different from him. She hoped he wouldn't find that offensive, because Joseph-Michel was funny and friendly and if she remembered correctly, handsome.

"Well then no matter what, I shant be offended," Etienne replied, and so Livie revealed to him everything about The Voice in her head that talked to her when she was troubled or in trouble or even on nice sunny days when nothing at all was happening. Having said that, she remembered the mice, Beatrice and Pierrot, who might or might not talk and who had occasionally helped her get out of trouble and told him about them and how they had come to their rescue in Prince Bullyboy's gopher hole. This made Etienne's eyebrows rise even higher. She wasn't at all surprised that he occasionally leaned towards her and frowned and touched his forefinger thoughtfully to his pursed lips; not to hush her but as if he was preventing himself from impulsively asking a question about something that might come up presently in the story. Livie had to admit to herself, many things in her story were unbelievable. Still, she decided, it was pretty nice having such a rapt audience, although Jeanine was quiet and attentive mostly because she was nearly asleep in the saddle. Then there was this dark feeling in the back of her mind that there was someone else there – someone following them but always one corner behind so that he could not be seen by them. Maybe Prince Bullyboy hadn't given up just yet. She interrupted her story and said so to Etienne.

"Oh, I wouldn't think too much on that," he assured her.

"You don't imagine he's following us?" Livie considered that if Prince Bullyboy's gang had indeed caught up with him that it was more than even Etienne might be able to handle.

"Oh, he probably is," Etienne said thoughtfully, glancing over his shoulder at the empty street. "But we'll soon be to the factory. The crowd there should frighten him away."

Livie could hear the rumbling hush in the distance, as if they were coming upon another of the Deume's rocky falls. But there was no bridge around the next turn. Instead, a long, low stone building ran along the entirety of one side of the cobbled street. The roof was made of wooden slats, tucked one beneath the other, sloping up to a peak. It was quite something; as big as Monsieur Picoult's barn. No, she corrected herself, this was much bigger. At the end of the building were great wooden doors.

Etienne was looking at her as she goggled at the enormous stone building.

"This is our factory, where we make paper."

Livie sniffed. Her mouth watered and she swallowed hard. There was something in the air, something good. The Montgolfier brother noticed and shook his head.

"I know. Usually it stinks, yes," he apologized. "That is the very nature of making paper, you see. You break down the wood fiber with water and chemicals and the pulp floats in a foul miasma..." Livie stared at him. She could see that he really was very smart, except that nothing stank at the moment and she wasn't sure what he was talking about.

"No, Monsieur," she interrupted. "Something smells wonderful."

"Oh! That. There's a boar roasting in the yard." Etienne was almost dismissive, until he looked at Livie, whose mouth hung open. What, Livie wondered, was a boar and why hadn't she ever smelled one before?

"Are you hungry?" he asked.

Livie curtseyed to Etienne.

"Oh, yes, Monsieur," she told him.

They walked down the street and around the next corner. The yard was an open green on the other side of the building, smaller than Papa's farmyard, but still large enough. A large cloth stretched out from the wall of the building as if it were drying in the afternoon sun, except that the loose ends were stretched out and suspended on poles stuck in the ground. People stood beneath the cloth in the shade. What a good idea that is, thought Livie. Sometimes it would be nice to get out of the sun, or even the rain, without going inside. In the shade created beneath were long tables with their own cloths covering over them and there were benches with women sitting at them, talking to each other, cutting fruit and slicing bread. Men stood about, talking, their voices rumbling. Nearby, two lone men stood at a stone pit. One wore a fine silver-trimmed tri-corn, only he had it on backwards, and the other had a yellow vest over his white blouse, but also a dirty rag wrapped around his head just above his brow. There were no flames in the stone pit, but smoke rose in ripples of heat from its center, over which was a device that suspended a great piece of meat. This was the boar, and it was blackened by the fire's heat. Livie knew without asking that this was the source of the heavenly fragrance. The two men were shouting at each other, waving their hands over their heads, obviously in disagreement about how the cooking should proceed. A handful of other more plainly dressed men stood nearby; watching, as men will, for something more to happen.

"Employees of the factory," Etienne said softly. "Actually, the one cook is our floor manager and the other the keeper of books." He put his hands on his hips and shook his head. No one seemed to notice him, or the horse, or the two girls, such was their attention to talking and cooking and arguing. One of the two men at the cooking fire balled his fist and waved it at the other, who stuck out his tongue at the first man.

"Are they going to fight?" Livie asked, her hunger getting the better of her with such a rude question. But Etienne only shrugged.

"Oh, I hope not. I suspect I should separate them," he observed. "but it is such an entertainment to have those two fools wrestle over that boar. And the boar roasts so slowly that some entertainment is called for. They are good cooks, despite their disagreements. Come, we will settle this."

He held up his hand to assist Jeanine down from Apollo, but the little girl had fallen asleep in the saddle, leaning forward clutching reins and horse's mane.

"I don't think I've ever eaten boar," Livie said wistfully.

"Well, then. That won't do at all," he replied. "Hmm. We can't leave her like this." The Montgolfier brother reached up and gently pried Jeanine's fingers free from Apollo's mane and pulled her over into his arms. Carrying her gently over to the table with Livie following, he smiled sheepishly at the bevy of women preparing food. Suddenly, everyone saw the newcomers and a great commotion erupted.

****

Livie smiled and juice ran out of her mouth. She swiped at it with the sleeve of her dirty dress. Her jaw fairly ached from chewing so much. She'd never tasted anything like it. She remembered the little piglets that Monsieur Picoult had taken to market. Not quite the same thing, Etienne had explained as the man with the dirty rag tied around his head carved tiny tasting-slices of pork from the carcass over the cook-fire. Right, the man with the backwards tri-corn hat had growled, boar has better flavor. Also, it's harder to come by, said Dirty Rag. Well, it's just that you have to hunt it, argued Backwards Tri-corn, and

Dirty Rag rolled his eyes and said of course you have to hunt wild boar, that's the whole point of being wild. But *where* will you hunt it? All of the land is the king's or the count's. Then the two men were fussing again, waving their hands and making faces at each other, completely ignoring Etienne and Livie, who escaped to one of the covered tables.

A fat woman with a spotless white apron held sleeping Jeanine in her arms and rocked her from side to side. She whispered a song but Livie couldn't hear the words. Dipping a soft piece of cloth in a bowl of water, the fat woman wiped at the dirt on Jeanine's face, all the time whispering and humming the song. When she wakes up, Livie thought, she's going to wonder where she is. *And who she's with*, said The Voice. *And why she's with her, and how she got so clean and how she learned that song.* Livie chuckled to think of all this.

"Where did you find these two sweet waifs, Monsieur Montgolfier?" asked another of the women, sitting on the bench shelling dried peas into a bowl. She had a pretty face, and although Etienne had already answered the question before, he didn't seem to mind answering it again. The Montgolfier brother blushed and started to tell Livie's whole story again, until he realized that this was what he was doing. He stammered and fumbled for words. Finally he pointed back the way they had come. The young woman didn't seem to mind Montgolfier's being flustered at all. In fact, she smiled at Etienne and nodded, as if he had been as clear about it as the summer sky. Livie looked at her, and at the blushing young gentleman, who bowed and then, realizing that he was sitting, stood quickly and almost fell over the bench in his efforts to bow again. The pretty woman seemed not to notice Etienne's clumsiness, as he backed away from the table and tried to go back to the cook-fire, where the two men still argued. Livie liked that she didn't giggle at Etienne, or make him feel small. Interesting, she thought. She likes the Montgolfier brother that doesn't even like himself very much.

One other of the women had brought another pot of warm water and a clean cloth and set to scrubbing Livie's face and wiping the mud from her neck and hands and arms. She had a comb and carefully worked the tangles from Livie's hair. No more flavoring your supper with dirt, she'd said in a gruff and friendly tone, nothing at all like Maman.

"Clean enough," the woman finally said after rooting around in her ears with a cloth-covered finger. "Don't tell anyone I said that, though," she winked. Livie grinned at her and picked up a pickled hen's egg from a bowl on the table. She'd never tasted one before, and took a brave bite. Oh! Her lips pursed and she clenched her eyes tightly shut and shivered. So...terribly sour, and sweet at the same time. How could this be so? Her eyes watered and she chewed carefully, lest the food burst from her mouth.

"I like pickles, too," said the pretty woman. Livie peeked. The woman's head tilted, looking curiously at her.

"We don't pickle eggs," Livie offered. "Maman says that they're dear."

"Aren't they, though?" said the pretty woman. "Your mother is so right. I only get them myself when the brothers have one of their company feasts." She nodded her head towards Etienne, who was waving his hands at the two men at the cook-fire to be quiet, because for heaven's sake couldn't they see that Jeanine was sleeping?

More folks emerged from the factory building, carrying bowls of foodstuffs the likes of which Livie had never seen. A man arrived with a big basket of bread. What a marvelous smell, Livie thought. It must be freshly baked! At the fire pit Dirty Rag and Backwards Tri-corn were finally working together, using a long knife to carefully slice pieces of the roast onto a large platter. A wooden plate was set before her by the woman who'd scrubbed her face, and a mighty slab of pork was dropped on it. This had to be for all of us nearby to share, right?

"If you like, I can cut that up for you, sweetie," said the pretty woman. "But it should actually be tender enough to tear apart with your fingers, now that they're clean." All of the people were sitting down to the tables now, and the rumbling thunder of talking faded as loaves were uncovered and broken and handed down the table. One of the long still-warm loaves reached Livie and she held it, but wasn't sure what to do.

"You can't be full quite yet, little one," said one of the men with a chuckle. "Snap off a piece and dig in!" Livie twisted the loaf and pulled off a fist-sized hunk. The others at her table cheered, and she blushed, handing the loaf to the pretty woman. The bread's perfume tickled Livie's nose. She bit down on the bread. It was crusty and chewy and sweet as if someone had put honey on it, but there was none there. Suddenly she felt as if it were Monsieur Picoult himself sitting right there, offering her a piece of bread to dip in her chicken soup. But it wasn't the old man. Instead, Etienne sat down beside her with his own plate of food, and tried not to make eye contact with the pretty woman, who as far as Livie could tell was openly watching him not looking at her.

"Won't your brother be worrying about you?" asked the Montgolfier brother, nibbling on fresh peas, which the pretty woman had just shelled.

"I guess," Livie replied. "He told me not to get lost." She could imagine how much trouble she was already in, and how that trouble grew with each passing moment. She took another gnawing bite on her slab of pork, rather than thinking about it any more. Better that she get in all of her good moments now, because they were going to be her last ones for quite some time.

The pretty woman's eyes were sparkling. She winked at Livie, then looked at Etienne with a mock-frown.

"Fix that, then, sir!"

Etienne stared at her. She kept frowning, but it was all make believe. They do like each other, Livie concluded.

"What?"

"Go get him! Fetch her brother."

"I can't," the Montgolfier brother said. "Everything's...here."

245

The pretty woman shook her head with a crooked smile.

"Oh, please. Then send one of *those* fools." She pointed at the men tending the cooking fire.

Etienne waved over Backwards Tri-corn. The gruff man was coated with sweaty smoke now, and smelled like roast pork.

"Enough of the two of you fighting," said the Montgolfier brother. He didn't tell the man that the pretty woman had called him a fool.

"Sorry, sir. No more, of it. Promise." The man, bowed and lost his fine hat in the process. Livie grinned.

"Fix your hat then and go over to Market, will you now? Find Olivia Bien's brother, the farmer, and bring him here." Etienne sounded very serious.

"Surely. Quick as you please," said Backwards Tri-corn. He picked up his hat and jammed it down on his head. He stomped off, but immediately stopped and turned around.

"And where'm I going?" he asked the Montgolfier brother.

Etienne and the pretty woman looked at Livie. She scratched her head.

"We have two oxen, named George and Louis. My brother will be with them. He is selling potatoes."

Backwards Tri-corn nodded knowingly, as if all of this made terrific sense. He held up a finger for emphasis.

"I'll be back in two shakes of a lamb's tail." And he stomped off down the cobblestone street, around the corner and out of sight.

After a moment, Etienne slapped his brow with his open hand. He gritted his teeth in frustration, then calmed down, because everyone was looking at him.

"Perhaps I should have given him Apollo to ride," he said softly. Then he looked at the others at the table and shrugged to their delighted laughter.

****

Jeanine finally woke up. The fat woman had set the little girl down on the bench, resting her head on the spotless apron and cover-

246

ing her with a spare tablecloth. Somehow she'd slept through every-thing until now, and Livie saw her sit up, rubbing her eyes with her knuckles.

"Livie?" Jeanine mumbled.

"Hungry?" Livie mumbled back through a mouthful of boiled potatoes. She'd never had potatoes except in soup, and didn't know that they could taste so good, salty and tangy with onion and still, somehow, sweet-flavored. She would have to tell Maman about it.

"Yes, please," the little girl said shyly to the fat woman who placed a bowl and a spoon in front of her without delay. Jeanine frowned a question at Livie. Livie didn't know which one, though, so she quick-ly told the story of everything that had happened since Jeanine fell asleep.

"Now what?" asked the little girl around a mouthful of potato.

"I don't know," Livie replied. She sighed. It was nice to be com-fortable and full of food and sort of clean, and drying in the after-noon's sun. Soon, she hoped, the backwards tri-corn man would fetch Jean-Charles, who would come for her, and then they could take Jeanine home. It seemed that everything else – the bullies, the chase, everything – was forgotten. But no one returned. Suddenly, there was noise on the street. Hoofbeats? No.

"Now! Now! It's time for the launch! The launch!" A man gal-loped on foot down the cobblestone street. He waved his hat in the air, dropped it, and skidded to a stop to pick it up. His shoes caught on the cobblestones and he toppled over onto his own outstretched hands. Everyone at the tables gasped. Etienne stood slowly, facing the strange arrival. The man sat on the ground, panting for breath. But it was not Backwards Tri-corn.

"No, no. I'm, alright! Come! It's time for the launch, Monsieur!" the clumsy man shouted between his panting, climbing to his feet and plopping his hat back on his head while waving off any fears that he had just hurt himself.

Livie looked quizzically at Etienne. Sometimes grown ups were so

247

strange.

"Stop shouting so!" the Montgolfier brother shouted back at the clumsy man, who came no closer than that spot where he had fallen. In apology, the man snatched the hat off his head again and bowed deeply. Doing so, however, he toppled over again, and once again received the gasps of everyone at the tables. Almost everyone. Some of the men were chuckling behind their hands. Etienne shook his head.

"Stand up!" he scolded the clumsy man, who this time stayed on the ground, still panting from his run through the streets. "Is it true? He is finally ready?"

"Yes, Monsieur! He said so, himself."

"And he is still going up himself?"

"So he says, Monsieur."

Etienne turned to the people at the tables.

"Come, everyone. Let us hurry. We don't want to miss this."

"What is happening, Monsieur?" Livie asked. Etienne frowned.

"It is Joseph-Michel. He is launching his balloon."

"Now?"

"Now!"

Chapter Twenty-five

And off they all went – everyone at the feast, just like that – traipsing down the cobblestone street following the clumsy man who limped
and rubbed the place on his head onto which he had toppled. Despite
his aches, he still held himself in a proud sort of way to be leading such
a parade of people. Everyone brought along whatever they thought
might be useful or necessary for a balloon launch. There were sconces
taken from the paper-bag factory walls, although the day was still perfectly bright. The women put food in baskets, which was a good idea,
Livie thought, because food with friends is always a good idea. And
because Backwards Tricorn was still gone on his errand, Dirty Rag
found another man to help him lug the remainders of the roast boar
still spitted on the iron pole and a couple of dogs appeared out of
nowhere to follow them, licking up the tiny scraps that fell from the
carcass. Etienne placed Jeanine back on Apollo, and she smiled and
clutched the horse's mane.

Livie had never been in such a procession, happy and noisy and full of purpose. As they walked, Etienne explained everything about Joseph's new balloon. One moment he sounded like he was complaining, but because the pretty woman was also walking with them he seemed to catch himself.

"You just wouldn't believe how much taffeta we've bought. And it's not like we could use linen or cotton-flax. Silk taffeta. Fantastic stuff. I swear to you, it is as strong as canvas, but light as feathers. The weave is so tight that it blocks the light of the sun. Oh, but so much of it, though. One hundred ball gowns. Probably two hundred. More..." Etienne shook his head and tut-tutted under his breath. He was talking to himself as much as he was to Livie and the pretty woman.

"But the truth is anything else would be too heavy, or would let the hot gas leak right through its weave. Joseph calls it 'the heavier than air conundrum'. If we couldn't get the taffeta, he'd be right back where he was before, with paper bags and glue. That was a mess, I'll tell you. Everything tearing into bits with the slightest breeze."

"Taffeta is so very dear," Livie said, so that Etienne would be reminded that he was still walking with the crowd from the factory, leading Apollo and Jeanine, and talking with the pretty woman and her. The Montgolfier brother stared at her for a moment – thinking, recognizing. He smiled crookedly at her. Then he was back to talking to himself, waving the hand with Apollo's reins in it. Fortunately, Apollo seemed used to this.

"Oh my, yes. You have no idea. And have I told you that it's all Lavoisier's fault? It is, of course. Grimy-fingered little man that he is he placed a surcharge on *imported* silk. As if there were any other kind. Does he think that I can grow it myself? And you know he does it just to spite us. But if you will ask me why, I will tell you that he is jealous of Joseph, of his balloons."

Livie nodded. This Lavoisier fellow must be the most frustrating man in all France. She remembered Joseph speaking about him. Another inventor. The one who talked of... she couldn't remember

250

what the words were. Demonstrations? Practical demonstrations! Practical demonstrations were necessary to prove what you claimed. But Joseph didn't mind the other man, that Lavoisier, so much as his brother seemed to. Etienne apparently saw things differently. Jealousy. It was perfectly reasonable to Livie that people would be jealous of the marvelous balloon she had seen on that day last Fall. Or jealous of one's success. Why didn't Etienne understand this? His own successes were obvious, but probably not so to him. Livie looked over at the pretty woman, who smiled back at her. Livie didn't even know her name. She wondered why Etienne hadn't introduced her. Was she listening to him? Grown-ups have different ways of seeing things. Perhaps, she supposed, if the pretty woman was paying attention to Etienne, it was just to hear him say the words, not thinking about what the words meant at all. Maybe they couldn't actually be friends, because she worked for him in the factory. Or because he was a gentleman. To let that get in the way of liking someone would be a foolish shame, Livie concluded.

The parade rumbled on, everyone appearing to have a good time; laughing and singing and talking, nibbling the food they'd brought along. Livie looked at Etienne, at Jeanine and Apollo, and the pretty woman. She realized to her surprise that she wished very much that her family was here with her. *I'll guess that you didn't expect to think that,* whispered The Voice. *That's what life is. A whole collection of unexpected moments.* No, Livie thought, not everything is coming around the next corner ready to surprise you.

Livie sniffed. Again, a whiff of smoke? No, it had to be the roasted boar the two men lugged between them. She frowned at the distant thunder, but guessed that this was the tromping feet and raucous talk of the parade of people from the factory. They rounded the next corner. She was wrong. Her eyes went wide and she stopped as suddenly as George and Louis did when they decided they didn't want to pull anymore. Etienne tugged gently on Apollo's reins for the horse to halt as well. He looked down at her but said nothing. He knew exactly

251

what Livie was seeing.

The church spire reached like a dark gray finger pointing into the sky. Livie knew it well, having seen it so many times from the top of her hill. But beneath the spire, she could see no church. Beneath the spire, indeed beginning to fill the church-yard, was a crowd of people, staring.

The balloon was enormous, its vast curve rising above the gathering like a mighty blue moon rising out of the churchyard. Or rather like a great blue lily bulb.

"Look!" she cried out to Jeanine, but the crowd milling about, joined by her own parade, was so noisy that everyone who wanted to be heard was shouting. She was drawn to it, felt her feet sliding forward, to push through the mass of people and be closer to it. *Now you've seen everything*, said The Voice. I have not, she thought. But I've seen more today than I believed I ever would. The fabric that Etienne had gathered for his brother was many different shades of blue, from the darkest morning sky when the sun is only just awakening, to the glare of a washed-out summer afternoon. Affixed to the broad curved sides were two great disks of shining golden cloth, like the sun and the grandest full moon of summer. Whoever had stitched each panel of cloth together must have known how it would look from a distance, because it dazzled the eyes like...nothing else Livie could have imagined. Was there ever before anything made up of so many types of blue? Only the very sky itself!

"Oh! Oh!" Jeanine kept repeating as she saw something new to gaze upon from her vantage high up on Apollo. Livie kept nodding, certain that they were seeing the same things. A sash of gold draped across the sea of blue like a falling star. Beneath the gold another sash of scarlet red. Silver ropes reaching up and over it all and stretching back down and into the crowd.

More people were wandering into the churchyard. No one was ignoring the launch of this balloon, that was for sure. Livie heard a strange sound – like the squalling of a baby.

"Oh!" Jeanine cried again, pointing. "Sheep!" Livie followed her hand and saw that there was in fact a small flock of gray-wooled sheep to one side of the churchyard. Like tiny oxen without horns and wearing blankets. They must come here to pasture, she thought. At the moment, however, they were pressed up against a bramble of thorn-bushes on one side of the churchyard and bleating their dismay at the confusion of the enormous balloon and the growing crowd, which Livie imagined was easily as large as the one which had gathered that day for market. It's probably the same people, she supposed, jostling one another and fussing and laughing, behaving as much like sheep as people could be.

"I don't see Joseph," Etienne shouted. "Count on him to keep everyone waiting."

As if in response to his brother's scolding, Joseph-Michel suddenly broke through the mass of people in front of them.

"Etienne! My good brother! I'm so pleased that you are here." To Etienne's discomfort, Joseph hugged his brother. When Joseph released him, the fussy Montgolfier fixed his hat and frowning at him mumbled 'and where else would I be?' Joseph didn't seem to mind his crankiness.

"Natalie, my dear!" Joseph saw the pretty woman and bowed to her, sweeping his hat on the grassy lawn. Ah, Livie thought. Natalie is her name! The pretty woman curtseyed, closing her eyes. When she opened them, she was looking at Etienne. See, Livie thought. She likes the quiet brother and he doesn't even recognize it.

Joseph looked at Jeanine riding on Apollo.

"Who is this princess on my mighty steed?" He said this in such a way that Jeanine giggled.

"Apollo is my horse, you scoundrel," Etienne shouted, but Joseph wasn't listening. He looked at Livie with a smile.

"I know you, don't I?" he leaned down so that only she could hear him.

"I am Olivia Bien," Livie said. She had been sure that he wouldn't remember her. It had been so long ago. "You told me to come to Market." Joseph had a quizzical look in his eyes, but then a wide smile.

"Good Olivia, hmm? Of course you are, yes, yes. The girl on the hill. My balloon rescuer." He held out his hand to her and she took it with a grin.

"I like your new balloon, Monsieur," Livie said.

"Thank you, miss. And so, you have come here to help me?" It was as much a statement as a question.

Holding her hand tightly, Joseph made his way back through the crowd. Such was the commotion, it was a good thing that he didn't try to talk with her or ask her any questions, because neither of them would have heard the other.

"Come on, scientist Montgolfier!" She heard one man shouting, his cry picked up by another.

"Yes! We haven't got all day!" At this Joseph-Michel Montgolfier held up his free hand, waving it as if the shouts were welcoming and happy. He's never flustered, Livie concluded. It must be nice to see everything as opportunity.

He gently nudged forward through the people, towing Livie behind him. Then, like breaking out of the woods through the laurel bushes, they were out of the throng, standing beneath the balloon.

"I present my *Globe Aerostatique!*"

Livie stared. The great blue bag – for she understood that's what it was, a bag still and beautiful and full above them – floated above the ground. And although she knew how it happened to do this, Livie was amazed anew. Silver colored ropes held a large blue-painted basket attached beneath the balloon. Below the basket, smoke drifted up and disappeared into the basket's base. Other, plainer ropes were tied to wooden stakes in the ground and held the basket in place.

"You see the coals?" Joseph asked. Livie nodded and pointed. There was a deep ditch beneath the balloon and it glowed a dull orange.

"Yes. That's where the hot air is made. It rises up into the balloon through a hole in the basket's center that is connected to the mouth of the balloon itself. It works best when there is no breeze to blow it away from the mouth, so as much of the hot air as possible goes into the balloon itself. Now that the balloon is full, the coals help heat the air inside even hotter, so that it lifts even more. It should be able to lift quite a bit of weight. See how firm the skin of the balloon is?"

"But it won't catch fire, will it?" Livie asked, watching at the ripples of heat rising from the ditch, like the cooking pit where the men roasted the wild boar.

"I suppose it could," Joseph pressed his lips together thoughtfully. "But I think we have it suspended high enough over the coals so that it shouldn't. The hot air diminishes the further you go from the source. The taffeta skin of the balloon holds it in for a while, enough to achieve lift in the cooler air. It goes up for a while, then comes back down again. Although can you imagine if it were made of paper? Whoosh! Up in flames, just like that." He waved his hand in a flourish.

Livie nodded again, although much of what Joseph was saying wasn't clear to her. The balloon had a mouth? Very strange.

"What are you doing there, Montgolfier? Quit all the talk and get on with it!" came another shout from a man in the crowd. Livie couldn't see who it was. His voice wasn't angry, but Livie thought it did sound impatient, much like Papa asking for a second time for something to be done.

Joseph waved again.

"Afraid it won't fly?" asked the heckler. He had an audience, because there was laughter at this.

"It's already flying, can't you see?" Joseph pointed at the basket tethered off of the ground.

"Well then, you and I sure have different ideas about what flying is," guffawed the man, and this time even more in the crowd laughed along with him.

Joseph walked over to one of the plain ropes anchoring the balloon and basket and grasped it, turning towards the crowd, with his other hand to his lips, as if he were carefully considering his next words.

"I do have a different idea about flying!" he shouted. The crowd hushed. But the man wouldn't be still.

"Ha! Growing wings like an angel?"

"Ah, well," Joseph said with a crooked smile. "Many of you know me well enough to agree that it is unlikely that I will grow wings like an angel, right?" That set everyone to laughing, and repeating to each other what Joseph had said.

"And I could explain to you the scientific principles of how my balloon flies," He laid his finger aside his nose. "But we're not interested in that, are we?"

Livie joined in with the crowd laughing and shouting "No, no!"

She felt someone beside her, and turned to see Etienne, his hat straight and his vest neatly buttoned. He nodded at her and leaned over to whisper in her ear.

"Joseph is well-loved, isn't he?"

"Oh, yes, Monsieur," she told him. "But he is not the only one, you should know."

"Who, then?" Etienne's eyebrows went up.

"Mademoiselle Natalie likes you," Livie blurted. "I would think it must be better to have a friend than to worry about anything other people might say." The Montgolfier brother put his hand on her shoulder and squeezed it gently.

"Do you really think..." he started.

"Etienne!" Joseph's shout startled them both. "I think we're ready. Would you give me a hand?"

The crowd hushed as Etienne dipped his head in a bow and walked over to his brother. How alike they are, Livie thought, and yet how different.

As Livie watched, the two men waved for others from the factory to come up and help them. Taking hold of the tether ropes, they carefully guided the enormous balloon away from the fire in the ditch, maneuvering it as if it were the balkiest of oxen teams.

Then, while Joseph instructed, the men from the factory pulled down on the ropes so that he could climb into the basket. His own weight in the basket sunk the balloon even lower, so that it scuffed on the trampled churchyard grass.

The heckler guffawed again.

"You, Monsieur, are heavier than air, that is for sure!" Everyone laughed at this, and Joseph nodded, with a purse-lipped smile.

"Too heavy. What then?" he asked aloud. He looked at Etienne, who shrugged almost unnoticeably. The people were still laughing, chattering with each other, bleating.

Bleating. Livie whirled around. Yes! What about...

"Monsieur Joseph!" she cried. "Monsieur!" Both Montgolfier brothers looked at her and she pointed over at the bramble where the sheep huddled.

Joseph's arms went up with joy. Etienne, hands on hips, was less enthusiastic. In a moment they had staked the balloon's ropes down again.

Of course, catching one of the shy beasts was a bit more complicated. The crowd watched bemused as the flock of sheep scattered and regrouped, trying to evade Joseph and the men from the factory. Finally, the clumsy man who had stumbled in the cobblestone street pushed through the crowd and tackled one of the small ewes, barely more than a spring lamb. Kicking and complaining she was carried to the basket.

"There, we are! Someone to go on this momentous journey!" shouted Joseph to the crowd. He looked more bedraggled now, but his smile was still winning.

"Quite the captain for your ship," said the heckling man, who neither helped nor went away. Unfortunately, Livie thought.

"A perfect passenger," Joseph retorted.

"So how will our little lamb tell of its experiences at journey's end?

No news is good news?" The man guffawed again with a haw-haw.

"It will not, but we will see by its calm return to the flock that the flight held no danger, and caused no pain. We will learn from this ewe," said Joseph, nodding to the man.

"You will learn from the ewe, not I," quipped the man, and the Montgolfier brother shook his head.

"I use science and you attempt wit. One of us is unarmed in this conversation. Perhaps I shall pause while you reload," Joseph replied with a wink to the crowd. For the first time, the laughter was aimed at the heckler.

While the two men shouted at one another, Livie watched the clumsy man struggling to keep the little ewe from escaping once again. The sheep was kicking and wriggling in his arms, so he took one of the staked ropes and with one hand made a loop to secure around the sheep's neck. Satisfied that now it couldn't run off, he let the rope go, leaning back and closing his eyes. Why in the world? Livie wondered.

"Kerchoo!" His mighty sneeze was part cough and part scream. Livie blinked. The little ewe, however, leaped into the air, hooves galloping full speed even before it hit the ground. The rope may have been tied carefully about the startled little sheep's neck, but it was only carelessly looped around the stake, and so came undone. The ewe was still securely attached to the balloon basket, but as the only creature holding on to a rope, and with the other ropes not securely fastened to their stakes either, something happened. The balloon began to rise, slowly at first, then more swiftly.

Livie ran for the little sheep. Snatching up the rope, she pulled as hard as she was able. She couldn't let the creature be dragged up into the sky. And she wasn't going to let the balloon take off without Joseph.

Chapter Twenty-Six

The balloon lifted straight up, just as the Montgolfier brother said it would. Had it just dragged her along the ground, Livie thought, then she might have let go - not wishing to get dirty all over again. But it yanked her off the ground instead and the feeling was strange and new and so she hung on. The little ewe, halted in mid-gallop and mid-bleat, went right up on the same rope by the thick wool around its neck.

The crowd gasped, its attention turned away from Joseph and the heckler and back to the balloon, the sheep, and the little girl. Nobody moved. Nobody even shouted or did anything at all for so long that when they finally did - when Joseph yelled for *somebody* to grab the ropes - nobody was able to reach them. The balloon carried Livie up above the crowd. The rope slowly twirled her and she could see that she was too high to let go now. The lamb squawked a frightened bleat.

"Climb, Olivia! Climb into the basket!" she heard Etienne shout. Then everyone in the crowd was shouting: Climb! Jump! We will catch you! Don't let go! All manner of different instructions were called out and it was like a wave of noise beneath her. *Yes, climb*, said The Voice, and she did, because she was a pretty good climber and the rope wasn't too slick. She let go of the rope with one hand and reached up. Someone below, - a woman - screamed.

One of Livie's *sabots* slid off her foot. Her left foot. Look out, she thought. She tried to look down to see where it went - if it hit any-one. Maybe the foolish man that kept bothering Joseph.

"I lost my shoe!" she called. She clenched the toes of her other foot so that her other *sabot* would stay put.

"Don't worry about it!" Etienne shouted. "And don't look down! Up and into the basket with you!"

Livie moved another hand up and pulled herself up some more. The basket was in her way now and she bumped her head, but she found when she slid her hand higher up the rope, her body followed along, right around the bottom edge of the basket. *Keep going*, said The Voice. With two more strong pulls Livie was able to grab the side of the basket, which was covered with taffeta, and climb into the thing, sliding down to the bottom, surprised by how tired the climb had made her. This has been a very long day, she said to herself. I won't be sorry when it is over.

A great cheer rose up from below, but it was different than before. She stood and peered over the side, then clenched her eyes tightly shut.

Oh, my. She was *flying!*

****

Once upon a time, Livie would have been happy enough just to keep her eyes shut. She was floating alone in the air. The balloon had climbed above the steeple of the church, and all of the trees in the town. But shehadn't gone through the storm, or come to Market, or stood up to the bully or crossed the roaring river to stay afraid of mean dogs and boys, and Papa's moods, and making new friends. That oldLivie would have missed everything. This Livie opened her eyes.

The balloon was a great blue sky above her, all of the shades separate now. Buttons, she thought. There are buttons on the silk, many many of them. Indeed the balloon looked like a fantastic gown, buttoned up and secure. Somewhat shakily, Livie stood, grabbed a silver rope to hang on and peered over the side of the basket. Surprising even herself, she waved down to the people far below.

"Don't worry, *cherie!*" someone shouted. It was Joseph, waving his hat at her. "You are the bravest one I've ever known! How magnificent! How wonderful! We will follow you!" He was on Apollo and the big black stallion was galloping along beneath the balloon, following the road.

"Halloo Livie!" came another shout. It was Jeanine. Livie laughed. The little girl was riding in front of Joseph, holding on with one hand as they bounced along and waving up at her with the other. "The lamb!"

"What?" Livie couldn't hear her very well. People were following the riders down the road, what appeared to be the entire crowd from the churchyard. There are a lot of people down there, she thought, and just her alone up here.

"The lamb..."

Of course! The little ewe was still dangling unhappily from the end of the rope. Slowly, Livie pulled the poor creature up; it, too, bumped the bottom of the basket before she could lift it over the side. Another cheer rose up from the ground. The sheep lay on the bottom of the basket after Livie loosened the rope around its neck, panting hard and far too frightened by everything that had just happened to even move.

Now Livie had a dizzying flurry of different thoughts. What about her brother? Who would let him know that she was up here? And who would tell him to take Jeanine home? She wiggled her toes - what about her shoes? Maman and Papa were going to be fierce about her losing one, even more than how grimy she was. Would Papa even let her tell about the adventure that today had become? She couldn't imagine it. It was more likely that Papa would look at her and grumble and then send her off to bed. Livie felt as if she had run around in circles until she'd collapsed. The balloon continued to rise.

There was so much for her to see. Houses of stone, shingled with slate. Light brown roads that led to gray bridges. The rippling green tops of trees. Fields of wheat and barley and rye, as many different shades of verdant springtime as an eye could detect. The Count's palace was to the west, beyond her Papa's hill, beyond Picoult's farm. And Paris and France's King Louis to the north. A breeze brushed the balloon, turning it to the west again. Stay this way and she would keep on going and going, and then the sea. Or if a different breeze changed its mind and blew to the east, then she would follow the curving, thundering Deume down to the wide and muscular Rhone. Which way then? The sea. For all rivers lead to the sea.

You see, said The Voice. *You already know a great deal about the world.*

The balloon – the Montgolfier Brothers' *Globe Aerostatique* – was now floating so high that Livie found that she wanted to squint her eyes closed again. She would peek with one eye, see the high clouds and close it tightly. Peek once again, and the ground had fallen a bit farther away.

Her hands hurt. She looked – her knuckles were bony white from gripping the rim of the basket so tightly. She let one hand go and shook it gently to get it to relax. Then she took hold again and relaxed the other. Soon they were both gripping tightly again. I suppose, she thought, that my hands might someday get used to flying, but not today, not yet. It was funny, she thought, peering alternately down and up and wondering at the feeling of giddiness that it gave her. At first rising into the sky meant that she could see things more clearly. The leaves on the trees, tiles on the roofs of houses, the rippling bends of the river. Climbing higher and all of those pieces become something even larger, the green of forests and pastures, the brown of rocky hills, newly-sewn fields and all cut by the river and by criss-crossing roads, so far beneath her that it was difficult to tell what was what and where she was. I wonder what I look like from the ground. For a tiny moment, she wished that she could see the beautiful balloon from down there. From the farmyard, perhaps, sitting with Maman shelling peas, pointing up and saying *my goodness, look at that, will you? Amazing!* But Livie decided that she wouldn't wish to trade places, not with anyone. She would rather be here. And where was here? She didn't know. Right now, she thought, *I'm lost.* Then, glancing over her shoulder, she was immediately able to find the point of the church steeple, although it was a small thing now, almost insignificant among all of the other shapes and colors. *I am here, somewhere, but I know where I am by seeing where I came from,* she told herself.

She felt a puff of a breeze on her face. The basket wobbled, and the taffeta skin of the balloon rippled and she could feel everything tilt more. Would she keep climbing? How high could this mighty balloon go? How far would she drift along? And where was she going to come down?

And the breeze didn't quite want to make up its mind, either. She felt it behind her now; cool enough to make the little hairs rise up on her neck. She shivered, then remembered Joseph's words – *when the hot air in the bag begins to cool, it descends.* Not just yet, if you please. Then the breeze turned around again, cooling her face and spinning the balloon slowly, so that everything was there for her to see. Trees, river, hills, fields. Everything, more than anyone had ever seen before at one time.

Another shout from down below, but she was too far away to hear. Somewhere down there was Joseph with Jeanine, riding like the wind on mighty Apollo to try and keep up with her. Did they turn around every time the balloon changed direction? Livie smiled to think of that. And Etienne watching them, possibly climbing up into the bell tower of the church for the best view.

The little ewe bleated softly and Livie turned to see. The lamb was sitting calmly on the basket floor, legs folded beneath it, looking back at her. *No wonder she is so calm, she doesn't see where we are.* Just another afternoon high in the sky. What happens next? Livie asked herself. Maybe you are Etienne's and he would let you come home with me. If not, we will have to take you back to the churchyard another day. It is probably too late for today.

Look down, said The Voice. *Hurry, Olivia!*

She peered down from the basket. There was a hill, fields thickly green with spring growth, a farmhouse and an outbuilding, connected to a road. The road came from behind her, and led off before her, although that might change with the next puff of breeze. In the field were spots so small that she couldn't be sure with her eyes that they were people working the fields, although she supposed that they were. Another spot came moving out from the farmhouse. Her Maman? Papa and her brother Guillaume? Atop the hill now, she could see a pasture, a place where no trees grew. *Look there,* said The Voice, sounding more like Monsieur Picoult's whisper now. *Do you see?*

Far below, was a square where the green pasture ended and small spots of red and yellow and orange reigned supremely. Livie couldn't help but smile, there was such a burst of colors, too many to see each individual hue. Her lily garden. But there was something else. Along with the lush green of grass and chicken weeds, were colorful blooms, spread across the pasture. How could that be? The deer! They had dug up the lily bulbs, and spread them, in their way. And the blooms had chosen this wondrous and strange sunny day to finally show their many beautiful faces. Oh, lilies! she thought, you are very fine, indeed. Looking back over her shoulder, a crowd of people was moving along the road, too far away and below for her to make out who was whom, but they would soon reach the farm on the hill.

Well now, Livie thought. Someone would have to explain to Maman and Papa that she was up here, flying in a blue one-hundred-ballgown taffeta balloon, and Papa would huff and puff and Maman would squawk and flap around the farmyard like a chicken. Some would probably stay at the farm while others, with carts and horses and wagons continued up the hill and over, following the balloon. They would eventually even reach Monsieur Picoult's farm, and possibly continue on. By now the falling-down man had finally found her brother Jean-Charles, who might have begun heading home after her in confusion with Louis and George and the wagon and the baskets and everything. Perhaps even a girl-mouse might hide along for the ride. You never knew. And Jeanine – would she be there waiting when this balloon came drifting down, somewhere? Livie hoped so, and for Maman to be there, too. "Maman," she would say. "This is my new friend." And Jeanine would probably curtsey, and Maman might even smile at that, patting the little girl on the shoulder. And later, Livie could show them both the lilies blooming in her garden, and pick a few to bring home. That would be nice. And maybe some of the people would stay to dinner, and there might even be some of the roast boar left, carried faithfully by Joseph and Etienne's men. The Montgolfier brothers themselves would be there, of course, with this wondrous balloon of theirs. There was also the next Market to think about, too, and the bullies. They would have to be dealt with, no doubt. But she wasn't afraid of them anymore. Not one little bit.

For now, Livie pushed all of that from her mind. She squinted ahead, occasionally closing her eyes to rest them, for now her balloon decided to follow the sinking sun, slowly drifting high in the clear sky almost as if it knew where it was going and that it was being followed and didn't want to get too far ahead of everyone in Ardeche, all running and riding and laughing and perhaps even dancing to see such an amazing thing.

The End.

Garrison Somers is a writer and editor of The Blotter Magazine and Corner Bar Magazine. He lives with his wife and daughters in Chapel Hill, NC.

Shelly Hehenberger is an artist and writer. She lives with her husband and daughter in Carrboro, NC.